Brought up in Kent and Norfolk, William Ardin was educated at the Royal Grammar School, Worcester, and won a Scholarship to Oxford. Much of his subsequent career with ICI was spent on Teesside, researching petrochemical markets. He and his wife now live in a hillside village in Galloway, looking down towards the ruins of Sweetheart Abbey, which was built by Devorgilla in the thirteenth century.

William Ardin's previous Charles Ramsay mysteries, SOME DARK ANTIQUITIES and LIGHT AT MIDNIGHT, are also available from Headline.

Also by William Ardin

Plain Dealer
Some Dark Antiquities
Light at Midnight

The Mary Medallion

William Ardin

HEADLINE

First published in 1996
by HEADLINE BOOK PUBLISHING

First published in paperback in 1996
by HEADLINE BOOK PUBLISHING

10 9 8 7 6 5 4 3 2 1

ISBN 0 7472 4483 9

Typeset by Keyboard Services, Luton, Beds

Printed and bound in Great Britain by
Cox & Wyman Ltd, Reading, Berks

HEADLINE BOOK PUBLISHING
A division of Hodder Headline PLC
338 Euston Road
London NW1 3BH

For Jill and Edward Ballard

Chapter One

Out on the wide flat sands the artist seems almost lost in the great wet spaces around him, in the flat landscape overhung with cloud. The only other vertical lines out there are the stakes of a salmon net away to his right.

The sunshine earlier in the afternoon had tempted Ian Lennox out with a false promise of good painting weather – a still day with plenty of light, he thought. He even allowed himself to take his time in unpacking his cartridge paper and making his choice of pencils and watercolours. Giving himself the luxury of being methodical for once he put all those into his favourite straw bag stained with paint and carried them in his left hand. In the other he had taken the light folding stool that he is sitting on now, the metal legs sinking into the wet sand; only prevented from going further in by the rails connecting them fore and aft although those are gradually burying themselves too. Two hundred yards behind him, on the dry beach above high-water mark, the rest of his gear lies in an untidy pile on a pale dune held together by coarse grass which is disfigured by one or two items of flotsam – a scrap of coarse blue net, the remains of an orange box. His bicycle, a heavy machine painted green, lies on its side with one pedal cocked in the air. Next to it his big umbrella, furled and tied with a piece of baler twine, because he doesn't need it today. It lies on top of a shabby leather portfolio which is so much larger than one might expect because it has to be big enough to take canvases, oil boards, even a couple of frames. The tin box which contained his lunch is empty now – so is the dark green bottle lying beside it. All that is flotsam of another sort.

With quick pencil strokes he outlines the silhouette of the Cumbrian hills on the other side of the Solway Firth, suggests a building here, a stretch of woodland there. Suggests only, because by now the mist has softened their edges and is beginning to obscure them. There is a squat pillar of rain hanging now in front of him. He notes its texture and is envisaging already the wash of thin colour that he will use to imitate it. Then suddenly the rhythm of his pencil changes as it sweeps over the page drawing the broad planes of the firth itself which can be called neither sea nor land really. It all depends on the state of the tide which soon will come hurrying in as fast as a man can run. He is aware of that. The knowledge hangs at the back of his mind, a warning like the raincloud and the mist sitting on the hills behind him.

From the outside this artist, Lennox, seems to be relaxed enough. A man who is confident in what he is doing and feels comfortable with it. On the inside, though, he is under stress for reasons which are all connected – which hang together in a web inside his head. Pick out the first of them, the most important reason. Tease it out and look at it. What is it? There isn't a drop of wine left in that bottle lying next to his lunchbox. That is the first reason. Two hours ago when he gulped the last mouthful of it he felt it satisfying, to begin with, the craving which nagged at his mouth, at his stomach. Then warming his cheeks and chest. Finally it took away the tremor in his fingers, gave him hands which drew with firm decisive strokes, released his imagination to work on the wild naked figure he is going to set against the scene he is sketching now. Later on, from this sketch he will distil the inner structure of the landscape, paring the lines and shapes down, reducing it to its essence – to serve as a background for another canvas in the series which he calls his Mysteries. It will be the tenth of them – *Mystery Ten*. He paints to get the means to keep his eye true, his imagination flowing, his hand steady. Red wine is best – a robust red wine at seven shillings a bottle. There is a little off licence in the town where they sell it. They know him there.

Seven shillings? How is he going to find it? Where?

The tactic is all prepared, ready to be implemented. In the holdall behind him is one of the other canvases in the series: *Mystery Four*, the best of them, he believes. A view taken in Glentrool forest embellished with a single naked girl – her body a ghostly thing, almost transparent yet retaining a vibrant sensuality. As you look at it you can see, even though her face is hidden in shadow, just from the way she is standing, what is on her mind. Sex – spelt gloriously S-E-X – that is the quickest word for it. No, she's not the spirit of the woods or any wishy-washy kitschy non-sense like that but a real woman – his woman, Jane, who has taken so much joy in the lessons he has taught her and can express so much more than any professional model – not that Ian Lennox can afford any extravagance of that kind.

Mystery Four – his favourite. However, he is a realist. It is also almost the only quick asset he possesses at the moment and since Robert McAllen, the laird over at Glengarrick, has admired the canvas so much, he is going to sell it to him for twenty pounds. And because he and his wife are people of discernment – broadminded people who can appreciate a painting as well as a bargain, they will buy it. Robert McAllen has said as much, given his word. Twenty pounds. After Lennox has paid off his slate at the pub and set a little aside for food it will leave him with enough to buy forty bottles of wine. He can visualise them in rows of ten. Four intact rows like guardsmen on parade. Beautiful. Enough to keep him painting at the top of his bent for a fortnight – plenty of time to get back into the swing of things. Painting, drinking and living, with warm Jane in bed beside him.

This is not the only hurdle facing him though. There is another to jump over. Today is Saturday – which means inevitably that tomorrow is Sunday, and in Scotland on a Sunday in this year of grace 1957 you cannot buy a bottle of alcoholic liquor, not of any kind, certainly not the heavy red wine that he loves. They won't even serve you a drink if you aren't a bone fide traveller willing to sign the book to that effect. Bona

fide traveller? They know him in every bar and pub
from Whithorn to Moffat and he owes money in half of
them. A traveller? They'd laugh in his face. It is not the
word they would use for him. They would throw a cruder
word at him.

So he doesn't have much time to get the picture sold to
McAllen and find some Christian ready to sell him a
couple of bottles before the dawn of the Sabbath. A
Sabbath without something to drink is bleakness itself.
The chilly Lord's Day.

The wind blows in his face, flicks at his skimpy tie as
he looks up at the sky, at the raincloud moving towards
him across the sands. His eyes narrow and his pulse
races. That is what he has been looking for. That is the
effect. Has he enough time to capture it on his sketch
before the rain gets to him? To lay down a wash and dab
away the surplus water? The tide has turned but it is
still a long way out. Far away – no danger there yet.
Hurriedly he reaches down beside him for his box of
colours, his bottle of water, rocking forward on his stool
so that it sinks a little more deeply into the sand.
Putting his pencil crossways in his mouth he tries to
unscrew the cap on the bottle while holding his pencil
sketch down firmly with his elbows. It is impossible to
shift the bloody cap. His hands are cold and clumsy now.
It's stuck.

In his efforts to get it to move he lifts one elbow off the
paper. And it still won't shift. Then he will have to stand
up and really get to grips with it; there is no other way.
The wind has dropped and there is a calm for a moment.
Right, he will take a gamble on that lull lasting. Laying

the sketch at his feet he stands up and takes a fresh purchase on the cap. His knuckles whiten, the knurled metal edge of the cap burns the skin of his palm. There, has it moved a little at last? Yes, it is shifting...

Then an unexpected gust of wind catches the sheet of cartridge paper at his feet and sends it cartwheeling over the sand. Engrossed in unscrewing the bottle top, it is a second or two before he realises what has happened. By that time the sketch is lying flat on a patch of sand twenty yards away. It will be damp now, maybe spoilt. Is it worthwhile trying to retrieve it or should he cut his losses, leave it to the wind and go off to Glengarrick straight away?

He knows it is good work and good work has been harder to achieve lately. It has caught something he needs for this next canvas of his and the sketch may still be salvageable. McAllen is a civilised, sympathetic man – he will let him dry it out at Glengarrick. Somewhere in the kitchen quarters – in a scullery or the maid's pantry. It won't take long. It is the sort of small service that McAllen would enjoy rendering to a man whose art he values.

So Lennox makes his decision – marches across the sand, his heels sinking into it – leaving deep imprints which fill instantly with water. The first shower of drops from the rainstorm blows into his face, unsighting him for a moment. When he has brushed the water from his eyes the drawing is no longer where he expects it to be. He looks round, his gaze travelling slowly over the sand, and catches sight of it thirty yards further on. Determined not to be beaten by the wind he pursues it doggedly. Again it is lifted up and bowled across the sand before he reaches it. Again he follows, finding himself labouring deeper and deeper in shoes which are wet now to the uppers, the turnups of his trousers flapping heavy and cold against his ankles.

Suddenly he topples to one side, lurching over as his left leg sinks up to the knee. He puts out a hand to steady himself and finds his arm engulfed as well, the cuff of his jacket pushed up against his elbow. There is nothing solid beneath his hand or his leg. And too frightened to delve deeper he holds his breath for a moment. Instinctively he puts weight on his right leg to try to lever himself upright. There is more resistance on that side, but he mistrusts it and stops pressing down. Then fear grips him and he has to spend a moment fighting, knowing that if he panics he will be lost. He tries to remember anything he has ever heard about quicksands. That one should relax and allow oneself to float to the surface as one would in the sea. He forces himself to think rationally. The density of the mixture of sand and water beneath him must be greater than that of sea water. More buoyant. All he has to do is to lie back and let himself go limp and the quicksand will release him. It is a question of willpower. Slowly he leans back and manages after a minute or two to release his left arm from the slurry of sand and water sucking at it. He shakes his sleeve. Good. He continues to lean back gradually. Fine, all he has to do now is to allow his feet to work up towards the surface. That is the first objective. Once he has done that and got himself into a horizontal position he will have to find a way of moving towards firmer ground. He will deal with that problem when he comes to it.

He pulls himself together. 'Come on, you old soak,' he chides himself. 'Relax and make an effort to float.'

He opens his eyes and, looking upwards, sees a trio of gulls wheeling and swooping into the wind. Free. He finds the sight exhilarating: he will find space for them in his canvas. All at once they decide to swerve towards the sea. His eyes follow them to the horizon, the line where water and sky meet, and that sight reminds him that the tide has turned. It is coming in now.

The thought floods into his mind like salt water, filling every corner of it.

Chapter Two

'A cannon!' Julia exclaimed and then laughed out loud. 'Fond as I am of you, Ethelred, a cannon is not the sort of thing I expect you to be looking for.' Ramsay silently agreed – it was much too macho an item to associate with her former boss. Not his usual line of trade at all.

'Who wants a cannon? Not Mrs Blennerhasset?'

He saw another giggle boil up inside her as she recalled the lady. When she had been Ethelred's assistant in his antique shop in Brighton Mrs Blennerhasset had been the bane of her life – the archetypal time waster who asked about everything and bought nothing at all. Every day she would come into the shop seeking advice, commenting on any new item, because she knew the stock almost as well as Julia did. Whatever it was – a papier mâché tray, a rosewood writing slope, a set of silver teaspoons – Mrs Blennerhasset's mother or her aunt or her cousin would have been sure to have owned something similar – but finer, older or more elegant.

Ethelred bridled. He didn't like being put down in front of Charles Ramsay. He had to admit that Mrs B had been ridiculous. Such a tiresome person. The memory of her made a sort of bond between him and Julia.

'I daresay one of the clan would have owned one, darling,' he grinned. 'Just the thing for the castle.'

Mrs Blennerhasset had been born in a castle. In Ireland somewhere. A fact she had mentioned almost every time she entered the shop. So had Julia, if it came to that, or as near as makes no odds, but she took things like that for granted. Some people were, some weren't – born in a castle. It wasn't a particularly comfortable place to be born, anyway.

'Spit it out,' she urged. 'Who have you found who needs a cannon?'

Ethelred was unwilling to divulge. He threw a glance at Ramsay and chose to be mysterious. 'I don't want any poaching,' he said. 'And anyway my client expects discretion.'

Ramsay grinned – at the idea that he and Julia would want to steal a client from Lewis. Their concern in Chelsea was on a far grander scale than his and they dealt with far grander people – at the top end of the market, with contacts in Zurich, New York, Tokyo, all over – selling items of unimpeachable quality and provenance to clients who had large and consoling supplies of money. Ethelred's business was much cosier – among the retired middle class on the south coast, mainly; people with time on their hands and a hundred or two to spend now and then. His official business, that is – Ramsay guessed that he had other clients out of hours who didn't ask many questions, answered even fewer and dealt in cash. Ramsay never touched any-thing like that. He was irreproachable.

Julia would have said that he was a prig who looked back nostalgically to a time that had never been, when honesty had been the best policy and a gentleman's word was to be trusted. She was careful not to tell him, but she thought the Ramsay family motto, *Probitas*, was quixotic – even rather pretentious. Nevertheless her partner seemed to live by it and it hadn't done the business any serious damage so far. If and when it did she might have to reconsider her position. These days, she was better placed to do so.

'What kind of cannon?' she asked, not really expect-ing an answer, turning back to the auction catalogue and wishing now that Ethelred would stop being a bore and take himself off. They weren't going to be able to help him, and while half an hour of his rather bitchy gossip was amusing enough she and Charles had work to do, decisions to make about bids for this sale on Friday.

'I'm not sure. I think it's for some sort of a display they're organising. One of these living reality things. You know,' said Ethelred, fluttering a hand, at a loss for the right word. The ring on his little finger flashed irritably with multicoloured light. He never liked to be pinned down. It always got inconvenient later on.

'Where?'

'In the north,' he said. 'They need a cannon for it. This man does.' Obviously he wasn't going to be any more forthcoming; perhaps it was a boyfriend and he didn't want the name bandied about to the other friends Julia

11

knew. He still showed no sign of wanting to leave, though. He began to wander round, glanced at the carved figure of a blackamoor supporting a lampstand, asked how much and winced when she told him. Wincing when he was told a price, any price, was a reflex with him. As good as. He was a master of the short sharp intake of breath – as though the figure spoken was so way out that it caused him a jab of pain. That too.

'It's heavily restored,' he accused.

'Find me one that isn't,' Ramsay came back sharply. 'We've nothing to hide.'

Pleased that he'd flicked his mark on Ramsay, drawn a tiny blob of blood, Lewis pretended that he hadn't. Adopting his we're-all-in-this-business-together voice he asked, 'Who did you get to do the work?' Julia told him.

'He's expensive. Still, he's done it quite well. And he's gone easy on the gold leaf. Quite tasteful really,' he conceded with another little wave of his fingers.

'Ethelred,' Julia told him, 'it's time you went. Charles and I are going away for a few days' well-earned break and we've lots of things to do before we go. Lots and lots of things.' With him you had to lay it on the line. The tact her mother had taught her was a waste of energy with Ethelred.

He knew when he wasn't wanted which was why he wasn't leaving. He picked up a silver table ornament in the form of a Chinese junk and was trying to preserve his dignity by studying the intricate rigging with a frown. An envious little frown; Ramsay could see.

'Going away. How intriguing. Where?' He put it back carefully with a sense of loss. When he had had his shop in the Arcade he had been able to sell nice things like that, to knowledgeable Americans with wallets full of credit cards. Not these days, though. Not in Brighton. There wasn't the dosh.

'Scotland,' Charles said as Julia settled down beside him and opened the glossy Crowthers catalogue, a notebook on her knee. 'A place called Glengarrick. In Galloway.'

If he hadn't been looking at a full colour illustration of a William IV maple wood centre table circa 1835 he would have noticed Lewis's well-manicured hand clutching the silver model halt in midair for a moment before putting it back.

'Bonny Gallowa'. Rabbie Burns and all that. Are you really?' he said absently – not really interested.

'Yes,' said Julia, 'to visit a friend of mine. Caroline McAllen. I knew her at school. She wasn't McAllen then – it's her married name.'

This information seemed to pass straight over Ethelred's head. 'That'll be nice,' he said, preoccupied, still lingering. Although he was trying hard to sound indifferent there was a flicker of interest in his next question. As if he actually wanted to know the answer. 'How long for?'

'Three weeks. It's time we had a break.'

Ramsay tacitly agreed. Getting the showroom up and running had been a struggle. Watching cashflow like a hawk, keeping the stock moving. Latterly, though, their fortunes had been improving because of a coup he had made at a run-of-the-mill country house sale in Warwickshire.

The first owner of the house, an envoy to the King of Naples during the Napoleonic Wars, had brought back several items of superbly decorated porcelain from the royal factory there.

At first Ramsay had ignored the porcelain, assuming that the specialist dealers from London would have it in their sights. Then he noticed that none of them seemed to be at the sale – the auctioneer hadn't been sure enough of the porcelain to describe it positively in his advertisement in *Antiques Weekly*. It was of undeniable quality, which was what had prompted Ramsay to bid for it. An oval tray painted with a view of the coast with fishing boats and Vesuvius smoking in the background, a pair of candlesticks each supported on the shoulders of three crouching satyrs, and several plates decorated with classical scenes. Although the local ring of china specialists could see its virtues, they were less confident of finding a market for it than he was. How many serious collectors of porcelain manufactured for the Bourbons of Naples were there in the UK? Not many and they didn't know who they were. Nor did Ramsay but he knew there would be a lot more in Italy, and he had good contacts there.

So he had bought the porcelain, every item, in the kind of silence which falls on any sale when something serious is being sold and real money is on the table. It soon became clear that the ring had been too cautious in fixing its bidding limits – hadn't set them high enough. Time and again the dealer bidding on its behalf had

14

shaken his head in chagrin as he noted Ramsay's successful bids in his catalogue, powerless at that stage to get himself more latitude from the others. Rings were too rigid, in Ramsay's view – not that he ever took part in that kind of illegal activity. He didn't need to, and he wasn't comfortable with it.

It wasn't just that he knew that it would make him feel grubby afterwards, as if he needed a bath; nor that he wanted to be able to look his father, Ernest Ramsay, in the eye, whenever he visited him at Bressemer, their home in East Anglia. It was the great dusty scroll in his father's study, the family tree hanging next to his father's desk with its rows of names going back for centuries, the whole thing surmounted by the Ramsay arms and the motto *Probitas* – meaning honesty, integrity, straight dealing. When Julia teased Ramsay about it he would agree that one or two members of the family hadn't lived up to it. However, he wasn't going to be one of them.

He had enjoyed making a clean sweep of the Bourbon porcelain. Julia had played her part. Had charmed some promising names out of Guido Falcone, his contact in Milan, and before long they had sold most of it to a wealthy recluse near Ravenna for more than twice what it had cost. The coup and one or two other breaks had made the profits look much healthier.

It was a pity, he felt, that this good patch of business hadn't come earlier.

Julia had organised their holiday – found a locum to take care of the shop. Ramsay should have felt pleased that they could afford to take some time off, and he didn't. He shouldn't have agreed to that deal with her mother. The woman had been given a lot of good cards, though. Morally, every way, and time had been on her side.

The door clanked shut behind Lewis and the big lift began its slow ascent. They said they were going to upgrade the Northern Line, he thought. It was about time. This station seemed much as it had been when he had first come to London in his teens. So many years ago – it hurt him to remember how many, when he'd had a stall in the Portobello Road, selling bits and pieces – prints, Sheffield plate. He'd made his way but the thought made him uncomfortable around the nape of his neck and he shivered. He wasn't easy in his mind and he knew precisely why. You could lose yourself here in London; in Galloway it wasn't so easy. Plenty of space but not enough people. And he hadn't realised they were going there for so long, for three whole weeks. Of course he could avoid the area himself but that wasn't the problem. Margaret Johnson was still up there and, worse, she had her husband with her. The irreproachable Ramsay might run into one of them and that was not at all desirable. At least there was time to warn them. Would it do any good? Would they take any notice?

Julia had told him something of her partner's deep involvement with the Johnson woman and, so he understood, it was Margaret and not Ramsay who had ended the relationship a year or two back, to return to her husband. No doubt that big win of Johnson's had been something to do with it, Julia had speculated, gossiping next to him in the Palatine when they were well into their second bottle of Macon Villages. She had not been drunk – no, never drunk – merely ready to confide. Shaking her elegant head, she hadn't been able to say how big a win it had been but certainly Johnson had been riding high at the time.

Now, though, brilliant craftsman though he was, Johnson was facing a recession financially – that was the reason why he had decided to stay on in Galloway after the job he'd been working on there had been completed, and Ethelred could well imagine that his wife, finding that she hadn't won a prize after all, was suffering from itchy feet again. If he just went to her and said, 'Look, Ramsay and Julia are going to be here on a visit in two days' time, steer clear of them, will you, and keep that man of yours out of their way?' it might have quite the opposite effect on her. For all he knew she might be just aching for a chance to cuddle up to Ramsay again, and if she did it would be a disaster from several points of view. Firstly it would put Julia's nose out of joint and Julia was a long time friend of his, even if Ramsay wasn't. There was another reason too, a reason that affected him much more closely and so carried a lot more weight with him since, fond as he was of Julia, he was much fonder of himself. What was to be done then? Hope for the best. He couldn't see what else he could do.

He clanged up the iron stairs into the market past the legend OPEN AS USUAL painted high up on the side of the railway bridge. They sold everything here, not just antiques and bric-à-brac as in Portobello Road in the old days, but clothes, batik shawls, candles, craft objects (he shuddered), cassettes, prints, books, you name it. Not much doing yet at nine o'clock on a Sunday morning – a ratio of about nine sellers to every buyer, he guessed – the crowds would come later; as yet only one or two well-dressed tourists breathing in the atmosphere, summoning up the confidence to spend a little money in a minute, while the regulars drank instant coffee out of polystyrene cups and chewed on cold ham rolls for their breakfast.

One or two of them looked dopey, inward-looking – drugs, Lewis thought. They had never been a problem for him – he came from a different time. He knew the signs, though, because of a boy he'd loved once – the love of his life, so it looked at the time. Teddy had reminded him of himself at that age – vulnerable, on the make – and he'd been destroyed by hard drugs. In the end he'd stolen even from Ethelred, his only friend. Things disappearing from the shop – nice things, and cash missing too. Ethelred had pretended not to notice at first. Then he'd seen something that belonged to him at a viewing, a little Moigniez bronze of a stallion, and that was altogether too much. There'd been a showdown. Tears flooding down his cheeks, Teddy had confessed – he was spending hundreds of pounds a day, stealing whatever he could and selling it. Feeling like death, as though the house had collapsed on him, Ethelred had doled out fifty pounds to him, counting the ten-pound notes into his palm in slow motion, and sent him packing. It was a question of his own survival – not the boy's; he was lost already. Completely changed, empty of feeling for anybody but himself, nothing to be done for him. He was as good as drowned. Ethelred had absorbed long ago the lesson Teddy had never learnt: how ruthless you had to be to survive – ruthless with others, above all with yourself. For a week or two after he'd shown him the door he'd felt quite dreadful. Then the wound had healed, more or less. Ever since then he'd walked by himself, though. You took your pleasures where you could and trusted nobody. Not a warm kind of a life but you knew where you were.

He came to a halt in front of a couple of big black hunks in dreadlocks who were unpacking their stock of CDs and slotting them in handfuls into place on their sales tray, labelled in sections – RAP, RAGGA, HIP HOP, REGGAE.

'Tell me,' he asked the larger one – he looked interesting – 'is Anny about?'

'Sure,' the man said negligently, neither friendly nor otherwise, jerking his head towards the indoor market. Ethelred made for the shabby swing doors and pushed through them magisterially. The sign said ANNY'S ANTIQUES. Another hand had added 'And Decorative', in a different script below. Ethelred wrinkled his nose. Neither description covered the fake, very fake, Preiss ivory and bronze figures in that glass case over there, so fake that they were an insult – like this bunch of canes with scrimshaw handles made of opaque plastic. Next to that was another vitrine containing a forlorn enamel clock. Fin de siècle. The card said tersely, 'French clock. Signed. £475.' What an optimist she was, Anny. She would never learn.

She was pointing out to a woman in a purple anorak the merits of what might have been a silver-plated sugar caster – it gleamed guiltily in the light from the powerful lamp at her shoulder. It was the purple anorak who saw him first, clearly bent on business, and hesitantly withdrew. Not best pleased at the interruption of her spiel, Anny turned mountainously towards him, her top storey swathed in several layers of knitwear, the colours swearing at each other. Hoarsely from deep inside it came the words, 'Hi, Lewis,' as she lit a cigarette. She proffered the packet.

'I don't,' said Ethelred. 'Haven't done for years, my dear. Not since you first had that clock.'

'Oh, that,' she barked and grinned fiercely, screwing up her eyes against the smoke, waiting for him to state his business.

'A cannon. I need a cannon.'

Cannon. He needed a cannon! Yeah. But she and Ethelred had a history of useful deals so she didn't venture a ribaldry – just kept the grin fixed firmly to her face.

'Any ideas, Anny? Can O'Leary do it?' O'Leary was her partner, who went out and found the heavy goods – anything ornamental made of metal – the larger the better as long as it was moveable: cast iron furniture, urns, embossed lead tanks, lead figures, gates. That was his field of expertise – going out into the highways and byways and procuring them. A large shadowy man who only came to the market when he had to. Ethelred had only seen him twice.

Anny's eyes ruminated through the cigarette smoke.

20

She fiddled with her gunmetal lighter, turning it over and over. Then her fingers stopped. 'Nothing down the yard, I know that. What sort?'

As he shrugged Ethelred felt put down. He hadn't thought to ask his client for a detailed specification. Militaria weren't his line so he hadn't ... the image in his mind had been sketchy – something with a muzzle and wheels and a carriage to keep them apart, that was all. He knew that pieces of ordnance didn't grow on trees, though. To find anything, but anything like that which didn't cost a king's ransom, would be a triumph. He wasn't fussy. Just a cannon. Something oriental, perhaps.

'A replica would do as long as it works – can fire a blank shot,' he amended.

'Give me a ring Tuesday,' Anny said.

Chapter Three

Lennox believes he may have sunk as much as six inches although he has made every effort not to disturb the sand, to give it any excuse to suck him down. He gathers his strength together and shouts out – as loud as he can. Better to call out less often and put everything into it when he does. He thinks he can just hear his yell echo from the hills behind, and that gives his morale a small flip upwards. He licks his lips, finding them salty, and for the first time for half an hour he thinks how good a drink would taste, a glass of that red wine. Mental abstinence for a full thirty minutes. Things must be serious. He can't raise a smile at the wry thought. There is silence except for the wind sighing – no sound from the sea. It is chilly.

He is facing out towards the flat sands of the firth and the hills of Cumbria beyond. He tries to twist round a little – gently – holding his breath again. So far so good. He feels himself slip an inch, half an inch, it doesn't matter. It tells him what he wants to know. Correction – what he doesn't want to know. He is only half supported, suspended in a mixture of sand and water which becomes more fluid when it is disturbed. There is a technical term for it, which he knows – it is on the tip of his tongue. No, he can't remember. It will come to him if he doesn't actively search his mind for it.

He bellows hard again and a gust of wind tears the sound out of his mouth. Ahead of him the damp sketch which he was pursuing when he got himself into this mess is suddenly lifted by the wind and flops back on to the wet sand, taunting him. Thixotropic, that was the word he was looking for, the property of becoming less viscous...

'Lennox. Is it you?'

A rough voice to the rear. He tries to turn his head to see who it is, shifting himself with care as though to avoid paining his back.

'Are you in trouble?'

He can't discern the tone of the voice but he knows who it belongs to – David Forsyth of Carrucate Farm. Not the man he would choose to come to his aid but he doesn't have the luxury of choice.

'Quicksand,' Lennox answers.

'Aye. You shouldn't have come out here. You saw the sign?' The voice has an edge of contempt in it for an incomer who can't look after himself. Lennox knows there is more to it than that.

'What sign?' he asks. What bloody sign? He'd seen none. His muscles are beginning to ache now with the effort of holding himself upright.

Silence behind him – then, 'Can't you move at all, man?'

24

'I daren't. I sink if I do. I sink.'

'You shouldn't have come out here. I'll get a rope.'

'You'll need more than a rope.'

Don't delay. Get on with it then, Lennox tells himself. He doesn't say that, though, not out loud, because he has a fraction of pride left. He isn't going to exhibit more fear to Forsyth than he needs to. He says again, 'More than just a rope.'

'Aye. I know that.' Not another word from Forsyth. No words of hope or encouragement, nothing. Is he still there or has he gone already? The man who is up to his waist in the quicksand, facing out towards the open firth, listens intently but can't hear anything. In any case David Forsyth's retreating footsteps would have made no sound on the sand.

It is more than a year since the farmer's brother was killed – Tam the para, taker of the Queen's shilling, who used to swank about the village in his red beret with Jane on his arm when he was home on leave. Openhanded in the lounge bar at night, which was how Lennox had come to meet her first – he was never loth to accept a drink when one was going. She was intrigued by him, a stranger from the city with something exotic about him – an artist who deserved the title, not just one of the local amateurs but a man with a skill – not well known but mentioned here and there in books. She persuaded Tam to buy her one of his watercolours, a sketch of a barn owl, which he let go for six pounds since he liked the look of her. He could've got more – birds always sold well. Her lover pulled a face because even though he got extra allowances, being a para, it was nearly a week's pay. Then he shamed Lennox into buying the next round and took ten shillings off him at the pool table, Jane sitting, sipping her drink, watching them jousting over the faded green baize. Not at all displeased.

A couple of months later Tam was dead. One of the few casualties of the Suez adventure – hacked down in a back street by an Egyptian teenager, who was given the chop himself in short order. 'We don't mess about with Gyppos,' his sergeant told them back at Carrucate after the interment. A life for a life. It made everyone feel a bit better as they consumed their farewell tea and shortbread in the dining room.

So Tam was wasted in a war that soon nobody was much wanting to mention and his girlfriend came to Lennox. Not his fault. He didn't set up the war – it was the politicians who were guilty of that. However, shrewd as he is, David Forsyth is not a rational man nor a forgiving one. Only thirty but tough as a buzzard. Just how keen is he going to be to rescue him? That is the question in Lennox's mind as the rain lashes at his face. It is getting colder and he can see a thin line of silver far off, near the horizon where the edge of the broad sands meets the sky. The tide.

Much the best idea to start early, at five, well before any real traffic, Charles Ramsay felt as he filtered the big blue car on to the motorway, cheerful at the prospect of a change of scene, a break, with no commitment at the end of his journey except to enjoy himself.

No buying, no selling, no negotiating. No telephone calls from Julia's mother. He settled down in the middle lane and Julia switched off the radio. Nothing worth listening to, he agreed – it was too early.

'It's time you briefed me about our hosts. Come on – tell all. Caroline was a friend of yours at school, I know that. And you've kept up with her. What else?'

'What else can I tell you?' She laid affectionate fingers on the back of his hand, lying relaxed on the driving wheel. A touch to remind him of the warmth they had shared last night. He gave her a grateful smile for the memory of it.

'Close friends, were you?'

'When she wasn't being close friends with somebody else and I wasn't feeling jealous.'

'Jealous? Why? You're not the jealous kind. You don't need to be.' She pressed his hand again in acceptance of the compliment and withdrew hers – slim and capable – to her lap.

'You are nice, Charles darling. That was when I was an ungainly adolescent, though, and she was incredibly beautiful – all the way through. You know how it is at puberty – you are clumsy, you bulge, you worry about puppy fat, greasy hair, your teeth, acne – all those things. She didn't have to bother about any of that. Just sailed through looking a dream all the time. Masses of fair hair, brown eyes, a sylph. Mummy said she was a secret anorexic but she wasn't – she used to have seconds of everything, even elephant's ears, and that rhubarb stodge they used to give us for supper every other Sunday.' Julia's eyes clouded at the memory.

'She had this incredible metabolism. Seemed to burn up calories twice as fast as the rest of us. Looked like an angel – she wasn't, of course.'

'I don't suppose you were either.'

His partner became judicious.

'I knew where to draw the line. Cal didn't always.'

'So she was a handful, was she? Out at night, smoking, that sort of thing?' he prompted idly.

'Sure,' she agreed, 'things like that. And other things more...' Wicked? Naughty? Unforgivable? She didn't elaborate. 'Mummy said she should have been sacked but Caroline seemed to have an in with Miss Vincent. She had this candid way of admitting whatever it was she had done – never tried to cover up. She never did anything to hurt any of the other girls either – she was never vicious or bitchy. Besides, I reckon the old bat fancied her.'

'Caroline didn't reciprocate?'

'No, no, nothing of that kind. Caroline was healthily normal. Too healthily, that was the problem – though I admit she was under a lot of pressure even in term time. Blokes were queuing up three deep. Mummy didn't like her coming to stay but couldn't ban her since I used to go to them. Said she was promiscuous. Rubbish – she didn't understand the setup. Then Caroline married James McAllen and all at once the sun shone out of her. You know Mummy.'

He nodded, not risking a comment. He knew Julia as well – she had very clear ideas on who was and who was not allowed to criticise her relatives. She was on the first list and everybody else on the second.

'So,' he said, 'James McAllen, a Scottish landowner. In a big way?'

'Yes, seriously rich. Several farms, one in hand I think, and miles of timber. And the family's been there since not long after the Flood.'

That was very much the sort of thing that counted with her mother, he thought, and found himself regretting, ungratefully, the money that lady had put into their Chelsea business. It created dissension and if not suspicion in the camp at least uneasiness. With luck they might be able to buy the old girl out in a year or two's time. Meanwhile he could handle it. He went back to his interrogation. 'How old is he?'

'About ten years older than her.'

'Any children?'

'Not as yet.'

'Any problem there?'

'Mind your own business,' she said evenly as though it had been a personal question directed at her. 'Who do you think you are, darling – her Relate counsellor? You haven't even met her yet.'

So there was a problem, which would be even more of a problem to someone like James McAllen, he guessed. Not a child of any sort, let alone a boy. No business of his though. She was right about that. Still, it reminded Ramsay of a conversation with his father, Ernest Ramsay, on his last visit to Bressemer to check up on him. The old man had suddenly seemed preoccupied with Julia – had kept coming back to her – her family, who they were; saying he ought to see more of Julia's mother, take her out to lunch when he was next in

London. Routinely they had taken their coffee into the study after the evening meal and his father had sat in his accustomed chair next to that family tree.

It was obvious wasn't it? His father was yearning to see some new names in crisp black lettering at the foot of it. The name of a wife to accompany Charles's own – Julia perhaps? That was what he had been fishing for. Most important of all, though, he wanted to see the name of a child, of children. Since Rodney's death on duty in Northern Ireland there was nobody else to provide an heir. So when was Charles going to make a decision about Julia? That was the unspoken question. A question which Charles was in no hurry to answer and certainly not out of deference to his father. Anyway, these days marriage was beginning to look old fashioned. Some of his friends hadn't bothered, at least until they had started a family, and he wasn't sure that he was going to – ever.

'Glengarrick. The house. What's that like?' he asked, turning to Julia. Head on one side, she was fast asleep. She was never at her best this early.

It gave him a few moments to think.

A series of container lorries thundered down on him in the opposite lane, one after the other, threatening him before they passed him by.

The problem? It was easily stated. A few months earlier his father, a Name at Lloyd's, had been in trouble with a large call he couldn't meet. Bressemer had been at risk. Charles had been forced to leave the partnership to Julia to run for weeks while he sorted out his father's problem. A good saleswoman, she was no expert when it came to buying stock and he had told her not to – it was his responsibility. They were close to their limit at the bank at the time and they had plenty downstairs in the stockroom. When he had been forced to go to Sweden to follow up the Lloyd's thing she had got it into her head that he wasn't coming back, that she was in sole charge. Then she had gone bananas, negotiated a short-term extension to the partnership overdraft and spent a lot of money buying the kind of furniture she liked but didn't understand. Some Dutch marquetry but most of it from France – nineteenth-century copies of stuff by the pre-Revolution ébénistes. Lewis had encouraged her. Told her she had an eye for it and made her feel like an expert. She had thought so herself – even thought that the French items were right. They were nothing of the kind. Flashy, sub-antique – the kind of newly polished reproductions smelling of shellac that they sold in those dubious shops on the edge of the flea markets in Paris. Not the standard he and Julia were supposed to be aiming for, nothing they could sell to their clientele, and selling was her department. Much as he loved her, she ought to have seen that.

When he'd gone downstairs to look round the stock-room on his second day back from Stockholm he had seen it instantly. Rubbish that shouldn't have been there at all. It was the first time ever he had shouted at her, really shouted – to his regret. Given time he could have traded out of the problem, sold the stuff off gradually on the Continent where there was a market, but they hadn't got time because the bank wouldn't extend the temporary facility she had fixed up. She had made a mess of that as well. It turned out that the local manager, a bit dazzled by Julia's 'I am a beautiful young aristocrat' act, had granted it without proper authority. Head office had rapped his knuckles so he wasn't playing cosy games any more when Charles went to see him. The partnership was given five days to raise the money. Ninety-six thousand pounds. She'd been crazy. He had made some money on the side in Stockholm but nothing like that amount.

What were his options? Dissolve the partnership and start again? And waste all the effort they'd put into setting up the shop, thinking up the concept, designing it? Having just weathered one crisis, he couldn't deal with another so soon after, nor with the aggression that would be unleashed. Besides, it was a sound business, or had been until Julia had been left in charge. He had to be fair to her – he couldn't blame her entirely. He had been at fault for running off to Sweden and not keeping in touch properly – he admitted it. She had felt that he had abandoned her and it had upset her, clouded her judgement. It was the only way that he could account for the aberration.

She was contrite, too, but that didn't solve the problem. Where were they going to get ninety-six thousand from? Julia had been distraught. Rang her mother. Don't worry, dear, she said. I'll sell all those gilt-edged in the family fund – the short-dated have been looking fragile anyway. Invest the proceeds in the partnership. She was a shrewd old person and her lawyer had tied it up tight. He had been tough, much tougher than Charles had expected – as though he was taking advantage of the difficulties Julia had landed them in. There was no time to argue. While they held off the bank she got her stockbroker to advance her seventy thousand on account.

So now Julia and her mother owned getting on for sixty per cent of the partnership. As Charles examined the chain of events yet again he couldn't see what he could have done differently. He'd confided in Dirk van der Meuwe, the monosyllabic Dutchman who headed the Crowthers office in Amsterdam. Dirk hadn't said much but it was plain that he thought Charles had been outmanoeuvred. What else could he have done, though? Julia wasn't subtle enough to have devised a scheme as complex as that. It was more likely that that wily mother of hers had seen the opportunity as the cockup had developed and had seized it with both hands. That was how people like her had survived since the Middle Ages. Grab your chances when you see them and don't be too nice about it.

No, Julia was innocent. Of course she was. He glanced across at her – sleeping, palms of her hands together as a cushion underneath her head – vulnerable and appealing. Of course she had faults – who hadn't? But she had virtues too and he loved her – not a fashionable word to use, but it was the apt one. Sometimes he was – what was the right word for that feeling? Enraptured. He found himself dazzled, holding his breath as she turned her head and looked at him, or walked with elegance ahead of him along the Embankment in the evening after the working day was over. She loved him too, there was no doubt about that. It was simply that when they were working she behaved differently towards him – and he was the same. They were matter-of-fact with each other – sometimes offhand or even harsh when there was a difficult decision to be made in a hurry and they couldn't agree. At night, though, it was different. She was warm and lovable – able to be loved ...

Anyway the change in the partnership was an accomplished fact now and he wasn't going to let it poison this holiday. When it was over, though, and they were back in harness, some fresh thought would have to be given to it.

He put his foot down. He wanted to be the other side of Manchester before nine.

Chapter Four

Lennox has been dozing on and off for an hour, it must be an hour. The dial of his watch is obscured with a smear of wet sand and he can't be fagged to make the effort to clean the glass. One good thing about the drowsiness – it has anaesthetised the ache in the small of his back from the effort of holding his body as still as possible. His breathing is slow, laboured.

When is Forsyth going to return? Does he know that Jane is pregnant? He's less likely to come back if he does. If he decides not to he won't lose anything. On this deserted coast it's unlikely anyone will have seen him and Lennox together. All he has to do if he is so minded is to go home for his tea and wait for high tide, sit reading the newspaper beside the kitchen range, scanning the latest prices for ewes. An easy revenge – one that wouldn't disturb his conscience much. If that's what he wants; if he can't stomach the idea of his brother's girl lying in the arms of a drunken artist or standing naked while he paints her. Anxiety settles heavily on Lennox at the thought – as unwelcome as the next raincloud moving in his direction from the west. He shuts his eyes again and tries to remember

Jane's warmth beside him in the iron bed. He can almost do it even though his loins are numb, compressed under the waterlogged folds of his trousers, and his privates useless; he can imagine them, shrunken and bloodless. Although he does his best to avoid reaching a verdict it is forced on him as the rain hits his face making him turn his head aside and take the force of it on his ear, his cheek. The verdict? Forsyth is not coming back.

His eyes close again. When he wakes up, a shallow saucer-shaped depression of sand has formed round his body and filled with water which is lapping now at the bottom of his ribcage, his sodden jacket.

Behind him there is a voice, 'Lennox! Here!'

He hears something splash behind him.

'Grab the rope, man, will you!'

Still half asleep he forces himself to react. Makes himself raise his chin from his chest and turns his head slowly as far as it will go.

Behind him Forsyth is standing yards away. It makes sense. It'll do nobody any good if he gets trapped as well. Taking a cautious step forward he picks up the rope and sends a violent wave skimming through it trying to bring it nearer to the head and shoulders of the man held in the sand, who opens his mouth to shout. He fails at first, coughs, clearing his lungs and throat, hawking up the phlegm and spitting it away from the wind. At the second attempt he manages to call, impatiently, 'I told you. I can't turn round.'

Far away at the horizon the gleaming ribbon of the tide is broader now.

Forsyth pulls in the rope hand over hand and busies himself with making a rough noose in it, hurrying over the knot.

'I called the laird on the telephone,' he calls out meanwhile. Turning to the big house for guidance in an emergency is what his father would have done, and his grandfather, whatever everyday differences they had with their landlord. 'He's coming.'

Over the dunes comes the boy from Carrucate leading a horse, an old Clydesdale, plodding steadily, harness jingling, its broad hooves thudding through the loose sand, past the pile of Lennox's belongings where he left them out of harm's way.

Forsyth has his noose ready. Inching cautiously forward, crouching with his gaze fixed on Lennox, he tries to fling it over his head and shoulders as though it were a quoit. He misses – and misses again. Angry at his failure he roars over his shoulder at the boy, 'Bring him here now, will you! Bring him here!'

Still only halfway from the dunes the boy, tall with a red face, trousers flapping at his ankles, can't get the horse to move any faster. It advances at its own pace, deliberate.

Forsyth has the noose in his hand again, the loops of rope in his left. Reluctantly he comes two, three, four paces nearer, testing each step with his boot, ramming the heel into the sand in front of him each time before moving forward again.

Deliberately he waits until the wind has dropped. Then tries again, sending the noose skimming through the air ... and succeeds. He has dropped it over the shoulders of Lennox who cries out. It is almost a cry of pain.

Forsyth watches until the man's arms move. 'Have you got it?' he shouts.

'I have.'

'A good grip?'

'Aye.' Lennox's voice sounds thin.

Forsyth begins paying out the rope, laying it on the sand. When he gets to the end of it he beckons to the boy to bring the horse over and back it up to it. The boy is wearing a military rain cape in drab green – part of Tam's army kit which he left behind – the rain streaming off its lower edges. He struggles to coax the horse forward, pulling on the leading rein. It won't stir. He curses and yanks at the rein. The animal jerks its head away and stands firm on huge hooves, then as soon as the pressure on the rein is relaxed it takes two backward steps, swerving to its right – its head rearing.

Looking behind him Forsyth sees what has happened. 'Bring him here you fool.'

'He's feared of the shore. He's not been out before,' the boy answers, and as he shrugs with frustration, arms wide, he loses his hold on the rein and allows the horse to retreat towards the security of the dunes. The boy gallumphs after him and Forsyth pursues them both, cursing. Together they manage to turn the horse, bringing its head towards the tide, and lead it slowly yard by yard towards the end of the rope. When it gets within twenty yards it halts and will not budge, its hooves sinking into a patch of ribbed grey silt where water is lying. Together the men drag at it but can't compete with its weight. The more they shout the more the horse resists them. They get it to advance another couple of yards and all at once it is up to its fetlocks, splashing, panicking, flailing with its hooves and scattering them on either side.

There is the roar of an engine behind them. An open truck is bumping over the dunes, planks, bales of straw bouncing in the back. It bounces down on to the shore and comes to a halt. A spare man gets out and doubles towards Forsyth.

'What the hell's that old horse doing here? Get it out of the way. Right out. Do you hear me?'

Now he has reached the farmer, his tenant at Carrucate, he looks him up and down. 'You've got a tractor. Why didn't you bring it down here, man?'

The tractor is new, expensive – it cost seven hundred pounds, a fortune, the price of a farm cottage. Supposing his shiny new machine got bogged down, caught in the tide? Forsyth wasn't going to risk it, that is why it isn't there. He stares steadily at Robert McAllen, the laird, and doesn't utter a word. He doesn't have to. He has rights, pays his rent, and he knows the other man has no time to waste on argument.

McAllen issues his orders. 'Move that horse and get it tethered. Then give me a hand with these bales. We need to lay them round him to get some support.'

The whole village knows why Forsyth has it in for Lennox and the laird is well aware of the story. He and his wife deplore the artist's lifestyle but have always managed to avoid noticing it. They have supported him in small ways – entertaining him, bringing his name into the conversation at friends' dinner tables to try to give him a boost – making the occasional tactful purchase when he has approached them, obliquely, signalling his need of money. And that isn't because they like him. It is because Jean McAllen, although an indifferent painter herself, has an eye for an artist with something to say and is sure that Lennox will one day emerge as a significant Scottish artist. She is convinced of his importance and so is her husband. It is McAllen's particular reason for wanting to save the man's life. A personal reason.

They have pushed bales of straw as close to the trapped man as they can, each bale wallowing halfway into the sand, and have laid planks across to one of them as a crude kind of walkway. McAllen lopes forward along it with agility, keeping his balance – and kneels as close to Lennox as he dares, speaking quietly, privately.

'Ian, I've come to get you out. Time's pressing but there's no crisis if we take it steadily.'

Most of Lennox's body is held firmly in the sand by now, his shoulders set square to the invading tide.

'What's the time?' he asks skewing his head towards the man behind him.

McAllen glances at his watch. 'Twenty past,' he lies without hesitation. It is much nearer high tide than that. 'I'm going to test the noose,' he adds. 'Let me know if it's secure.'

He retreats, back to the sodden end of the rope, picks it up and heaves at it experimentally. 'Is that tight? Can you feel it?'

'Don't feel anything. Nothing,' Lennox calls back. 'Can't feel.' His head is lolling to one side.

McAllen gestures to the two others to join him. He shows the boy how to fold the rope around his shoulders as though he was the anchorman in a tug-of-war team. Stamping their heels into the sand they take the strain.

Then McAllen shouts, 'Heave.' And again, 'Heave.' Their feet can't grip the sand and as soon as they begin to pull in earnest their boots slip. The boy at the back falls on his rear and sits splay legged while Forsyth gives him a tongue-lashing. Then they break up one of the straw bales and stamp chunks of it into the surface. They try again. This time the rope tautens. Lennox cries out, 'I'm shifting.' Keeping the tension up, taking half a step backwards and forcing their feet down again on the crude pads of straw they pull on the rope, their hands burning with the strain. At that moment it slackens and they topple again – the noose has failed. McAllen drags the rope back, refashions the noose, tests it and goes forward along the walkway for the second time, inching forward to get as close to Lennox as he can. He manages to get it over the man's head. Clumsily, too slowly, Lennox manages to push it down, get his arms through it, but in doing so he has paid a price. He has sunk further into the sand. McAllen hurries back along the walkway, then sprints past the others until he reaches the open truck. Getting in, leaving the door hanging open, he flicks the gear lever into reverse and begins to back it towards the rope. Leaning half out of the cab, eyes urgent, intent, he

41

shouts to Forsyth. 'Hitch it to the tow bar, will you.' Forsyth does so, looping it twice, trebling the knot this time.

Meanwhile McAllen runs up towards Lennox. 'We can't get you out by hand,' he yells. 'I'm going to try and use the vehicle. I'll take it slowly. Give me a shout if you've got a problem.'

Running back to the cab he swings into the driving seat, changes into first gear and revs the engine. The rear wheels begin to dig themselves into the sand sending gobbets of it spraying backwards. Forsyth and the boy have already pulled up armfuls of wet straw from the ground and are beginning to pack it against the wheels. Then they scramble round to the front of the truck and push, with McAllen reversing, in order to shift it on to the platform they have created. More straw is put down ahead of the wheels. McAllen guns the engine again and the wheels spin, catch, spin again. Smoke pours from the straw. Then a flame spurts upward, against the tyres. Cursing, they kick at it to scatter the burning straw and get it away from the fuel tank.

They take one of the planks remaining in the back of the truck and poke it under the chassis, ramming it hard up against the rear tyres and holding it there to give them some purchase. The tyres slip and knock the plank away, then sink deeper and deeper into the sand. They can see the patch of tide growing broader every minute. So can Lennox.

McAllen makes his way towards the walkway again, more reluctantly this time. This isn't a job he can shirk. Who else is there to do it? Not the boy certainly and it would be the ultimate cruelty to allow Forsyth to take it on – he might even enjoy it. McAllen is dubious about him. He can't accuse him directly of being half-hearted in bringing help but he knows very well that this sullen tenant of his has been dragging his feet. Unconsciously? Never. Forsyth isn't a fool. So why wasn't the rope long enough? Why didn't he bring his tractor down? Its broad rear wheels would have coped easily with the treacherous sand. And why didn't he get more men down here? His wife could have phoned round and got them out.

McAllen knows that he isn't without blame himself. As soon as he arrived he should have made an appreciation of the situation, as he was taught to do in the army. Make an appreciation. Next a plan. Then give your orders. He should have taken Forsyth back to Carrucate straightaway and made him bring the tractor down here instead of wasting time on that abortive attempt to pull the man out by hand. Then he should have...

He puts the thought out of his mind and prepares himself for the difficult job he has to do next. He has reached the walkway and is taking it carefully. All of a sudden the plank beneath him subsides as its supporting bale of straw shifts. He doesn't risk going any further along it. Instead he goes down on one knee, then onto his belly to get his centre of gravity as low as possible.

'Ian.'

There is no reply from Lennox. Only his head and

the top of his shoulders are protruding now from the surface of the sand.

'Ian? Can you hear me?'

'Yes I can.' The voice is unforgiving.

There is a sudden flurry of wind and McAllen waits for it to subside because he has to ensure that Lennox hears him clearly. It is important that he gets the message immediately, the first time the words are spoken. The *coup de grâce* must be administered cleanly – there must be no need for a second stroke.

'Ian. I'm afraid we aren't going to be able to get you out.'

The trapped man says nothing. McAllen adds, 'The bloody vehicle is stuck. There's nothing we can do.'

'I know that.' The reply is scornful.

The gleaming edge of the tide, reflecting the sky, is still a long way off but they both know how fast it is moving.

'Mr McAllen.' Lennox had never got used to calling Robert McAllen by his first name. 'Cover my head with something, for God's sake. I don't want to see the tide.'

A jacket? McAllen isn't wearing one. What else is there? Rolling over on his side he begins to tear at the loose straw from one of the bales. 'It'll have to be straw. It's all there is.'

McAllen can feel the plank shifting again underneath him. He has gathered a heap of straw together and holds his arms round it to stop it blowing away. When the wind has died down he pushes it briskly over Lennox's head, reaching out as far as he dares. He gathers the residue together and pushes that out as well. Then he retreats, bringing his weight back to the centre of the plank. Although it is better balanced now he can feel danger underneath him. Nevertheless he has to make the offer.

'Look, I will stay here. As long as I can, if you want me to.'

His words make McAllen feel self-conscious – he doesn't like heroics. That doesn't matter. It's the last thing the other man cares about at this moment, his head hidden under that incongruous pile of wet straw. The wind carries a stray wisp of it away. It is starting to get dark.

Lennox speaks, his voice surprisingly strong this time. 'You'd do better to take yourself off. Away with you, man.'

That's all he says. McAllen has failed him. Why should he give him any thanks, any comfort, having none himself?

McAllen raises his head and calls out, 'Goodbye then.'

He feels that something else needs to be said. Although he is an agnostic, and has been ever since his service in Korea, he adds, 'May God keep you.'

It makes him feel a little better as he crawls backwards to safety. He has no idea what the words may have done for Lennox, if anything. No idea if he has heard them even.

He walks across to the two other men standing well back, watching the straw-covered hump which is all now that marks the trapped man's position.

McAllen catches a greedy look in the boy's eye and says sharply, 'We've lost him. There's nothing more to be done.' He begins to march up the shore. The others follow him, stubbornly reluctant to move despite the incoming tide. They pass his truck, its back wheels deeply embedded. There is no hope of rescuing that either today. McAllen has no idea how much damage will be done by several hours' immersion in salt water. If the worst comes to the worst he can well afford to replace the vehicle. But he vows to himself that tomorrow he is going to force Forsyth to come down onto the shore with his precious tractor and drag the truck back. He is entitled to that service at least.

The wind hammering in their ears, they reach the loose sand of the dunes at last, and the place where Lennox's belongings are lying – the artist's umbrella, his big portfolio, the tin lunchbox with the empty wine bottle beside it. The boy goes off to untether the horse.

Forsyth stops and turns to look out at the heap of straw in the distance.

'Come along,' McAllen orders. 'We'd better be going.' The last thing he wants to do is to stand there and watch the tide pass over Lennox's head as though he was Judge Jeffries at Wapping, observing with curiosity the pirates he had lately condemned, writhing in their chains below high-water mark – seeking an extra minute of life.

'I'm staying,' Forsyth grunts, adding self-righteously, 'somebody has to watch over the poor wee man.' The boy has led the horse over and looks from one face to the other, hoping that he too will be allowed to stay and witness the end. McAllen's body clenches with anger – he masters it and doesn't reply. There is nothing he can do to prevent them from indulging themselves.

He looks down at Lennox's belongings piled together next to his deserted bicycle. With a grin, Forsyth puts out a boot and gently kicks the empty bottle. It rolls over once or twice and comes to a stop. The action conveys his opinion of the artist more precisely than any words he would be capable of stringing together. If Lennox hadn't been on the bottle he wouldn't be out there now, up to his neck, waiting for the tide to drown him in a few minutes' time. He has got what he deserved. Forsyth follows this up with a piece of hypocrisy. Solicitously he picks up the big umbrella tied with baler twine, and places it next to the portfolio. Then closes up the lunchbox and puts that with it too. He is not going to allow the laird to accuse him of being unfeeling.

'I'll see to all this. I'll take it all up to Carrucate later.' That service he can do as well, since McAllen has no transport now, and has no intention of returning to Carrucate with the other two. Nothing would persuade him to go back there to listen to Forsyth recounting the tragedy to his wife. He can imagine her – larger than usual because she's six months pregnant – a pious woman tut-tutting over each detail, trying to keep her pleasure hidden. The thought crystallises inside McAllen all his dislike for the pair of them – his callous tenant and the sly wife. There is no way that he can evict them from Carrucate; their rent is paid regularly and their tenure guaranteed by law.

However, McAllen comes from a farsighted family. That is how they have held on to the Glengarrick estate and made it prosper for so long. He thinks thirty years ahead. If that woman is carrying a son he will make sure that he doesn't take over the tenancy. There will be no Forsyths at Carrucate Farm when his own son inherits. He will spare him that.

McAllen turns to them and says curtly, 'I will leave you to your Schadenfreude.' Of course they have no idea what the word means. It is merely an unpleasant-sounding German word to them, though the contempt in his voice is obvious enough.

Forsyth looks him up and down and says, challenging him, 'You'll be away then? I thought he used to visit up at Glengarrick.' Visiting the big house. Not a privilege which has ever been accorded to any member of the Forsyth family.

Out there the tide is approaching Lennox's head now, moving steadily forward, not seriously ruffled by the wind and rain, getting closer. McAllen asks himself how it must feel, the cold water rising against the face. First the mouth, then the nose, filling the nostrils, splashing against the eyes. How long does it take to drown? He shivers.

'Damn you, Forsyth. Go to hell,' he snaps and straight-away regrets the outburst. It sounded foolish and has put him at a disadvantage. Forsyth makes things worse by ignoring it. In any case he is intent on what is happening out on the shore. The termination of a life.

McAllen pushes past him and steps out for the road.

If it takes him twenty years, he will get the bloody Forsyths out of that farm.

Chapter Five

'... And that,' concluded James McAllen, 'is why, when David Forsyth died, the tenancy of Carrucate was not allowed to go to his son Malcolm. Robert McAllen, my father, made certain of that.' Head tilted to one side he inspected the well-roasted joint of Galloway beef awaiting his attention on the sideboard, and began to carve it unhurriedly. He laid a generous slice on the first plate in front of him. 'One could say as well, I suppose, that it's why Malcolm Forsyth went down to England to seek his fortune, like so many Scots before him.'

'And found it there,' the man next to him chimed in – a man with jet black hair and a pale skin, echoing the black and white of his dinner clothes. Having accepted the role of honorary waiter he was standing beside his host ready to pick up the plate and carry it to one of the guests. 'Who's this for?' he demanded.

'Julia.'

It was delivered to her sitting at her host's end of the ample Georgian dining table. Charles Ramsay looked along its polished surface and approved of it. Once it had been installed in this dining room – what was the age of the house? In the early 1850s – it had never left it, he'd been told. So it had been in the same room for getting on for a century and a half. The chairs too, amply proportioned. Some would say they were too late, too heavy; others might scorn them as just 'brown furniture', the day-to-day fodder of the saleroom, but he respected them for what they were: honest, unpretentious and exactly right for this room. A solid, high-ceilinged dining room in the baronial-style house which a Scottish laird had had built the year before the Crimean War. It wasn't used often, he guessed, and he warmed to the McAllens because they had gone to the trouble of opening it up and laying on proper dinner to welcome their visitors. They had obviously put some thought into how it should be done. Halfway down the table they had set a silver centrepiece, not a stag at bay or a highlander in full gear as one might have expected, but three statuesque women facing outwards, dressed in Greek robes. About the same date as the table. Good, and right.

He had volunteered to act as wine waiter. In his hand he had the first bottle of Pauillac. After taking a precautionary sniff at the cork – no problem there – he began pouring. First he filled Caroline McAllen's glass, attentively. As she rewarded him with a smile he had to agree that she was ravishing; quite as beautiful as Julia had led him to expect. He had come here as an arrant disbeliever; he knew his partner was prone to exaggerate the attributes of her friends – their intelligence, their achievements, their wealth. That in particular. She was good at selling – it was where she made her main contribution to the business – and that touch of hype was all part of her saleswoman's equipment, her box of tools if you like. She could create around herself an aura of success which would reassure the client, make him or her more ready to open a cheque book and part with thousands of pounds for a pair of library globes or a tiny George II tripod table.

She didn't have to bother to impress him though, not him – not the whole time – and he wished she wouldn't.

So he'd been sceptical. Nobody could come up to her glowing description of their hostess, he thought – and he'd been wrong. There she was, slim and dazzling, just as advertised. The genuine article.

Maybe Julia had changed her ways, because she'd probably been right on another count too – James McAllen's financial status. She'd described him as seriously rich, an expression which she used much too often, so of course he'd taken that with a pinch of salt too. And he was wrong again – as far as he could see.

Operating in the upper reaches of the antique business he had developed a nose for the circumstances of the people he dealt with, particularly when there was something they might want to sell. It was not so much the state of the houses they lived in – a sort of shabby splendour was often the order of the day with landed people who turned out to be very comfortably off – nor the size or age of the cars they drove; that merely showed how ready they were to spend money, their own or their bank's. It was the condition of their estates that told him what was what: the state of their farm buildings – whether the roofs, gates and fences were in good order; how well the woodlands had been looked after. Those were the clues.

And from everything he'd seen since their arrival that morning it looked as if Julia hadn't exaggerated. The place was a model – well cared for in the areas that mattered, the areas that generated income. He knew from his experience with Bressemer what that meant in terms of resources and effort. Glengarrick was properly managed; it had a well-organised feel about it. He very much doubted if McAllen would be seeking his professional advice, not on the selling side at least. Unless he was a member at Lloyd's or something crazy like that. Charles felt a chill between his shoulder blades at the memory of his father's recent escape from that particular mantrap.

Having done the rounds with the bottle he sat down in his place next to Caroline and received a plate of beef from the man with black hair. Over pre-dinner drinks in the sitting room he had introduced himself as Cameron Rae – an incomer from Edinburgh, he had said with a deprecatory grin. A lawyer, apparently.

'So. A man caught in a quicksand drowning by degrees. Not a comfortable situation to be in at all,' Charles Ramsay commented, 'and the dreadful irony is that he died far too early. Poor old Lennox. If only he could have stayed alive to benefit from what his works fetch nowadays. Pictures aren't my line and I can't remember exactly how much *Mystery Three* made at Crowthers last year, but I do know it was a pile of money.'

James McAllen had brought his own plate to the table and sat down. A big sanguine man; ten years older than his wife, Julia had said, and he looked at least that.

Reaching for the gravy boat he nodded vigorously. Perhaps he did keep in touch with the art market.

But to Ramsay's surprise it was Rae who came up with the actual figure. He didn't look like a connoisseur of modern Scottish painting at all.

'A hundred and eighty-five thousand pounds. Comfortably above the estimate. Wasn't that right, Arabella?' he asked the woman opposite.

'Yes,' she agreed and sipped her wine with discrimination. It was the only word she had spoken, but she showed no sign of shyness. She was alert, amused – and quite ready to let others do the talking. Arabella Knight she was called. Thirtyish and attractive in a rather capable way. Apparently she was knowledgeable too – an artistic person.

'That's a very respectable number in today's market,' Ramsay said. 'He's really taken off.' He glanced towards McAllen. 'Do you have anything of his?'

'My mother and father bought a few of his drawings and some of the watercolours of birds—'

Caroline interrupted briskly, 'Tell him the story.' She spoke as though this was something she knew her husband would insist on getting off his chest – a story which had to be told, a ritual which had to be gone through; so he might as well do it now. The others looked at him expectantly. McAllen laid down his knife and fork.

'It doesn't count as a story really and I can't vouch for all of it. It was like this. Just before the accident my parents had been expecting Lennox to bring them one of his pictures, to sell to them. Everything was handled very tactfully. It was to meet some unexpected expenses – that was the way he put it – mostly drink of course, everybody knew that, but he had his dignity to preserve. Mind you he had every right to – he was a bloody good artist.

'Now, although my father had agreed to buy the painting he didn't know when Lennox was going to turn up with it. The man was pretty erratic – very much a law unto himself.'

'Which one of the series was it?' Ramsay asked.

'*Mystery Four*. My parents took a great fancy to it and Lennox himself claimed that it was by far the best of them – the one that had most of him in it. His particular contribution.

'Afterwards, my father became convinced that the artist had been on his way to Glengarrick to deliver the painting on the day he was drowned. That, cycling along the coast road with it, he'd suddenly seen something he wanted to sketch and had stopped off to catch it while there was still enough light. There was no particular hurry. He knew he was welcome at Glengarrick at any time. My parents were a laid-back couple.'

'Did your father have any evidence?' Charles asked.

'Yes. Some. Scaup Bay, the place where Lennox was caught in the quicksand, is on the way from the village to Glengarrick. More to the point, though, the picture couldn't be found anywhere in his rooms when his landlady cleared them out after his death. And she said she'd seen it there the night before. It stuck in her memory because she didn't care for the painting. Not a bit. Mrs Cameron was a strait-laced old girl, very much a pillar of the kirk, and the picture was...'

'Raunchy?' Julia suggested.

McAllen grimaced when he heard the word. Raunchy? His parents hadn't been people like that – not at all. 'Joyous, I think would be a better term,' he said, 'or uninhibited perhaps. A celebration of life. Its theme was certainly outside Mrs Cameron's experience.'

'Sensual, would you say?'

'Yes, OK, sensual.' McAllen allowed that word.

'So what had happened to it do you suppose?'

A voice on his right broke in, speaking excitedly. The words seemed to tumble against each other. It was Caroline. 'Robert always maintained that it must have been among Lennox's bits and pieces lying on the shore; his painting gear and so on that David Forsyth took back to Carrucate. But my father-in-law wasn't a reliable witness where they were concerned because he couldn't stand them. We don't think much of them either, as a matter of fact.'

'He must have asked him if he'd seen it,' Julia said.

'Yes. Forsyth said he hadn't of course – pretended not to understand and my father couldn't press him because he'd no hard evidence that Lennox had had it with him. He was sure he had, though, and that Forsyth kept the painting not because he thought it was worth anything but simply out of spite.'

'It's worth a lot of money now.'

'Yes, but very little then,' McAllen pointed out, 'and besides we don't know how good it was. I've only my father's word for it. The whole thing happened just before I was born. That was another reason why he was so angry with Forsyth. My mother was eight months pregnant and he wanted to give it to her as a present to celebrate my arrival.'

'And he had agreed to buy it?'

'Yes he had. No money had changed hands, though,' his host admitted.

'Then he couldn't prove any right to it?'

Ramsay raised an eyebrow. Rae's tone was too abrupt for the occasion. He sounded like one of those solicitors who specialise in petty crime with a steady flow of legal aid cases, trying to browbeat a shop assistant into admitting that she hadn't seen his client actually putting the blouse into her shopping bag. Perhaps he was indeed that kind of lawyer. Nothing wrong with that, of course, except that this was a dinner party, not a sheriff court in Glasgow on a Monday morning. Time to intervene, Ramsay decided.

'I think morally speaking he had a claim on it,' he put in mildly, trying to draw Rae's fire on to himself and lower the temperature a little.

'But certainly not legally,' Rae returned.

'However unfamiliar some of us are with the law of contract in Scotland we don't need a solicitor of your undoubted ability to tell us that.' James McAllen smiled. The put-down was firm but friendly. McAllen could look after himself. Charles Ramsay liked his style.

'Has anybody any idea where it fetched up in the end?' he prompted. It was intriguing: the idea of such an important painting going missing, neglected, given away perhaps. A canvas worth a couple of hundred thousand hung over a cottage mantelpiece by somebody who was totally ignorant of its value. Ramsay amended the thought – in this part of the world he guessed it wouldn't be on display. More likely to be hidden away decorously in a cupboard.

'David Forsyth probably put it on the fire. He loathed Lennox and could never have admitted that any painting of his was worth keeping. I daresay he just got rid of it. My father and I had a quick look through the house and buildings at Carrucate after his widow quit the place but there was no sign of it. That was twenty years later.'

'Still, it might be worth searching the place more thoroughly,' Ramsay said.

'Can't be done,' James McAllen answered. He didn't elaborate and his tone of voice said that he didn't want to talk about it any more.

Helping herself to horseradish sauce Julia cheerfully ignored the signal. 'Why not?'

'Because we don't own Carrucate now,' Caroline replied in a level voice. Her husband shot a concerned look at her and then seemed to decide that the only thing to do was to get the explanation over with.

'I sold it to Malcolm Forsyth. My father's refusal to let him take over the tenancy was the best thing that ever happened to him. He took a degree at the local agricultural college and went down to East Anglia as a farm manager – arable farming on a big scale, completely different from what we have here. They don't buy the land, they rent it – huge acreages – and put their capital instead into the enormous machines they need to work it. It's not traditional farming at all. It's on an industrial scale. Simply to exploit the CAP subsidies.'

Ramsay nodded. It was familiar territory for him. His father had hated the trend, having to watch centuries-old hedgerows being uprooted to create a dull prairie empty of trees, people, life. He had fought for years, was still fighting, to prevent Bressemer going the same way.

James went on, 'Then he decided to launch out on his own. It was risky. He borrowed heavily and it paid off. He did very well indeed, apparently. After ten years down there he was in a position to retire, so last year he came back here to Galloway.'

'And bought the farm where his father had been tenant,' Rae elaborated. Yes they had gathered that. He seemed very good at telling you what you already knew, Ramsay thought. He could easily imagine how Malcolm Forsyth must have enjoyed returning in triumph, as the new owner, to the farmhouse which he and his mother had been forced to leave.

'He's restored it, put in an extra bathroom, a sauna, built a huge conservatory at the back with humidity control and I don't know what. Huge great jungly plants, succulent and sinister, that look as though they're going to eat you. As big as this,' Caroline said, suddenly pushing back her chair and jumping up to demonstrate how high they were. The sleeve of her sea-green velvet dress caught the heavy silver-handled knife on her plate and knocked it to the floor.

'That's very high,' agreed Ramsay, ever polite, stooping to retrieve it. Her sudden eruption of enthusiasm didn't seem to faze the others. McAllen smiled indulgently, Rae glanced at her and then away again. Only Julia scolded, 'Come on, Cal. Do behave.'

Caroline resumed her seat and looked pained before riposting, 'I'd really rather you didn't call me Cal. School was a long time ago and I've grown out of it. Caroline's the name now, if you don't mind.'

'Of course not,' Julia soothed her. 'You should have said. No more fifth form nicknames now that you're a grown-up lady. It will be nothing but Caroline from now on, I promise.'

Charles Ramsay looked around and found some more oil to pour on troubled waters. 'You were telling us about Malcolm Forsyth's house.'

'Yes,' said Caroline, 'so I was. He's spent a fortune on it. A completely, but completely, fitted kitchen. Yards of units. I wish we could.' She glanced at her husband and then away again as though she knew she shouldn't have said that.

Julia asked, 'What about the decoration?'

'Oh, expensive and ordinary. You know what farmers are. Malcolm Forsyth is no different from the rest.'

Rae made a sympathetic grimace and turned to Ramsay. 'You'll gather that the man hasn't made himself terribly welcome here.'

'Not since he put Jeannie out of her cottage,' McAllen said.

Caroline put in indignantly, 'She'd lived there for forty years and two generations of her family before her, and he gave her a month's notice. Said he wanted it for his keeper. His keeper! He makes himself ridiculous. He

61

hasn't got a real shoot – just a few acres of woodland down by the burn. Poor Jeannie. We had to find somewhere for her.'

Arabella Knight put in a word on Forsyth's behalf. 'You may be too hard on him. I do know that her cottage was a pigsty when she left it – really nasty – and it took a week to clear it out.'

Rae said, 'Jeannie's very old. She couldn't cope with it, that was all.' Then he added, as if to tease her, 'You're just defending Forsyth because he's putting up the money for your pageant.'

Arabella said sharply, 'I don't like him any more than you do, but we can't afford to look a gift horse in the mouth. I do wish you'd keep quiet about the guarantee. He particularly asked that it shouldn't be publicised, and he can get awkward. You know that.'

'Sure,' Rae returned, 'he wants to remain anonymous but not too much so. As long as somehow the right people know about it. Let me tell you this – it's going to take a lot more than that guarantee for Malcolm Forsyth to be accepted locally, and I've heard one or two whispers in the Sheriff Court that make me think it's never going to happen. Of course the man did collect a lot of loot in his foray south of the border, but he has a bad name in the town. There are other theories about how he made his money.' At that point his lawyer's discretion silenced him and awkwardly, as though he had gone further than he should, he concentrated again on the plate of food in front of him.

A pageant? Ramsay thought. It sounded old fashioned. Pageants belonged to the early years of the century –

before that, even. There was a pageant, wasn't there, in Trollope somewhere?

Arabella seemed more interested in the pageant than in Forsyth's reputation. 'At least we're trying to do something. And to scoff at it is really bloody of you. It's a spectacle of sound and light.'

'How grand,' said Rae. 'Is that what you're going to call it on the programme?' He was ignored.

'Spectacle?' Ramsay enquired.

'Yes. At Steilbow Castle. I'm producing and directing it. Everybody's going to be in it. James is appearing as a Scottish Captain in the siege sequence – the castle was taken by the English after the Scots were routed at Solway Moss. The man Forsyth is Bonny Prince Charlie...'

'He gets the plum part because he's guaranteeing the costs. Spectacles of sound and light come very dear,' Rae put in.

Caroline enthused, 'And I am going to be Devorgilla, who founded Sweetheart Abbey. A very rich and lucky lady until her husband died.' Her eyes suddenly sought her husband's as though seeking assurance that the words hadn't brought bad luck on him. He grinned and she gave a half giggle as if relieved of guilt.

'I wanted to play Mary Queen of Scots,' she went on, 'but somebody else was given the part. Such a romantic lady.'

'Which reminds me,' her husband said to Ramsay, 'that I have something to show you while you are here. Something that should interest you quite a bit...'

Julia cut across him, talking to Caroline. 'When is all this going to happen?'

'On Friday week.'

'Good, then we'll be able to come and support you. I'd love to see you as Devorgilla. It all sounds most diverting.'

'Don't buy your tickets in advance,' advised Rae. 'It'll be rained off. Nobody but the wildest optimist would put on an open-air production in Galloway.'

'We've been through the records for a hundred and fifty years and chosen the month with the least rainfall,' retorted Arabella. 'It's all been gone into. Besides, the audience will be under cover, thanks to our sponsor.' She didn't sound very grateful, Charles noticed, although it was obvious that Forsyth had been generous. He must be more than anxious to ingratiate himself locally.

At that moment the lights went out – all of them – and they found themselves in pitch darkness.

'A power cut,' announced James McAllen. 'Matches, somebody.' Nobody had any because nobody smoked.

'I'll get the candles,' he said. Ramsay could hear the door open.

'It's time they gave us a new power line, an underground one. It's probably Forsyth's bull at Carrucate that's responsible again. It knocked down a pole during the final of the World Cup last year and blacked out the village, which didn't add to his popularity at all,' Caroline complained loudly in the dark. It didn't sound as though she wanted to rush to assist her husband.

Ramsay sensed that she was still sitting next to him.

He could smell her perfume, a light flowery scent. Then there was a muffled tapping, repeated regularly. It took him a moment or two to work out what it was – her fingers drumming on the table with impatience.

A woman's voice said, 'I've got a torch in the car. I'll go and get it.' It was Arabella. She must have knocked into Rae on her way out because she apologised as she passed him.

Out of the gloom Julia asked him, 'Do you have to put up with much of this?'

'It used to be a lot worse,' Rae replied, 'and sometimes it can't be helped. A tree comes down in a high wind and brings the line down with it.'

The soft drumming on the table beside Ramsay had stopped. Then he had a surprise. He felt a warm hand – it had to be Caroline's – touch the side of his face. He could feel the rings on her fingers as the back of her hand brushed his cheek. Next it changed direction and her palm stroked downwards against his hair, lightly against his ear, in a gentle caress. Then the hand withdrew and she waited for him to make the next move. Madam was bored with a country life, or her husband, he supposed, and looking for some fire to play with. He wasn't going to offer any. He sat, immobile, making no response at all. Then he decided to stand up and make for the door. 'I'll lend them a hand with the lights.' But when he reached it he saw James already returning along the passage with a branched candle-stick of silver flaring in each fist. He was carrying them high above his head, the candle flames almost blowing out because of his haste. Triumphantly he set them down on the table, on either side of the imposing centrepiece, and stood back. 'There.'

Caroline called across to Julia, 'He's a good go-getter, you know.'

James looked benignly at her. 'Go-getter?'

'Getter of illumination, of course,' Caroline answered without hesitation. 'So quickly, and such beautiful illumination too, my love.' When Charles saw Julia smile knowingly he knew that something else had been intended. What had Caroline really meant – that her husband was merely a gofer, a fetcher and carrier who was useless for anything else? What private code were they using, she and Caroline? What were they up to? Julia gazed dreamily at the flames and said, 'It's a cliché, but candlelight makes me feel romantic. Don't you find that, Cal?'

'Not Cal. I told you before,' Caroline replied and started a giggle.

'They're back in the Upper Fifth. Both of them,' James observed, seeming to have noticed nothing, as Ramsay picked up a bottle and went his rounds with the wine again, wondering why the wife of his host ran a risk like that with someone she had only just met – the risk of a minor rebuff, or a larger humiliation, perhaps, if she had struck unlucky. It wasn't normal behaviour – even for a bored young wife.

It was past midnight and a shower was beating against the window of the bedroom they'd been allocated. Julia was sitting at the dressing table, a bunch of tissues in her hand, wiping off her makeup with slow, efficient strokes, cleansing her pores, revitalising the skin. Ramsay was already in bed, watching her.

'If I had been the laird of this estate,' he mused, half to himself, 'I don't think I would have sold that farm to Forsyth. James McAllen was wrong to do it.'

'Why?'

'It smells of disloyalty.'

'Disloyalty. Goodness. To whom?'

'To his father. Robert McAllen. He wouldn't have wanted it.'

'It's nothing to make a thing of. Robert's dead – he can't complain. Anyway, James may have had a more stormy relationship with his father than you have with yours. Perhaps he just wasn't into being fathered.'

'I don't get that feeling,' Ramsay objected.

'Then maybe they just had to sell at that moment. I don't know.'

'But they didn't have to sell to him. To Malcolm Forsyth. There's plenty of money up here looking for farms, Irishmen selling their farms in the Republic and coming over here – a big demand. They would have had no problem in finding someone else to sell to. So why him? It doesn't ring true. It's obvious that they don't like him.'

'People change. Besides, maybe he made them a colossal offer which they simply couldn't bring themselves to turn down. If he wanted to buy the place really badly.'

From what he'd been told of Forsyth he sounded much more hardheaded than that. And James McAllen, was that the way he operated? He doubted if the extra money would have been so important to him. Surely he could afford to pick and choose and would have done so. Why? Because his family pride wouldn't let him accept Forsyth's offer. Because the Forsyths had been anathema to his father and once they were back at Carrucate, owned the place, they might be there for ever.

Perhaps, though, he'd had no option but to sell the farm because he'd used it as security for a loan and he'd been forced to by his bank. But that didn't wash. He had plenty of other assets – hundreds of acres of mature woodland, which meant he had lots of room for financial manoeuvre. It didn't add up.

Caroline's behaviour too had indeed been odd – abnormal, tinged with mania. That didn't sound too extreme. He wondered if she had always been like that, but it wasn't something he intended to mention to Julia, even though his own reaction to her had been exemplary. What a smug guy you are, Ramsay, he thought, and grinned to himself.

He felt the bed bounce and there was his barefoot partner sitting beside him looking delicious. She put out a hand and laid it on his forehead.

'Penny for your thoughts, old mole,' she said.

'Nothing in there,' he replied. 'Not worth a halfpenny, even.'

'Worried?' she asked. The question was unexpected – she was perceptive.

'Absolutely not. A bit uneasy, maybe.'

'You were thinking about Caroline, weren't you?' It wasn't a reproach. He nodded.

'As I said, she's always been something of a handful,'

she mused, then leaned across him, perfumed by Guerlain, to turn out the light.

'Anyway I have other thoughts on my mind,' she said. 'Why don't you tune in to me?'

That was a much better idea.

Chapter Six

Ethelred had reached a decision. He'd gone back down to Brighton but things were still very slow down there, and sitting hour after hour in the shop, wondering what was going on in Scotland, made him edgy. It wasn't so bad when a client came in and he could put the charm on or have a natter but there weren't many about at the moment. Clients. They'd all migrated to Marbella or the Dordogne or wherever the wrinklies went in the winter and he wondered sometimes whether his move to Brighton had been wise. He hoped the shop wasn't becoming boring for the ones who had to stay behind. Even Mrs Blennerhasset had only been in once in ten whole days, havering over that teacaddy with the boxwood stringing – truthfully not boxwood but slivers of a slender hardwood section at 25p a foot from the DIY down the road; a neat, cheap job, he'd done it himself. A razor blade, sandpaper, a little bit of instant glue, a smidgeon of ... he hadn't lost his flair for inexpensive restoration. It was a long way from his days in the Arcade, he thought with a pang; still, what the eye doesn't see the heart doesn't grieve over. Mrs Blennerhasset's eye certainly hadn't seen ... not that she ever seemed to be the grieving kind. Besides, she owed him a purchase now and then in exchange for all the free entertainment his shop had given her ... and his cheerful conversation as well.

What the eye doesn't see ... that hit the nail on the head, indeed it did. Very true. Charles Ramsay's eyes had to be prevented from seeing the Johnsons. It was vital, he saw that clearly now, even if it meant running a risk. Prig Ramsay might be, but he had never been a fool, and he would be suspicious immediately if he ran into those two, which was all too possible as long as they stayed up there in Dumfries licking their wounds. He couldn't leave it to chance. He had to warn them, and impress on both of them the full extent of what was at stake. Johnson wasn't the problem, she was. He had to convince her that whatever she thought she wanted she ought to play ball. Get right away from there for the time being and put off any designs she might have on Ramsay to a later date. And after all, he reminded himself hopefully, he didn't actually *know* she had any, did he?

A phone call wouldn't be any good. It didn't give you enough scope to set out your stall. He'd have to go up to Galloway himself – oh lack-a-day and dammit. There was no other choice, though.

Margaret Johnson was a loose cannon. You didn't know which way she was going to slide. Cannon. That was the other point. Procuring that piece of artillery was the only deal of any substance which he had on hand at the moment. He'd been given no time at all to find the bombard, demi-culverin or whatever it was they wanted, and if he made a mistake he'd be landed with it because Anny's terms were money up front and no refunds. At least a trip to Scotland would mean he could check up on the specification at first hand. And there might be other trade to be done up there – you never knew. He had a car now, a middle-aged Japanese estate, and it had to earn its keep in the business. He would drive.

The woman who answered the door wasn't Margaret Johnson. There was a child behind her who was staring at him – insolently, Ethelred thought. He couldn't guess what gender it was. He didn't care either.

'Up the way,' its mother said. 'OK?' Her voice was loud, defying him to assert otherwise.

'Upstairs, you mean?' Ethelred queried smoothly. 'You mean the upper flat?'

'Aye, mister.' Her body was tense as though the forty seconds of her time she had given him so far was already more than she could spare.

'He's awfy daft,' the child observed, as though to ingratiate itself with her.

'Who're yew shouting your mouth off?' the mother yelled, bundling the child back into the corridor and slamming her door. A door faced with off-white hardboard strewn with fingermarks – closed and barred against an incomer with an English accent.

Ethelred mounted the stairs and rang the bell of the flat above.

There was a kind of music in Margaret Johnson's voice when she spoke his name. 'Mr Lewis! Do come in.'

Oh, that was better – that was soothing. To be with a civilised person. She was an attractive woman, her casque of fair hair shining even in the dimness at the top of the stairs. A faded scarf of Chinese silk knotted at her neck gave a touch of elegance to the loose blue jumper, the casual slacks. Neutral as he was towards women in general, of course, he could understand why she had appealed to Ramsay, why Julia might fear her as a competitor, however airily she pretended to dismiss the threat.

'Ian is out at the moment,' she said. 'Will I do?' She watched him with candid eyes, standing in the rented living room with a looped pile carpet and cheap stretch covers which must have bothered her every time she entered it. That crisply carved walnut side chair in the corner, though, must belong to her. Tasty, he thought. For a moment he wondered whether to, whether she might be ready to sell it – after all, they needed money. No, this wasn't the moment for huckstering.

He gave her the case he had prepared in his head while on the road from Annan – spelling out the risks and underlining them. As he spoke he wasn't sure that it sounded as convincing as he had hoped it would. She listened, without interrupting though, and when he had finished, instead of raising objections or arguing with him, she simply said, 'When Ian gets back I'll tell him what you have told me and we can discuss it.'

Her tone was non-committal. Ethelred knew that if he went back over the arguments he would weaken them. Leave them to work their way through, to penetrate – that was the best thing.

He held back for a few minutes in the hope that her husband would appear and he could force a decision out of him instead; it would save so much time. Then the pauses in the conversation grew lengthier until he felt that he couldn't keep the pretence going any longer. He had other things to do. He would come back and discuss the problem with Ian when he was at home. Of course, she agreed, without pressing him to wait. Goodbye. She closed the door behind him quietly and with finality.

When Ian Johnson arrived half an hour later she told him what Ethelred Lewis wanted them to do, over the takeaway meal he had bought plus a bottle of the supermarket's wine of the month. That new tipster on the radio was a star, he said. He'd come up with an outsider at long odds and he'd been the envy of the betting shop as he collected his winnings. How much? she asked. Not that it made any difference to her; it would soon evaporate again. Thirty-five pounds, he told her jauntily. His first win in a fortnight. It wasn't like the days when he had ridden high in Monte Carlo or the clubs in Mayfair. Still, it was a favourable omen, didn't she think?

She didn't reply. Simply stared at him with steady eyes, amazed at his capacity for self-delusion – and not only about his gambling. She spooned another helping of chicken biryani onto his plate to spare the tablecloth, then, just as carefully, some more rice. He tended to be erratic if he helped himself – after the fourth glass.

'This message from Lewis might be an augury too. What do you think?'

He was capable of reading significance into the most everyday events. He was losing touch with the real world. It was all part of that.

She looked blank. Deliberately. Forcing him to explain his flights of fancy sometimes brought him back to earth. Not this time, though.

'An unexpected visitor in the afternoon – telling us to leave. It has a psychic feel to it. I am persuaded, anyway.'

'Persuaded of what?'

'That we ought to. There is nothing more for us to do here and it's time we made a move.'

'We have to wait. You know that. Money. We've barely enough to keep us going until the . . .' She broke off, not as though she couldn't find the word she was looking for, but rather because she didn't want to speak it out loud.

'And you want to put that at risk?' he challenged her.

Very well – that she was prepared to consider as a reason.

'Where would we go?'

'London.'

She was incredulous.

'London! Come on. We can't afford London.'

'It is the time to go. I know it. We don't have to stay long. Just get away for the next three weeks, as Lewis says. We can manage three weeks. We have to. I can feel it in my bones.'

She turned merciless eyes on him. 'Your bones? You ask me to trust the feeling in your bones. How many times have you said that phrase to me? And where has it got us?' she demanded. She looked round her, at the reach-me-down furniture, the orange-juice stain in the corner of the carpet – a present from the previous tenant.

'Where has it got us? To this cesspit,' she concluded, speaking the word with a kind of academic precision that gave it extra force as a statement of fact.

'It's easy enough to be negative when we've had a run of bad luck.'

'We? You've had a run of bad luck,' she corrected. 'You don't need to include me.'

His next words were predictable. She had heard them so many times.

'You were happy enough at the Hôtel de Rome.'

There was no point in pursuing him down that well-worn cul de sac. She retorted, 'You want to go to London for one reason and one reason only. To gamble at that club of yours. The answer is no.'

He put out a hand and took hold of her wrist. Gently. It reminded her that he had never used violence towards her. That at least. And after the miscarriage too he had been kind to her even though he had known all along it wasn't his child.

'No,' she repeated.

'Look,' he admitted, switching smoothly into his confessional mode. 'We have a little more than I thought. How much will it cost for three weeks? If we go easy? How much would you say?'

'Five hundred a week at the very least,' she replied, confident that the figure was well out of reach if he wanted to gamble as well.

'Margaret,' he said, 'I'll make a bargain with you.' That was a well-worn phrase too. 'Wait a moment.'

He disappeared into the bedroom and returned a minute later with a roll of notes with an elastic band doubled round it. Since the bankruptcy he preferred to handle cash. He put the thick cylinder of money on the dining table between their used plates, the smeared cartons.

'There is two grand,' he said. 'You can count it if you like. You take charge of it and pay the expenses out of it. Put it in an account in your name in a building society. You don't even have to tell me which one. OK?'

His look said, 'What could be fairer than that?' He was a traitor, though. He had never told her he had that extra money hidden away in the bedroom. Where? Probably inside one of those black shoes with pointed toes, the pair he had disliked as soon as he had bought them but couldn't be persuaded to send to a charity shop. What other secret caches did he have?

She picked up the roll and weighed it in her hand. It was surprising how heavy it was. Real money – not transparent promises. Turning and crossing the room she put it into her shoulderbag hanging from a peg on the outer door.

'Very well,' she said, 'I agree. We go.' She kept all her reservations to herself.

It had started to rain again. Ethelred switched on his windscreen wipers as he drove down the lane towards Carrucate Farm. A clutch of sheep in the field on his right stopped plucking at an iron manger full of hay and turned their heads towards him in unison. Then one or two of the cleverer ones returned to the business in hand. He didn't see them – he was too busy peering through the windscreen for his first sight of the house and he wasn't much interested in sheep in any case.

There it was – and behind it a mass of farm buildings, mostly businesslike rather than fancy. A large sectional building clad in corrugated steel painted green dwarfed the farmhouse, which was ample, stone-built and white-washed. An attractive building he thought; vernacular. Sad about that hangar thing behind it.

He got out of the car, pulled his raincoat out of the back and put it on, suddenly conscious that it wasn't a very countrified raincoat. It made him feel conspicuous – more of an outsider from England than he needed to. He looked southwards away from the house and caught the view: the sweep of the flat sands and, halfway to the horizon, the gleaming edge of the sea. Beyond that the hills of Cumbria clothed in a blue haze. Untamed. Not at all like Brighton.

He went up to the front door carved out of some exotic hardwood – all wrong for that style of building and the knocker didn't compensate for it either – a brass knocker in the form of the head of a Greek goddess. An expensive pattern but not at all special. It didn't look as though it was meant for use so he pressed the doorbell and waited. Again he tried it and waited ... It was the sort of house where the doorbell ought to work, but perhaps...? Experimentally he lifted the head of the goddess and let it fall. Bang. And then bang, bang. No response.

He sidled up to one of the ground-floor windows and peered through it, one hand shading his forehead to cut out the reflection of daylight on the glass. It was a drawing room furnished with a pair of huge button-backed sofas in white leather. He saw a modern gilt and alabaster table with a chandelier to match. Although it was not an interior that he could have lived with, it was nevertheless a comforting sight because it looked as though this Forsyth man had plenty of money. Where was he, though?

The back door perhaps? He went round, skirting the new Victorian-style conservatory – costly tiles on the floor, he noted and smart cane furniture – and found it locked. Nobody came to answer the bell there either.

As he turned back into the farmyard it began to rain in earnest; a real downpour. He called out, 'Mr Forsyth? Are you there?' Suddenly a tethered dog ran out to the length of its chain from a kennel next to the cowshed and began barking. If Forsyth was around that should raise him.

Ethelred eyed it; black and white with a heavy curved tail. Probably a sheepdog since there were sheep every-where. What you had to do was make sure it knew you weren't afraid of it.

'It's just me,' Ethelred assured it. 'Good dog.' It stopped barking which made him feel pleased with himself. Then it turned back into its kennel and lay down, its head on its paws, quelled by the force of his personality. Or perhaps it just wanted to get out of the rain. That was more likely – the downpour was getting worse. He needed to take shelter too. The cowshed would be the easiest but it meant running the gauntlet of the dog. Whatever breed it was it didn't look wholly civilised. He glanced round him. Over there was a cow byre which must have belonged to the original farm. He would try that. Forsyth couldn't object since the rain was really pelting down by now. He pushed at the door and it wasn't locked so he went in.

Now this *was* interesting. Stacked inside was a whole lot of used furniture. The penny dropped in Ethelred's head. Forsyth had cleared it out of the house when it had been renovated and instead of sending it to a saleroom had stored it. Presumably to give himself time to choose what he wanted to keep.

Ethelred's eyes darted here and there, assessing it all. This dining-room suite. No. Mass-produced, thirties. Shipping furniture, not for him at all. Nor the brass bedsteads. Rather good – ornate. He shook his head. They wouldn't go on his roof rack and he hadn't the space in the Brighton shop anyway.

The decorated ewer and basin set was passable – blue and gold, the kind of thing some of his customers fancied. He looked inside the ewer and saw a long dark crack which didn't show on the outside and shrugged. Never mind.

This late Victorian wardrobe was too big too. Nice crystal handles, though. Out of habit he turned one of them and pulled the door open. Hm, well-fitted inside, lined in red satin, smell of mothballs. Two drawers with inset brass handles below and a shelf above to take hats. He ran his fingers along the edges, searching for damage – reached up to feel along the high moulding

which surrounded the top. What was that? His fingers
had hit something. Something loose which had shifted
as they pushed against it. So it was something light –
and flat. What the hell was it? He was intrigued. His
fingers groped again but couldn't get hold of it until it
had been pushed right across the top of the wardrobe
and was caught at the end. But he still couldn't get
sufficient purchase on it to be able to reach it down. He
found a chair and climbed up on it, knocking his head on
a beam as he did so. There, he had it at last.

A canvas. A picture. Ethelred, what a find!

He felt a shiver of anticipation. Then he thought –
don't be silly. It'll be nothing – somebody's amateur
daub or a machine-made copy. All the farmers bought
them probably.

He took it to the window to look at it. Even there the
light wasn't good; still, there was enough to see what it
was. Yes, he could see. Yes indeed! Oh this is nicely
painted. Ethelred, he thought, I love you. You are
beautiful. You – have – made – a discovery.

A view of a forest, the outlines of the trees – evergreen
trees, pines, firs, or spruce. Unable to name each sort he
was still able to recognise them, even though the artist
had refined their shape and abstracted their essence
from them. Against that background, pale and almost
transparent, was posed the nude body of a girl. Although
naked girls did nothing for him, he understood the
message well enough. It throbbed out of the painting. A
painting of quality, even an important one. He considered it again for a moment, his eyes searching the
surface for damage. Now, Galloway and particularly

Kirkcudbright had been the haunt of celebrated Scottish artists since the turn of the century. He trawled his brain for some names – Jessie M. King, Hornel. No, this was not the work of either of those. Couldn't be. Rawlston Gudgeon? He pursed his lips – that was getting closer – he shook his head. No.

It was absolutely obvious, though, that this painting was much too good for the philistine who owned it, who had left it neglected in this outhouse. Ethelred felt quite indignant at the thought. This painting should be in the hands of someone who appreciated and understood it. Somebody of discernment ought to be allowed to take charge of it, and research it, make sure it was preserved for future generations – find out what it was worth.

Somebody like himself.

The first thing was, who had painted it? He narrowed his eyes, trying to make out in the poor light the signature in the right-hand corner. There was an L there and an e. I. Lemmon? Lerner? There was a name on the tip of his tongue. Damn. He shook his head, and gave up.

He jumped – what was that? The engine of a vehicle changing into a lower gear as it pushed up the lane to the farm. He cursed himself for lingering too long. It had always been one of his vices. If he hadn't wasted time looking for a signature, the painting could have been safe in the boot of his car by now, and nobody any wiser. He peered through the window spattered with rain. He couldn't see the vehicle in the yard; it was probably at the front of the building. He heard it stop.

Now what was he going to do? He looked with

yearning at the canvas in his hands for a long moment. Too long. Quickly he returned to the wardrobe and put the painting back on top of it. Coming down from the chair he almost toppled over in his haste, but managed to regain his balance. He returned the chair to its rightful place. He had to hurry. Forsyth, if that was who it was, would see that the door of the building was open and might come to check straightaway. Ethelred had to establish his innocence. He couldn't afford to be caught snooping.

He marched out into the yard and came face to face with Malcolm Forsyth coming round the corner of the conservatory. Putting out his hand he introduced himself with an honest smile.

'Mr Forsyth? My name is Ethelred Lewis. Lewis – you remember? I was just trespassing,' he said breezily, 'taking shelter from the rain – in your furniture store.'

Forsyth ignored his hand and waited to hear more, so Ethelred went on, 'I'm here today because I wanted to have another word with you about the cannon. For this historical spectacle you are directing – it sounds most fascinating. You needed a cannon, you said. You rang me a fortnight ago.'

The other man still said nothing.

'You do remember? I'm sure you do,' Ethelred insisted brightly. 'Well, here I am. In person. I want to make sure that I have got your requirements exactly right, clear in my mind.'

Forsyth said, 'If you needed to get out of the rain you could've sat in your car.'

He turned a sour eye on it, as though it belonged to a

poacher. Not a good start, Ethelred admitted to himself. For a moment he thought he was going to be told to get out. What the hell, he could cope with verbal violence, he always bounced back from that. He'd had plenty of practice; he was the original india-rubber man. Physical violence was another matter altogether – he didn't care for that. When he had worked in the Portobello Road as a young man he had been able to look out for himself. However, he wasn't young any more and Forsyth looked perfectly capable of being . . . well . . . aggressive. It was a good thing he hadn't caught him inside that building.

'You'd better come in now that you're here,' he said, turning on his heel and leading the way to the house. He didn't have the air of a Galloway farmer: close-cropped hair, expensive leather jacket and black trousers, a thin gold chain at his neck – whatever was on the end of it was tucked into his shirt. A macho look about him. Ethelred wondered fleetingly if perhaps he was the same persuasion as himself. Truly rough trade. He wasn't going to risk making an overture, though. Well, not yet. No, no, not at all. He backed away hastily from the thought as he watched Forsyth go lithely towards the front door. Once it was open he went up the steps and into the house in a single flowing movement. The man was an athlete. Uncertainly, Ethelred followed him and was led to the drawing room.

'Wait here would you,' Forsyth told him. 'I shall be back.' Ethelred did as he was told, decided not to sit down on one of the white leather sofas, and wandered to the window and looked out at the great expanse of the Solway Firth. Grey sky faced him and the wind sighed now and again in the chimney behind the reproduction marble fireplace. As far as he could see there was nobody else in the house – no partner. Just silence. He looked down at his feet and there was a surprise. A circular rug, in sombre colours. Around its edge were pictures, like the signs of the zodiac or the symbols on a pack of tarot cards, in strong colours – crimson, yellow, dark blue: a dead child flanked by a bloodstained sword. A man hanging – by an arm and a leg. A nasty item, Ethelred thought. Of course there was a market for things of that kind – in the wilder reaches of the pop music scene, for example, but not among his clientele; his full lips puckered in a smile at the idea. It would have been woven in Persia – Tabriz or Isfahan – commissioned from Europe by somebody with a taste for cruelty – some time ago, too.

A voice said, 'That rug is not for sale.'

Forsyth's footfalls had been deadened by the thickly piled carpet. He was standing behind Ethelred who bumped into him as he straightened up from his inspection.

'Oops. Sorry ... I didn't imagine for a moment ... I was just ... interested.'

'Aleister Crowley had it made for him in Persia,' Forsyth said, pausing to allow Ethelred to register amazement.

'Did he now?' breathed Ethelred, and made it sound too tame so he added, with extra enthusiasm, 'How exciting!'

Crowley. Who the hell was Crowley? Then his memory was unlocked. A rich dilettante who had dabbled in

Magick, as he called it. The Beast – The Book of the Law – had celebrated unmentionable rites with his followers. The Black Mass and I don't know what. Oh dear, so old fashioned, but unpleasant – a man who had tainted and destroyed everybody who had come close to him. He looked at Forsyth with something like pity in his eyes.

'I found it last year at an auction in Perth. It wasn't dear.'

No, thought Ethelred, it wouldn't have been. 'An interesting find,' he murmured – and as good as unsaleable except to a specialised market which he had always avoided. SM – chains and leather – horrible, and so vulgar. It was a nasty thing, that rug, and it had put him right off its owner.

Forsyth had a book in his hand. He removed a marker and laid it open on one of the gilt and alabaster tables. Ghastly table, Ethelred thought.

'This is the kind of cannon I need.'

Ethelred inspected the photograph. Oh, that was all right. That couldn't be too difficult. Just as he had visualised – the barrel of the cannon, a carriage to put it on with a pair of big wheels with spokes. If he'd had a fax machine he could have saved himself the journey, he thought. But then he would have missed discovering that painting. The thought of it made him feel hot and cold.

'Can I take a copy of this?' he asked, picking up the book. A book about military uniforms and equipment in Tudor times. Bold pictures – a book not for the historian but for the kind of person who painted model soldiers or liked to dress up at weekends and carry a pike to mock battles; almost a child's book.

'A copy? I'll get you one.' He took the book and went off. It didn't take long. 'There. Can you find me one?'

'I guess so,' said Ethelred.

'You have to be certain. We need it by the first of June.'

'That's only ten days. It's going to be tight.'

'By the first of June,' Forsyth insisted. 'And it's got to be capable of firing a blank shot.'

'Yes, so you said,' Ethelred replied. 'The first of June? I can try. It's going to cost, you know.'

'How much?' The question was abrupt.

Ethelred considered. He didn't like Forsyth much; the man was arrogant, success had made him a bit of a bully. He had money, though. If that had been all, Ethelred would simply have indicated an outrageous figure, take it or leave it. Enough to compensate him for having to deal with this bullying person whom he didn't care for. It wasn't so simple, though. There was the painting on top of the wardrobe in the barn to take into consideration, crying out to be rescued from somebody who obviously didn't appreciate it. Unlikely to sell it, though. Still, there were other possibilities aside from outright purchase, a commission deal of some kind . . . It would be worthwhile just to keep in touch; one never knew what opportunities might arrive. He mentioned a figure large enough to cover him, which took into account the lack of time. Not over the top but solid.

'Done,' Forsyth said. 'You understand, though, it had better be here on time.'

'I understand one hundred per cent,' Ethelred assured him. 'It will be here.'

'I wouldn't be in your shoes if it isn't.' A jocular threat. 'Don't worry.'

'I never worry,' Malcolm Forsyth replied. Then he became a little more agreeable. 'I think you'd better come over to Steilbow Castle with me one day this week, and see where we're going to put it,' he decided. Ethelred wasn't keen but he didn't bother to argue. Forsyth went on, 'I want you to get me a good one because when we've finished with it for the spectacle I'm going to have it here, in front of the house.'

I guessed you might have that in mind, Ethelred thought, but he said only, 'Mmm. Out there. It'll make an impressive feature.'

There was no accounting for anyone's tastes and certainly not for those of Malcolm Forsyth.

Chapter Seven

Ian Johnson sat at the table, his breakfast roll eaten, his coffee drunk, reading the racing page. With a masterful ballpoint, he jotted a couple of names on the pad at his elbow. Margaret was clearing the table. As she took the tray to the kitchen his voice followed her. 'I'll help you with the packing when I get back.'

She didn't bother to reply. She knew he thought that by then, by the time he returned from his stint in the betting shop, she would have everything ready for their departure – suitcases in the lobby, the power switched off and the spare key handed over to a neighbour. His only task would be to carry the luggage down to the taxi. The easiest way to dodge a job was to be out of the house when it had to be done.

He tore the slip of paper off the pad, the slip with the horses' names and the odds on it, and slipped it into his wallet among his folding money. It seemed that there wasn't enough of it in there for comfort because he went into the bedroom to top it up.

Returning he made straight for the door. 'Kiss the rabbit's foot for me.' For luck. The rabbit's foot he kept on the mantelpiece – a soft dead stub of a thing which she couldn't have brought herself to put to her lips. Kiss the rabbit's foot – an empty phrase. She knew it and so did he. Of course she wouldn't, had never done so – but he needed the pretence that she had accepted this habit of his and was prepared to connive at it. 'See you later.'

Rinsing their breakfast plates in the kitchen she didn't reply. As he opened the door she heard a voice raised in the ground-floor flat and a sudden wailing from the child who lived there – cut off as he slammed the door behind him.

When the new money came – when it came – how long would it last? It was his to do what he liked with, since he had earned it. He would insist that they went abroad, somewhere warm, in the Caribbean perhaps, for a long orgasmic gambling session for him. She didn't rule out the chance that when he gambled he might win. There might be another upward climb in their volatile finances – another high. Rooms with a view out to sea, ice tinkling in the misted highball glass, attentive waiters, and she knew that if there was another upswing it would be followed just as surely by a sickening swoop downwards again. It was in the nature of the process that it never came to a stop. It gave him the everlasting roller-coaster ride through life he seemed to crave. Up and down and round and round.

When the crockery was put away and the worktop wiped she went into the bedroom as though to start packing. But she didn't look in the bottom of the wardrobe for the suitcases. Instead she held herself back and waited for a moment, standing stock still in the centre of the room. Then her gaze went slowly round it, staring first at the bed with its lime green candlewick cover, then the stained pine dressing table which didn't match the wardrobe – and under its glass top the faded patch of Regency silk embroidery which she had brought with her as a kind of reminder, to give her courage. Next, with detachment, she observed the crudely flowered curtains which barely reached the sill, examining them as though she was a scientific researcher trying to prise their inner meaning from them.

She straightened up – she had made her decision.

Before she began to search the room she went to the drawer where she kept his shirts and removed their official cache of money hidden at the bottom – the one that he acknowledged and that she had known about all along. She counted it and found that it was all there. That went into her handbag.

Then she started. First she looked for the pair of black shoes that he never wore. They were empty now. She placed them, soles upward, on the bed. That was where she would put everything that she had looked at so that she wouldn't waste time going over the same ground twice. Then she stopped. The bed itself, the carpet under the bed – they had to be investigated first. She heaved at it, arms rigid, pushing it on its castors into the corner, then rolled back the carpet to reveal the strips of underlay smelling of rubber and dust beneath it, and underneath that, old newspapers, dried out, flattened. She peeled one of the strips back – nothing. Rolled it further, tight against the bed and plucked at the newspapers. She pulled them clear and flapped them in the air. A twenty-pound note fell to the floor – a second – and another. There were more under the black underlay. Standing up, she pulled the bed up on its side, and the mattress sagged down against the wall. There would be nothing hidden there, since it was always she who had to make the bed.

Inside the mattress, perhaps? No, she had to be systematic – the floor first of all. She would take all the bedding out of the room – bedclothes, mattress, pillows. Clear it right out.

It was an interesting harvest. She collected nearly eight hundred pounds from the floor alone. An investigation of the base of the bed revealed that the hessian backing was loose in one corner. Putting a hand in there, she found a stout roll of five-pound notes tied inside one of the coiled springs.

After she had cleared the wardrobe and piled the bed high with his clothes her eyes lighted on a large carton of books wedged between the end of the wardrobe and the wall. She pulled it out and tore it open. Notes fluttered from the pages of the second book that she opened and shook. Between the pages of the books. What a naïf she had married!

When she had finished with the bedroom, put the clothes back where they belonged and repositioned the furniture, she turned her attention to the living room . . .

She had made up neat packets of notes, sorted by denominations, each one encircled by an elastic band, with a scrap of paper at the front of it noting how much was there. She put them all into a large manila envelope and placed it inside a plastic bag from the supermarket. Then she went to the kitchen cupboard, took out some of the items she had bought there a day or two earlier and put them on top. A lettuce, a packet of cornflakes and some onions in a bag – nothing heavy. It seemed to be a sufficient disguise – anyway there wasn't a serious risk of being mugged in broad daylight here in Dumfries.

When she reached the building society the boy behind the glass at the false marble counter made no comment as he made out her passbook and took charge of her offering, counting the notes. These days such people were serious, too impressed by the need to appear efficient, to be meeting the terms of the 'Society's promise to you the customer' to venture a cheeky aside. She wanted him to ask, 'Have ye won the lottery today then?' so that she could reply, 'No, not at all. I think my husband has lost it.'

He handed her the pristine book with the figure at the top of the first page, newly printed by the machine: £9360. Four clear digits that bore witness to her husband's treachery. They brought painfully back to her mind the economies he had forced on her because she had to make sure that they could survive until this new money came in – cold rooms and routine food.

She consoled herself with a short but expensive spree in the supermarket, rounding it off with a visit to the bookshop to buy a copy of a novel which had been hyped in the weekend reviews. A hardback copy – an extravagance at last. She also bought a manila envelope and sealed the passbook inside it, writing her name and address in bold capitals on the outside. Then she went down the cobbled street to her bank and handed it over to them for safekeeping.

She permitted herself as well a taxi ride back to the flat. Chatting to the driver about the rain, the flooding of the Nith again, she felt the yoke of frustration lifted from her shoulders. It was the first time in months, since her loss – she chose that term deliberately because she couldn't bring herself to think the word miscarriage, let alone speak it ... the first time since then that she had felt herself turning and beginning to swim back against the tide.

When Ian returned just after three she was still lying on the sofa, absorbed in the novel. Looking up, she saw at once from his long face that his day had been a failure.

'I need a drink.' He poured himself a glass from yesterday's bottle, his mind so taken up with his defeat in the betting shop that he seemed to have forgotten that they had been due to leave that afternoon.

Her gaze worked its way down the freshly opened page, her eyes flicking back at the end of each line. She came to the end of it and turned it over, smoothing it down with her hand to make it lie flat. Waiting.

Standing preoccupied beside the fireplace he took a quick gulp of the wine. Put the glass down on the mantelpiece and looked round. Suddenly he woke up and it struck him. 'Hey. Aren't we supposed to be leaving this afternoon? Haven't you packed?'

'No.'

'Hell and damnation. We'd better get started.' He was peevish, faced with the task after a bad day.

'We aren't going.'

'What do you mean? Why not?'

'Because I have decided that we are going to stay here.'

'The decision has already been made. We've talked about it and agreed. We have to leave,' he asserted. 'You know as well as I do that this deal of mine is crucial. We can't afford to compromise it. We're going. That's it, I'm afraid.'

He stood above her, his body threatening her, her poor blowhard husband. She was convinced that the threat was empty, that he wouldn't strike her, and if she was wrong she didn't much care. A blow would strengthen her position.

He realised that and released the tension inside himself. Then he reasserted himself. 'If you won't leave, I will,' he announced, making for the bedroom. The door slammed behind him.

'Do as you wish,' she called after him, closing her book and putting it down on the table behind the sofa. She lay back, watching the door, waiting for him to come back into the room, wondering what his first words would be.

There weren't any. When the door opened he simply marched across the worn carpet from the bedroom towards the door of the flat with his eyes turned away from her. He had not changed his clothes nor packed a bag. She could see what that short, exposed walk was costing him but he couldn't avoid it – there was no other way out of the flat. She heard his feet on the stairs, then the door below opened and slammed shut. When he was hungry he would be back – diminished and silent. Her husband.

She was determined not to give way to tears. Instead she picked up her book and began to read it again.

Chapter Eight

'They start to lay about the first of April. We incubate the eggs and this is the result,' said James McAllen.

Charles Ramsay, Julia and Caroline looked down at the result, a scurrying mass of pheasant chicks penned in a big cage faced with wire netting. 'After six weeks they will have reached a reasonable size.'

Both of the women had been brought up in the country to accept country pursuits. Neither of them took exception to the fate that awaited the tiny blobs of fluff next winter. On the other hand, at least neither of them said, 'How sweet'. They weren't hypocrites.

'The shooting has to pay for itself,' McAllen said.

'It does a lot more than that,' Caroline chimed in. Ramsay didn't doubt it. The more he saw of Glengarrick the more he admired the way it was managed.

'How many birds last season?' he enquired.

'About nine hundred, all told.'

'And how many shots expended?' Ramsay asked, perhaps mischievously. That ratio told you how competent the shooters were.

'Three or four to one. But many of our guests don't

shoot often – they have more serious ways of occupying their time. On a good day McPherson and I can do one on, one off.'

Ramsay nodded his acknowledgement; that wasn't at all bad.

Caroline said, 'James is pretty good with a gun so woe betide any unauthorised person who shoots one of these when they are grown up.' She put an arm round her husband's waist and looked up at him with admiration in her eyes. It seemed to Ramsay that she meant it. Why then had she flirted with him on the night of their arrival? Perhaps she was an accomplished actress and this was just part of a new gambit of flirtation. He wasn't playing so it didn't matter much.

'Unauthorised people get short shrift. Don't they, darling?' She turned to Ramsay. 'James has been known to take a pot shot at such people in the past, so watch it,' she giggled. 'But I'm sure James will be looking for an extra gun some time next winter. Why don't you come up for a weekend and have a day's shooting?'

'What could be better?' James agreed. 'Why don't you? I think you'd enjoy it.'

'We'd love to come!' Julia enthused.

Ramsay accepted with grace since his host seemed genuinely willing.

Turning to James he asked, 'What's this I hear about taking a shot at "unauthorised people"?'

'He was a poacher after deer ... with a shotgun,' McAllen confided, disapproval in his face. 'He ought at least to have had the decency to use a rifle.'

Caroline giggled. 'The funny thing was that James loosed off at him with a .303 Lee Enfield Mark Four. Sort of poetic justice.'

'A service rifle?' Ramsay tried not to be astounded.

'Left over from my grandfather's stint in the Home Guard. We forgot to hand it in,' James explained. 'And Caroline exaggerates. I didn't loose off. I took the utmost care to shoot nowhere near him – aimed well over his head. Gave him a fright, though. I certainly made him accelerate.' He grinned.

'The next thing was that the peasant had lodged a complaint with the police. They came round, would you believe? Here,' Caroline complained with indignation. Then her tone changed completely as she declared, 'He's a reckless one is my beloved James. Absolutely reckless – but I love him as he is. He's really good to me, most of the time. Aren't you, darling?'

James didn't seem to know how to handle that scrap of badinage. There was a moment's pause before he said, 'If you're going to that rehearsal of yours in town why don't you take Julia with you? How would that be?'

Julia picked the message up immediately – he wanted to talk to Charles in private.

'Love to,' she said. 'But, Cal, before we go I want to see the damask roses in the walled garden.'

'The name is Caroline,' the other girl said sharply. Again.

There was a moment's pause before Julia came in with, 'Absolutely. So sorry I forgot,' and allowed her to lead the way down the path, past the Thomsonii rhododendron, its grey branches full of waxy crimson

101

blossom, towards the secret garden enclosed by high granite walls topped with sandstone where the McAllens who had built the house a century and a half ago had grown the figs, pears and peaches which had been among the privileges that went with the estate – available nowadays to anyone who can push a super-market trolley.

As Ramsay sauntered back to the house with his host, McAllen explained, 'We have made over the walled garden completely to roses now. It's an ideal place for them – those high walls are just the thing to keep the deer out. There's nothing they like better to browse on than young rose leaves.'

No doubt he gave the bullet to those would-be poachers too.

They paused at the entrance to glance at the crest carved in the lintel above the massive front door, and underneath the single word, *Osons*.

'We dare?' Ramsay ventured.

'Yes,' McAllen smiled. 'I wouldn't say the family always lived up to it, particularly after the Act of Union. We were always good at backing both sides. It was said of one of my ancestors that he was a Catholic when he left Glengarrick and a Protestant by the time he reached Edinburgh. An instantaneous vicar of Bray. Daring wasn't his strong suit at all.'

Now they were proceeding up the ample staircase panelled in red pine.

'Is your family burdened with a motto to live by?' McAllen asked over his shoulder.

'*Probitas*,' said Ramsay, 'that's our motto.'

'Lord – very much a tough one,' McAllen sympathised. 'How do you manage with that?' He avoided saying that, in his business, Ramsay might find it difficult.

'Some of the family have done better than others – like the members of your shoot. But on the whole we've achieved a reasonable score.' It was an understatement; the Ramsays were a byword for honesty in their part of East Anglia, a fact that made it ten times harder for him to relax his standards. It was that which made him toe the line, not the word, chosen centuries ago by some ancestor, probably on a whim.

They had reached the second-floor landing and he was following McAllen to a room at the end of the passage. A turret room. Having neutralised an alarm system, his host drew a key from his pocket and unlocked the heavy door. Inside the air was stale, as though the room was rarely visited.

'Let's have some light in here,' he announced, switching on a single powerful bulb with an old-fashioned green enamelled shade hanging in the centre of the ceiling. The room was circular, its single window framed by steel shutters. There was no furniture except a small table in the middle and a shelf which curved all the way round the wall with cupboards underneath it. They matched the panelling in the corridor outside – put in when the house was built, by the look of them.

McAllen began to explain. 'In the Middle Ages when money was often needed at short notice – to pay a ransom, to buy weapons, or to bribe one of the king's servants – it became the family's habit always to keep part of its wealth in cash. It paid off time and time again in times of trouble – persecution – anarchy.'

'Fine, except that the currency could be debased,' Ramsay objected, 'and often was, I daresay.'

'Right,' McAllen allowed, 'and later on, when banknotes came in, my great-great-grandfather lost a small fortune when a major bank failed and its notes weren't honoured. So he decided to spread his risks by supplementing the hoard with valuable items other than cash – jewellery, art objects and gold. The family had collected a fair amount of such loot over the years anyway, here and there. He bought a lot more and when he built the house he installed this strongroom to keep it in.'

'In the middle of the last century? Surely by that time he could have found some bank that he could trust.'

'He wouldn't have agreed with you. He'd had his fingers badly burnt,' James McAllen replied, 'and I think he was right. I don't trust them – not one of them is safe. Even the most respected name can be brought down in a matter of weeks. You don't know what goes on behind closed doors. They speculate in derivatives, futures, options. With your money, mine.'

'So you have a bank account?'

'Of course I do. I have to. But I hold the estate's balance down to a workable minimum and I keep the bloody bank at arm's length, I can tell you. I never borrow, and any surplus on the estate goes straight into assets which are under my control. Property, gilt-edged or these.' He nodded his head towards the cupboards.

Ramsay wasn't convinced. And as for the hoard . . . he

was much too polite to say so but the idea was wrong-headed. OK, gold was all right – it was a commodity. You knew where you were with that. But other things. Jewellery? He wouldn't like to be holding those when the erstwhile Russians flooded the market and torpedoed the cartel. Objects? What happened when you needed to find a buyer to raise money in a hurry? You would be skinned by any dealer you approached. Go to an auction house and you would forfeit twenty-five per cent in commission and premium – and it might be months before you laid hands on what was left of your money. Over the long term the price of antiques had kept pace with inflation, but he could reel off a whole range of things whose value had fallen in real terms: famille noir porcelain, Georgian drinking glasses, almost any Japanese porcelain in the last few years, some ivories … Antiques as a store of value? He could give a lecture on the subject. But not here and now, he thought, his gaze travelling round the room.

McAllen was drawing a small bunch of keys attached to a chain from his pocket and went to kneel down and unlock one of the cupboards. As he did so Ramsay glanced out of the window and saw that he had a view straight down into the privacy of the walled garden. There were Julia and Caroline, deep in conversation. The subject, as far as he could see, was not the roses – they were being ignored. They both had their backs to them. Julia looked up towards the turret where he was standing – he saw her face, white against the dark foliage behind her. His fingers made a small salute but she didn't see him.

'It's the tradition, you see. I feel it's important to keep it up,' McAllen confided with boyish enthusiasm over his shoulder and Ramsay suddenly remembered that the man was childless, so far at any rate. His wife was young, though. There was plenty of time, although he couldn't easily see her in the role of mother. No more than Julia, who seemed to possess no maternal instincts at all. Not a shred. She said it herself and it was a pity. People change, however.

His mind jumped back to what McAllen was doing. He hoped he wasn't going to be asked to provide any valuations because they were always liable to give offence. You gave an honest valuation and the owner never thought it was high enough. No, he assured himself, there was no danger of being dragged into that. His host was much too sensitive to ask that kind of question merely to satisfy his curiosity and he scarcely needed to sell anything, did he?

'Look at these,' McAllen said, taking a tray out of the cupboard and placing it on the table. There was nothing more sinister in his voice than simple pride of ownership.

On the tray were netsuke, the small toggles usually made of ivory, metal, or wood which the Japanese used in former times to anchor the pouch containing their belongings into the obi or broad sash which was worn to keep the kimono in place. Pouch at one end of a cord, netsuke threaded on the other and that end tucked into the sash. Simple and elegant.

He knew that netsuke of a primitive kind had been in use for centuries, the earliest being made typically from scraps of wood left over from the carving of Buddhist images. Then in the seventeenth century the samisen became more popular – a stringed instrument which was plucked with an ivory plectrum. When a plectrum was carved from a tusk, the offcuts were used to make netsuke, many of which were triangular, being carved from the unneeded tip of the tusk.

Over the years netsuke had become more elaborate and sought after. Most of these on the tray dated from the last century and were katabori – the figure carvings popular with Western collectors. He guessed that McAllen's ancestor had bought them all at about the same time.

Instinctively he tried to put a value on them. Most of them could be bought at auction in London for less than two hundred pounds – there were a few which might make five hundred, and one or two which were worth much more. Ten thousand pounds would buy the whole trayful.

When he looked up McAllen asked, 'What do you think of them?'

His voice was careless but it was clear what he was hoping for. Ramsay made it a point never to overpraise what he saw out of politeness. After all he was being asked for an appraisal, however informally, and it behoved him not to mislead his host. Besides it always led to trouble in the end.

'A respectable collection,' he said brightly. The three words were meant to convey his meaning with the least discomfort and it seemed they had succeeded.

'That's what I thought. Interesting though, aren't

they?' McAllen replied. If he was disappointed he didn't show it.

'Did your great-great-grandfather collect them himself?'

'I doubt it. He wasn't a connoisseur, you see. He had many interests, but collecting netsuke wasn't one of them.'

So it was somebody else's collection which he had bought purely as an investment. Never the best way.

McAllen brought out the contents of other cupboards and laid them on the shelf above. It was much the same story. Good, run-of-the-mill items: porcelain figures which were not Derby or Meissen; miniatures which were portraits of men rather than women, and lateish at that. Nothing there to set the blood racing. The sort of thing that looked good in a local collection – would impress the uninitiated, but wouldn't cut much ice in a London saleroom. He could imagine that McAllen's ancestor had relied on the advice of a local dealer, only half-expert himself, pushing his own stock probably. Of course there was another possibility. That once upon a time the collection had been richer and more extensive and somebody, years ago, his father or grandfather, had been forced by sudden shortage of cash to sell off the best items.

Since McAllen obviously wanted his opinion on the collection, he gave it – making no mention of money. He never did that unless he was asked the direct question, and in any case, he thought, he probably didn't need to. McAllen seemed to be subtle enough to pick up that information from his tone of voice alone.

Then the man sprang his surprise. He went straight to the cupboard that faced the door. This time he didn't search for a key in his pocket, but to open a combination lock. He rose to his feet with a narrow tray in his hand and laid it on the table.

'I think you'll find that this is a bit more special.'

The tray was steel, and clearly belonged to a small safe which, looking past him, Ramsay could see had been set right into the granite wall of the tower – concreted in.

McAllen slid open the lid of the tray and took out a flat box. It was covered in dark brown leather tooled in gold with fleur de lys that had faded. Gently McAllen pushed aside the tray to make space on the table for the box. Then he opened it and said proudly, 'There. What about that?'

Something golden in the case caught the light and flashed it back into Ramsay's eyes, dazzling him for a moment.

A large medal – a medallion, that was what it was.

'May I?' he asked. McAllen inclined his head.

He put out his hand to bring the case in range. Yes, there was a gold medallion in the centre of it and there was no mistaking the portrait upon it – Mary Stuart, the tragic Queen of Scots: a full face portrait of her wearing the cap of mourning for her father-in-law, Henry II of France.

It had not been struck but cast, like many early medals, moulded by the lost wax process, cire perdue. Lying on either side of it, on a bed of satin, once scarlet, now faded to a dusty pink, were the two moulds which had been used to make the impression, front and back, on the wax disc from which the medal had been cast. Those moulds were miraculously detailed – engraved in the finest intaglio. What material were they made of? Was it boxwood? That had often been employed, Ramsay knew. No, it was stone.

'That medal is the only one in existence,' McAllen said seriously, 'and it has been in the possession of my family since it was cast.'

'Who made it?'

'Nicholas Hilliard.'

Ramsay knew the name well, but only as the artist who had painted portrait miniatures of leading figures at the court of Elizabeth I. He remembered one of the Earl of Leicester in his prime, dressed in black with a high proud ruff, a thin gold chain around his collar.

'That's more inspiring than the rest of the gewgaws isn't it?' McAllen demanded.

'Magnificent,' said Ramsay. It wasn't a word he used much; he was a man who preferred to keep his judgements sober. This was different, though. For a moment there was a thrill in the air, a kind of electrical charge of excitement as they gazed down at it.

'Yes,' breathed McAllen. 'I thought you'd like it.' Then he added briskly, breaking the spell, 'There's a story to it. Let's go and have some lunch and I'll give you the background.'

First, though, he had to go through his ritual in reverse, putting away the medallion in its safe, locking first the cupboard door then the door to the room. Pocketing his keys he led the way downstairs to the kitchen. As he followed Ramsay glanced out of the window again, down into the walled garden. Julia and Caroline were no longer there. Just then a thought flashed through his mind, almost dreamlike really. The medallion, its sharp outline, that surface completely innocent of any blemish, because gold was incorruptible. It did create a problem. He recalled a reliquary which contained the skull of some saint or other, in the museum beside Siena Cathedral not far from the huge open square where the dangerous race for the Palio took place. Silver gilt, that reliquary, and it could have been made sometime this century certainly, but the little ivory label on the case said – 'No, doubting Thomas. This was made six hundred years ago, give or take twenty years.' The authorities in Siena would have documents to prove it.

In the kitchen McAllen delved in the refrigerator, rattling off the choices for lunch. 'Soup? Cheese? Beer?'

'No, yes, yes,' Ramsay fired back. McAllen chuckled as he searched for the breadknife. He carved chunks of wholemeal bread while Ramsay pulled open the cans.

'So,' he prompted, as he poured his host a careful mugful and handed it to him, 'the medallion?'

'Are you prepared for a brief history lecture?'

'Try me,' Ramsay answered, taking a swallow. Canned or not it was good beer, bitter and not gassy.

McAllen considered where to start. 'I don't have to tell you about Mary Stuart. You'll know all about her. Hopeless as a queen but because she was a woman, frail and foolish, needing protection, she commanded loyalty from many of her subjects long after they should have known better – and among them an ancestor of mine, John Guthrie. He was one of those who brought her safely to Kirkcudbright after her army was defeated by the Regent at Longside and then to Dundrennan before she crossed over the Solway to England in an open boat with the Lords Herries and Fleming and a few attendants.'

'John Guthrie went with them, I take it.'

'No, he stayed this side of the Solway and made his peace with the Protestants.'

'Then why the medallion?'

'A fit of guilt later on,' said McAllen helping himself to Stilton. 'Although he stayed behind he'd been one of those who advised her to seek sanctuary in England. During the next twenty years, while Mary was shuffled from prison to prison by Elizabeth, he prospered. To begin with he lay low here, simply improving and enlarging his estate, because the times were hazardous. The Regency often fell into the hands of people like Morton who pushed the interests of England against those of Mary. However, that all changed after her son James was crowned King of Scotland in 1577, at the age of twelve.'

'Only twelve? I didn't realise that.'

'Yes, he was always precocious. At any rate, when that happened Guthrie judged it was safe to go back into public life. He returned to Edinburgh, set himself up in lodgings in the Royal Mile and found work at court. A fairly humble job at first, but in 1585 he accompanied Patrick Gray to England to negotiate a treaty of friendship between the two countries ... Help yourself.'

McAllen interrupted himself to gesture at the cheeses. 'More bread?'

He went on, 'Part of the deal was that Mary was to be released from imprisonment and returned to Scotland. In fact Gray didn't try – he didn't want her back. Instead, so it was said, he deliberately poisoned Elizabeth's mind against her. Guthrie did his best to push for her release but he wasn't in charge of the mission. Then of course, the following year, after the treaty was signed, she was implicated in the Babington plot. A special commission in the Star Chamber tried her for treason and condemned her to death. That was when Guthrie was sent to Elizabeth's court a second time, again as Gray's assistant, with another man called Robert Melvil, to try to get her off. With Gray doing the talking she didn't stand a chance. I don't know how much James knew about where Gray's sympathies lay. Indeed, he might have been selected for the job because the King knew that he would deliberately blow it.'

'You may have a point,' Ramsay mused. 'James was only twenty years of age, a Protestant, and next in succession to the English throne after his mother. She was a Catholic who had been involved in more than one intrigue against Elizabeth, and was bound to cause trouble if she returned to Scotland...'

McAllen sat up suddenly; a fresh thought had struck him. 'The letter,' he said.

'Letter? What do you mean?'

'The letter – it's well known – that Elizabeth wrote to him six days after Mary's execution. I have it somewhere, in a book in the library. Yes, I'm sure it's there.'

While he went to find it Ramsay took the opportunity to pour himself another beer. He was enjoying this minor bout of historical speculation in the congenial company of James McAllen. He was back in a minute or two with the volume open in his hand.

'Here it is,' he said. 'To begin with she sounds genuinely sorry – "My dear Brother, I would you knew (though not felt) the extreme dolour that overwhelms my mind for that miserable accident (which far contrary to my meaning) hath befallen..." and so forth.'

Ramsay remembered; he put in, 'She'd signed the warrant for Mary's execution but told Davidson it wasn't to be put into effect without a further order from her. And it was. She claimed—'

'Wait. Listen to this.' Hand outstretched in his enthusiasm, McAllen overrode him. 'Later on, when she's got the apologies out of the way, she says, "The circumstances it may please you to have of this bearer, that is to say, the messenger carrying this letter will give you the detail." Then she goes on, "And for your part, think that you have not in the world a more loving kinswoman, nor a more dear friend than myself; nor any that will watch more carefully to preserve you and your estate."

'We don't know whether this was written for publication or not. Now a third party reading those words at the time would have taken them as no more than a formal assurance of good wishes. The sort of thing that any prince of the age might have said when winding up a tricky letter to a brother monarch. But suppose James had told Gray to say one thing to Elizabeth in public and

114

another in private. Something like – my master is a dutiful son who is anxious that his mother should not be executed ... on the other hand if you don't see fit to reprieve her there could be considerable advantages to both sides ...'

Ramsay broke in, 'Like making sure, in the year before the Armada, that the Protestant cause remained in the ascendant in Scotland and her northern frontier was secure. So her letter is saying in effect, There it is, I've done what we agreed and be assured I shall continue to look after your interests.'

McAllen said, 'Of course it's only a guess – nobody will ever know for sure. Remember, though, that James was taken from her when he was two years old and later told that she had connived at the murder of his father. He had no reason at all to feel any affection for her. Why should he have? There was no bonding between them. And if Guthrie understood what was going on, it would help to explain the medallion.'

'How is that?'

'What happened was this. While he was at Elizabeth's court, Guthrie is said to have met Nicholas Hilliard. Then two things happened. Mary was executed and in the following year the Armada was defeated. Now Hilliard designed and executed a medal in gold to celebrate that event – a magnificent medal with a grand starchy profile of Elizabeth on it. It was then that my ancestor Guthrie decided to ask Hilliard to make a similar medallion to celebrate the tragic death of Mary, the queen he idolised. You can imagine his feelings – guilt at having deserted her twenty years earlier, frustration at being unable to save her, anger at the cold political calculation that led to her losing her head. When he approached Hilliard, however, the artist wasn't at all keen to take on the commission. To begin with Elizabeth was quite capable of ordering his right hand to be struck off if she found out – a considerable disability for a miniaturist. He finally agreed in return for a big payment up front and a solemn undertaking from Guthrie that the existence of the medal would not be disclosed until after both he and Guthrie had gone to their graves. Guthrie was so obsessed with the idea that he agreed. In any case, it made sense to keep it secret from James as well. So that's it. Coffee?' he enquired, jumping up to fill the kettle.

'And the medallion. It's been in the family ever since?' Ramsay asked him. 'An heirloom?'

'Yes. Guthrie's daughter married a McAllen and it came as part of her dowry.'

There was a silence. They seemed to have reached the end of the topic, until McAllen said, 'There is one thing I would like to know.' He put the steaming mugs of coffee on the kitchen table. Ramsay helped himself to milk. He knew what was coming next – something he hadn't expected to hear.

'I sometimes wonder, you know, what it might be worth. To a collector.'

So that was what this was all about. The build-up, the brisk trot through Anglo-Scottish diplomacy in the late sixteenth century. Ramsay had taken pleasure in that and now he felt slightly let down.

What was it worth? What did it matter? He didn't

know its market value of course – he couldn't be expected to. Run-of-the-mill silver coronation medals, even quite early ones – Charles II, for example – could be had for a few hundred pounds; but they had been struck in their hundreds. This medallion was in a class of its own, a completely different item. For a start it was the only one, unique, and cast in gold. Next, it had a fascinating history and provenance, the original moulds were there ... Hilliard had been a brilliant artist ... anything with his name to it would be sought after.

'Obviously it is very desirable. You need an expert in the field to tell you what it might fetch. I know who they are if you want to contact them.' Golver would be the best people to go to, Ramsay thought. There was a new specialist there whom they'd invited to the opening of their Chelsea showroom, he remembered. What was her name? Helen somebody. Julia would be able to find it. She'd dealt with the guest list.

McAllen said, after a moment, asking a favour, 'Could you handle it for me, do you think? You'd know what questions to ask. I'm not sure that...'

That he wanted to descend into the market place and put himself at a disadvantage, perhaps. He wasn't the shy type, but proud. Yes, he was certainly that.

'No problem,' Ramsay assured him. A phone call or two was all it would take; a small thing measured against the hospitality he was receiving here, the prospect of a weekend's shooting next winter. Nothing. However, McAllen had asked the direct question, and not, he judged, simply because he wanted to know how much he should have the prize item in his collection insured for. Young as he was Ramsay had been in this situation often enough to know the signs. McAllen might want to sell. If so, and if he was going to ask Ramsay to get more seriously involved, to handle the sale, he might have to be told that there would be a commission involved. He'd put it to Julia; they were her friends. He didn't imagine that she would allow that to make much of a difference, though. Favours of that size weren't Julia's style. It would be strictly business with her. Whatever they decided, it looked as though he was in for a busman's holiday.

Chapter Nine

Built of dull red sandstone, Steilbow Castle could be seen from the air as a triangle set in a wide moat. At its apex a causeway led into the main gate guarded by a tall cylindrical tower on either side. The high walls running along from each tower were still intact, but the one which had once defended the base of the triangle was in ruins. It was over there in the wide grassy space next to it that the spectacle of sound and light was to be held: the Pageant of Galloway – a present to its people from Malcolm Forsyth, the local boy who had made good.

The castle had been taken at the end of the thirteenth century by Edward I, after a long and difficult siege. As a salute to the courage of the defenders of the castle he hanged a good few of them when it surrendered. Later on a Renaissance dwelling house had been built in the interior, backing on to one of the curtain walls. Although roofless now, its delicate frontage was still intact, with three rows of windows each surmounted by a worn baroque lintel. Those dark empty windows offered scope for all sorts of theatrical effects and Arabella Knight intended to make full use of them in her production.

She was sitting now in her directorial chair, clipboard on her knee, with Malcolm Forsyth and Ethelred Lewis standing beside her. She said, 'The cannon will be dragged on from stage left by two soldiers who will position it over there with its breech towards the audience. When they have laid it, the third soldier carrying the linstock will light the touchhole and the blank charge will go off. Bang. Simple.'

Forsyth objected. 'Is the audience going to see it, though? There's no point in Mr Lewis going to all this trouble to find us a cannon if the audience is only vaguely aware of it. Will it be properly lit? I thought that corner was going to be in darkness in this sequence. Where's the lighting plot?' he demanded, reaching for her clipboard.

Arabella whipped it out of reach. 'No problem. I'll make sure there's a spot on it,' she answered cheerfully. Her patron's need to throw his weight about was a small price to pay for the joy of directing this great spectacle.

Waiting until the battle of wills had ended in a draw Ethelred made his contribution. 'Are you going to have only two men to pull this cannon? I haven't procured the piece of ordnance yet but I'm sure it will be heavy. They'll have to be pretty brawny if you're only going to have two of them. Four would be better. Preferably hefty.'

Calmly Arabella Knight made another note. This man at least was constructive.

Then Julia came through the great gate and saw him.

'Ethelred,' she cried out with every sign of surprise and pleasure, 'what on earth are you doing here?'

He looked startled, at a loss for words for a moment. Then, 'I'm here to be briefed. About my cannon,' he said with dignity.

'Why didn't you tell me?'

'I did.'

He didn't argue any more. Instead he launched into a bout of amazement at the coincidence – that he should be there and she should be there. That they both should be there at the same time. There were exclamations, explanations, introductions and Arabella beginning to get discontented because they were using up precious rehearsal time. Malcolm Forsyth looked all ready to niggle again because attention had shifted away from him. Then instead he cut loose from the group and ostentatiously began to pace out a triangle in the corner of the main acting area. Looking up at the façade, he saw a lighting electrician working on the topmost floor, setting up a spotlight in one of the empty window spaces, leaning outwards to check the alignment. Forsyth strode into the building and climbed the stone stairs to get to him, then started to ply him with questions about the problem of getting light on to his cannon.

Since her rehearsal seemed to be disintegrating anyway Arabella Knight clapped her hands and announced a break for coffee. Under a chilly sky the members of the cast queued up to collect it from an urn on a trestle table. A pair of men came marching down from the gateway carrying lengths of iron scaffolding and dropped them with an officious clang. They had come to erect the seating.

From above, Forsyth's voice shouted, 'Bring me a coffee, Cal, will you?' It was not a request but an order. Julia's eyes followed Caroline's movements with surprise as she collected two mugs and made her way up the stairs. She did seem oddly familiar with that man, Julia thought.

A breeze blew up from the Solway Firth across the deserted marshes where in winter there would be thousands of hungry geese. Julia and Ethelred took their mugs and sheltered in the lee of a ruined wall.

Ethelred said, 'I haven't taken to him.'

'Who?'

'That yobbo over there. The one your friend is acting as waitress for. He's going to be a pain to trade with.' He nodded towards Forsyth.

By now Caroline had climbed the stairs and reached him. As she handed him his mug they heard him burst out, 'You didn't bring one for Bill, ye gadgie. You'd better give him yours.'

The voice was harsh, and louder because it came from high up, echoing over the heads of the chilly group of actors, extras and technicians standing around below.

'Ye wee maddy. Ye fule.'

There was a sudden silence. They stood and watched the pantomime, high up in the window. First Caroline offered her coffee to the lighting man. He gallantly refused it. Next Forsyth grabbed it from her and pushed it at him, insisting, 'Here, take it, man. Take it.' For the sake of peace the technician took it.

Turning her head Caroline looked down at the people

watching her humiliation. 'He must have had a rough night last night,' she called out, and eased the tension a little – there were one or two uncertain laughs. With dignity she came down the stairs, found a clean mug and poured herself a coffee. The others began to move, to resume talking, and the contretemps was slowly dissipated.

'There you are,' said Ethelred. 'Have you been to his house? Carrucate? That farm he has?' he asked.

'No. I hear it's dire,' Julia said.

Ethelred hesitated for a moment while he agonised. Should he share his discovery of that picture with her or not? While his own interests warned, *Hug it to your bosom, Ethelred. This is a big opportunity. Keep it to yourself*, he had the ravenous need of a lonely man to talk about it, to unload his triumph on to somebody else. Now that he had met Julia by accident she was the obvious person to tell if anybody was going to be told, and at least she was secure; the safest person he could think of, in fact.

She would want her share. Yes. But he owed her a favour, didn't he? And she might be useful with this. Two heads were better than one. The painting was important, his nose told him it was, and he, Ethelred, had discovered it. He had to admit to one impediment though – he had no idea who had painted it. Perhaps she could help with that.

Julia said, 'If you don't like him, why have you got yourself involved over this cannon?'

'One has to earn a crust.' Should he tell her? Should he? Well, yes, perhaps he ... 'And there's something else.' There – he'd done it now really, hadn't he? Because she could read him like an open book. She looked calmly at him and waited to let him tell her in his own way.

'When I went up there to Carrucate, I was a bit early – you know me, ever Mr Punctual – and Forsyth wasn't around. There was a dog – one of those black and white farm dogs – chained up, but no client visible – no Forsyth at all. It began to rain, really quite hard – it did, you know – and so I took refuge in a convenient outbuilding. I had to, I mean...'

'What did you find there, Ethelred?' she asked in the mock severe voice she knew she could use with him.

He looked at her speculatively. 'This is just between us. You and me – you know – Scout's honour?' Ethelred hadn't been a boy scout but he understood the concept.

'Of course, love,' she assured him.

He was suddenly assailed by doubts and felt a panic need to backtrack.

'No, it's probably nothing. I'm making a fool of myself. It's just a print of some kind.' That was hopelessly unconvincing. He might not be Anthony Blunt, thank goodness he wasn't, but he could tell a print from an oil painting at a distance of fifty yards. He knew he couldn't take the words back now, so he'd said it, hadn't he really? – about the picture.

'You've found a picture, haven't you? Up at Carrucate.'

He shrugged and smiled and wagged his head from side to side – half teasing, half annoyed.

'Come on, Ethelred. What's it like? Who's it by? Where is it?'

Ethelred giggled. 'Tucked away on top of a wardrobe.

Late Victorian, quite nice, too big for the shop, sadly. He might not even know he has it – the painting, I mean.' Lips close to her ear he told her all about it in a breathy undertone. He concluded, 'I don't know who the artist is, my dear, I haven't a clue. There's a signature but I didn't have much time to inspect it. It was all in rather a rush.'

'You mean he surprised you in his outhouse? Snooping about? Is that why you don't like him? He didn't order you off the premises? He can't have done or you wouldn't be here today.'

'No, of course he didn't,' Ethelred answered pettishly. 'No, no, it wasn't like that at all. All very dignified and *comme il faut*.'

Something had struck her; she looked at him with a wild question in her eyes and asked, 'Did the artist's name begin with an L?'

He pouted – it was his turn to tease. 'Could be, love. Yes, it did as a matter of fact. How did you know that?' It was his turn to be amazed. 'Yes, an L. It did look like that. And there was an e and a couple of n's or m's, but you see the light wasn't at all good . . .' He looked across to see if that registered with her.

'The name of the artist,' she said slowly, 'I'm almost sure . . . the name of the artist is . . . Lennox.'

'Lennox? Why should it be that?'

'Ian Lennox. Yes, I bet you it was.'

'My dear Julia, why, for goodness' sake?'

'Because . . .' She began to explain sketchily about Lennox and how he had been drowned and how Forsyth's father had taken away his belongings afterwards, and how some people thought that there had been a painting among them, and what that painting might fetch these days. When he heard the last bit Ethelred felt contentment fill his mind. Even though what remained of his coffee was cold and bitter, and the wind had changed direction and was chilling their faces, he felt his body suffused with a special warmth, because he'd made the right decision in trusting her. She'd told him just what he needed to know.

It was an artist called Lennox, one he'd never heard of. Now that he had his bearings, that gap in his knowledge could be filled at the local library. They would have the information he needed. And then he had a friend, Duncan, who lived in – where was it? Peebles – who was very well informed about Scottish art and where it could be disposed of if it was a little overripe. Head to head with Julia, he was engrossed in what she was telling him when he looked up and all at once saw Caroline McAllen – only a few yards away – and the dreary man Forsyth right behind her.

He hissed in Julia's ear, 'I spy strangers.' She stopped speaking and looked up calmly at her friend and the dark man whom she had to accept was another friend of Caroline's, or close to her at least. Not somebody she would have chosen for her.

Caroline asked, 'Secrets?'

'Yes, trade secrets,' Julia replied easily, turning to Forsyth to explain. 'Mr Lewis used to be my employer. I worked for him until I launched out on my own. He taught me everything I know.'

'Everything?' Forsyth had picked up some trite little

double meaning in the phrase and his voice was mocking it. An odious fool, she thought.

Ethelred's face was set in the mask that he used to convey that he had heard nothing and understood nothing. He was used to shrugging away these minor slings and arrows and anyway his mind was on other things. Correction, an other thing. Made of wood and canvas. He needed to know a lot more about Lennox before he could decide how best this find could be exploited; this valuable truffle he had found buried in the dark damp earth. Richly scented. Scrumptious.

If he stayed he might get more stuff on it from Julia. It was obvious she knew a lot more which she hadn't had time to tell him. Forsyth was the problem though – it looked as if he was going to stay around; and besides Ramsay might be coming soon to join them and it would be altogether better if they didn't meet. However, at least Margaret Johnson and her husband had taken themselves off. She was a sensible soul who would have taken his warning seriously. They would be well away by now.

No, it was a pity he couldn't hang about a few minutes longer. Never mind. Duncan would know about Lennox, he'd be able to advise. He'd phone him. This thing needed to be done in stages. Formulate his strategy, how to play it, that was first. Then have a chat with Julia about sharing out the proceeds. Seventy/thirty would be fair he thought – thirty for her. He needed to phone Anny too, and get the search for this bloody artillery piece going. There wasn't much time to see to it.

He told Forsyth he'd be in touch, nodded a polite nod at Caroline, pecked Julia on the cheek telling her to take care, and went on his way.

Arabella Knight clapped her hands, resuming command. 'Can we have everybody in the council sequence please? The council sequence.' Bodies began to move reluctantly. One of the blue-denimed workmen behind her dropped a bag of scaffolding clips. 'Would anybody who is not in the council sequence please leave the acting area. Thank you.'

Forsyth turned back to watch the rehearsal.

James McAllen drew a sharp knife from the beechwood block at the rear of the worktop and cut the first tranche from the middle cut of wild salmon lying in front of him. Ramsay was scrubbing new potatoes under the tap.

'You'll find a packet of petits pois in the freezer,' James instructed as he poised the knife for the next cut. A large gin and tonic, freshly iced, stood at his elbow. First deal with the salmon, though.

'The sauce,' he said judiciously, 'is of my own devising. It involves white wine, dry of course, capers, slices of lime and other delicious ingredients known only to me.'

Ramsay was only half listening. He was counting the potatoes – two more, he thought, would be enough. It had been James's suggestion that they should prepare the evening meal before the girls got back from the rehearsal. A good idea. It made them feel virtuous and it ensured that they would get fed sooner rather than later.

McAllen was laying the pink steaks neatly in the grill pan. He turned round to find the bottle of Meursault he had uncorked a few minutes earlier.

'Charles,' he said. The timbre of his voice had changed and it made Ramsay listen. McAllen was concentrating on pouring out exactly four fluid ounces of wine – not looking at him. 'I'm glad you and Julia have been able to come up to see us. It's been very good for Caroline – the company.' Now he was searching in a wall cupboard for a particular spice, looking hopefully at the label on each small cardboard cylinder. He went on, 'We lead a very orderly life up here. Not an exciting existence perhaps for her, having no children and feeling left out because all her friends have started families. It's a problem for her.' Something else hovered on his lips but he pulled it back.

'After this performance is over she ought to come down and see us in Chelsea,' Ramsay offered. 'Julia's planning to run a small exhibition of Regency furnishings in our showroom next month. Caroline might like to give her a hand with putting it together. It'd be fun. Julia would enjoy it and she'd be a huge asset at the opening.'

'It's an idea. You might like to put it to her.' McAllen sounded doubtful. He started to cut up the lime, dropped a spare slice into his gin and tonic and tried it. Not bad.

Twenty minutes later the two of them arrived. Caroline slumped into a chair, exhausted she said, hand outstretched for a drink. Drinks were supplied, compliments passed on the cookery. They would eat in the kitchen, informally knee to knee.

Elbows on the table, wineglass in hand, Caroline exclaimed to Ramsay, 'Malcolm Forsyth had somebody in tow at the rehearsal. Guess who.'

He saw a flash of annoyance cross Julia's face then disappear, wiped away in an instant.

Guess who. He thought for a moment. Arabella Knight must have been there since she was directing the show. No surprise there. He'd only met one other local since they'd arrived so it had to be him. 'Your solicitor friend – Rae. Who was here last night?' He had been very anti the whole idea of the spectacle so maybe it was a surprise to see him at a rehearsal.

'Nope,' Caroline said with a decisive shake of her elegant head.

He couldn't think of anybody else. There wasn't anybody. 'Give up.'

'Your friend Ethelred Lewis,' she announced triumphantly. 'They need a cannon and he's going to find one for them. For Malcolm Forsyth that is, since he's paying the piper.'

'Ethelred Lewis?' Ramsay was puzzled.

Julia put in, 'Yes. You remember, he told us he was looking for a cannon. For somebody in the north.'

'The accepted meaning of "the north" is the north of England – if you mean Scotland you say Scotland,' Ramsay objected. 'Besides he told us it was for a display of some kind, not a pageant.'

'A smokescreen. You know how evasive he can be.'

Yes indeed he did – that adjective was Ethelred's very own. Why hadn't Lewis said this client of his was in Galloway? He'd known they were going to be here. Was that the reason? No; he was odd, but he wasn't as paranoid as that.

'Who is this evasive man?' James enquired.

Julia didn't respond, so Ramsay filled in carelessly, 'More a friend of Julia's than mine. A dealer she used to work for, with a shop in Brighton. It's a coincidence his being here. A big coincidence.' He glanced at the faces of the other three, from James, to Caroline, then at Julia. What was this about? It wouldn't be the first time she had got up to something on the side with Lewis. She looked back at him with no hint of uneasiness in her eyes. Perhaps she was . . .

'A real coincidence,' she said, 'truly. None of my doing.' She took a sip of wine. 'You know, this meal is really good,' she said brightly to James, who bowed.

'I'll leave Julia to tell you the really important thing. Go on, Julia, tell him,' Caroline urged.

'I promised I'd keep it to myself,' Julia objected.

'You told me. That's not keeping it to yourself.'

'That's different. I swore you to secrecy.' They might have been back at school.

'I have no secrets from my darling spouse,' Caroline replied. Julia was about to come back on that but didn't because there was a challenging look in her friend's eye. This game of theirs had its rules.

'If you won't tell them, I shall.'

Julia looked annoyed but decided to give in. 'The story you told us the other night, about the missing painting. Ian Lennox. Well, Ethelred had to go to Carrucate Farm – is that the name of the place where Malcolm Forsyth lives?'

'That's it,' James replied.

She paused, reluctant to go on.

'Well, come on. Tell us,' Charles Ramsay prompted.

Caroline said to him, quietly – it was unlike her, 'Mr Lewis, Ethelred, had to shelter in one of the sheds and what do you think he found in there?'

Julia took a gulp of wine before saying it. 'The painting. *Mystery Four*.'

McAllen looked at her sharply. '*Mystery Four*? How do you know it's *Mystery Four*?' He sounded almost angry, as though she was being presumptuous, invading his privacy, trespassing on ground which was as much the property of his family as the estate.

That didn't worry her. 'I know it is, from Ethelred's description. A nude girl against a forest background – evergreen trees. Stylised.'

Ramsay chimed in, 'Come on, Julia, that's hearsay – terribly secondhand. You can't possibly be sure. You haven't seen it. Nobody's seen it for nearly thirty years. I bet Ethelred has never heard of Lennox.'

'Fair point,' she said. 'He knows a good painting when he sees one though. Do admit.'

McAllen said slowly, 'I am very reluctant to disagree with you, Julia, but let's be clear. Nobody living actually knows what this picture looks like. It was one of a series which all had much the same theme. And Lennox took pupils, you know. It could very well be a copy of one of the others in the series done by a pupil who was a particular fan of his. Or a copy of *Mystery Four* itself.'

'But it was found in Carrucate Farm, where Malcolm

Forsyth's father was tenant – the man you told us took the original painting after Lennox drowned.'

'It wasn't there, though, after Forsyth's widow quit the house. We searched it afterwards, my father and I together, remember? If it is the painting, the son must have brought it back with him,' McAllen answered patiently.

Julia knew she had taken the argument far enough. It was time to withdraw in good order. 'OK, OK, I have to admit, it is a bit too good to be true. Nice idea though, wasn't it?'

Caroline poured herself another glass of wine. 'Well, I think Julia's right. It is *Mystery Four*. And if it is, it belongs to us,' she asserted flatly.

'Your friend Cameron Rae didn't seem to think so,' Julia reminded her.

'Cameron Rae! You wouldn't expect—' Caroline began before James McAllen interrupted.

'I am absolutely convinced of one thing. If it is *Mystery Four*, it doesn't belong to bloody Malcolm Forsyth.' His voice had become harsh – too emphatic, as he must have realised, because he brought it under control. 'OK,' he offered, 'I'm afraid the Forsyths get under my skin rather. Charles, it's time we produced the next course.'

They turned the lights out, then proudly they produced it: bread and butter pudding Glengarrick, flambéed in whisky.

The girls had left for the drawing room. As he was stacking the dishwasher McAllen asked thoughtfully,

'If the medallion turned out to be valuable, what would be the best way to sell it? At auction I suppose?'

'Possibly.'

McAllen mused. 'It might be a good idea. Some people would ask, what's the point of keeping it? It's too risky to put it on display and it's not doing much good sitting in that safe.'

'What's the problem?' Ramsay asked, head bent over the coffee maker, 'Lloyd's?' Although he was ten years younger than McAllen he felt he knew him well enough to ask such a question without offence.

'No, no, absolutely not. We've kept totally clear of that nonsense. In the eighties the bank thought I was mad. The obvious way to increase the return on Glengarrick, they thought. Ten per cent a year extra on it without lifting a finger – that was what they told me. No thanks, I said. Oh, I'm not claiming I was particularly wise. I just don't like taking on liabilities that I can't quantify.'

While he wasn't offended, that was as much as he was prepared to volunteer about his financial situation. Somewhere there was a problem, but he was giving nothing away.

Ramsay said, 'To go back to your question. You might get more competition going for the medallion if you sent it to one of the auction houses, but of course their charges would take a big slice of the money.'

The older man made a gesture which said he was aware of that pitfall. He said, 'It's too public as well. The media might well get hold of it. The medallion has the sort of history that would get it the full treatment on the

134

arts pages of the Sunday broadsheets. And once it gets around that you're selling something like that it can have a fallout that you don't expect. I don't want that. I don't want it known.'

By whom? His banks of course. But before he'd claimed that he owed them nothing. So what was the problem?

'Of course. Understood,' Ramsay said although he didn't really understand.

'We're a small community here and one likes to keep things like that to oneself.'

Come on, thought Ramsay. *It's not a big deal. Some people might welcome the publicity.*

McAllen was searching in an overhead cupboard for the coffee cups. There they were: Limoges porcelain – attractive; well used though. He carried them carefully to the table and looked round for the tray.

'If you want to sell, I think the best thing might be to approach Golver plc and see if they can fix up something private for you,' Ramsay suggested.

The coffee maker gurgled as it completed its task. With deliberation McAllen added glasses and a bottle of malt whisky to the tray. The bottle looked intriguing.

'Golver? I thought they were traders in bullion.'

'They are, in a big way – gold and silver, hence the name. They also trade in noble metals which go mainly into industry – platinum, palladium, rhenium – for catalysts and so on. But Golvers have always had a department dealing in retail gold, jewellery, objects, medals. Although it made a decent little profit, its main function for years was cosmetic. It was good for their image, could be used in the corporate publicity. Then the gold market went dull and the recession hit demand for catalysts so they've put a lot more effort behind it. The company has offices world wide so they have plenty of wealthy contacts to be exploited.'

'Could you fix it for me?' James McAllen asked. 'The sale. A private sale?'

'Sure ... it could be done.' He spoke slowly and paused, because it wouldn't be done as a favour. Not this. He was a professional and McAllen wasn't a pauper. While it had cost him nothing to cast his eye over the items in the tower and give his opinion, finding a buyer for the Mary Medallion was something else.

McAllen sensed the point straightaway. 'You'd take a commission of course.'

'I'd expect to.'

'How much?'

Ramsay told him.

'That seems fair,' McAllen said.

'It is,' Ramsay replied with a grin. He wanted that understood too. 'Yes, Golvers, I'd try them first. The man in charge is called Andover, Sir Anthony Andover. I've never taken to him much and you may not like him either – he's smooth, condescending and a bit larger than life, but he knows his job and he goes down well on the other side of the Atlantic. You don't have to meet him if you don't want to. I can deal with the whole thing myself.'

'Lord no,' said McAllen, 'I don't need protecting.' Tray in hand he led the way down the corridor to the drawing room. 'Keep it to yourself though, would you? Not a word to Caroline or Julia just yet, if you don't mind.'

'Understood,' Ramsay said, following with the glass coffee jug, watchful to make sure he spilled nothing on the Shirvan runner in the passageway. A mite worn now, but still sacred. Irreplaceable.

Chapter Ten

Though the McAllens were the friendliest of hosts, Ramsay was a wise enough guest to give them a break and the next day he insisted on taking Julia off westward to explore the coast, to visit Dundrennan, perhaps to go far enough to inspect the extraordinary collection of plants at the Logan Gardens. First, though, Julia wanted to see Carrucate and the place where Ian Lennox had died.

'Ghoul,' accused Ramsay.

'Not at all. Do I look like a ghoul?'

'No. You're a touch too healthy.'

She yelped disapproval. 'Not translucent like Caroline?'

'No. Really wholesome. Not like her.'

'Caroline's wholesome too,' she protested. Julia had sprung too fiercely to her defence, he thought, and realising that he'd touched a nerve he left it at that. They both knew that something was adrift with Caroline and neither of them wanted to say it.

To cover up she decided to talk inconsequences. 'After the story of the loss of *Mystery Four* I need to absorb the feeling of the place – sense the atmosphere,' she announced. 'It's no more ghoulish than visiting Dun-drennan. That's a sad place too. Poor Mary, holding her last council there, trying to make up her mind which of her advisers had it right, what their motives were, whether she should go into exile.' She shivered at the bleakness of that spring day in the abbey.

'OK, you're completely right,' Ramsay capitulated. On a sunny morning like this he wasn't going to quarrel. 'There is something else,' he said, watching the open road in front of him. One joy about driving in Galloway was the lack of traffic, even in the summer.

'What something else?' she asked idly, glancing at a hawk hanging in the air to her left.

'Ethelred,' he said.

She looked at him in mock dismay and implored, hands locked in prayer, 'Don't let him come between us. Please.'

He wasn't willing to play. Instead he was sceptical, because this was business. They were locked together in a partnership and he had to know what she was up to.

'Come on,' he scouted her, 'Ethelred Lewis up here? At your rehearsal yesterday? That's no coincidence.'

'Of course it is. I told you it was,' she said pretending now to take offence.

'I don't believe it.'

'I swear to you I had no idea he was going to be at the rehearsal.' Her voice was harder now.

'You knew he might be around, though.'

'Look, that sparrow hawk,' she cried out with excite-ment. 'It's stooped.' It was so like her to know the correct word for a hawk descending on its prey – and like her too to stage a diversion to give herself time to decide how much she was going to tell him about Ethelred Lewis's non-coincidental presence in Galloway.

'They do,' he said. 'Sparrow hawks, now and then, otherwise they wouldn't eat.'

'Not particularly penetrating of you,' she responded decisively, resting her gaze on him while he kept his carefully on the road. He didn't have to look at her to know that she was still thinking; that neat little cogs were revolving busily in her head as she decided what story to tell him – which one would cause least fuss. Which she could get away with. He didn't want a story, he wanted the truth.

She drew in a big breath. 'Well, it was like this,' she said. 'A week or two before we left London I rang Cal about the arrangements, you know how one does, whether there was anything I could bring and so on, and she said no but had I any idea where they could get a cannon because Malcolm – Malcolm Forsyth, that is – was looking for one and they hadn't got much time to find it. So I said of course I do and put her in touch with Ethelred. You know how he likes bustling about looking for things – if there's money in it – and I knew trade was slow for him in Brighton.'

'So why the charade when he came into the showroom that time? About Mrs Blennerhasset and so on.'

'I know you don't like him,' she said, 'and I did want to do him a good turn. I'm really fond of him. Truly. I'm allowed to be, aren't I?' she challenged him. 'And I thought, well, if you knew that he was on the loose around here it would spoil your holiday, and you deserve an unspoilt holiday.' Yes he did, he thought, after a couple of days being harried by Blenkinsop, that solicitor of her mother's, over the fine print of the new partnership deed.

'Because I knew you felt sore over Mummy and the extra money and that deed she insisted on,' she went on. 'It was like that. Truly, truly. Then of course Cal and I ran into him and I had to introduce her. She likes him, by the way. There are people who do, you know. She thinks he's fun.'

Not at all a bad effort he thought. Very plausible. Five point nine for both technical merit and artistic impression. She had a creative mind and she was a skilful actress, with all the beauty and charm a woman needed to survive on the professional stage. She could have done so if she had wanted to, he reckoned, though he had to admit he was biased in her favour. He looked across at Julia and gave her his absolution. The intervention of Blenkinsop had been her fault in a way, but she hadn't planned it and at least she'd had the grace to recognise that the deed rankled with him. Yet there was something else cooking he decided – some side project of hers and Lewis's that she didn't want him to know about. The last time that had happened they had ganged up on him over a Canaletto painting, a real one. He'd been prepared to wear it at the time, just prepared to, because he was a fair man and his own behaviour had provoked the thing to some extent – and because she was Julia, slender and sensual, and her beauty was his. Lips, eyes, smooth thighs in the darkness of the bed, slim fingers.

Anyway she'd burnt them that time, her fingers,

which served her right. It had been good for her. He wasn't going to put up with anything like that again though. Their relationship had plenty going for it and besides, they made a good business team. They complemented each other. He had the expertise and a flair for buying. She was a born saleswoman who had the contacts and knew how to handle clients. A good organiser, too. Yet none of that counted if she cut him up again. Certainly not. Very well, she was allowed to give Lewis a helping hand if she felt she had to, though he couldn't understand why it was necessary – the guy was more than able to take care of himself. He would even be prepared to pretend not to notice some private venture of theirs as long as it didn't do him or the partnership any harm. Partnership – he'd come round to that again, and the word brought the memory of that bloody man Blenkinsop flooding back – Blenkinsop sitting in the flat with a glass of their oldest Islay malt on the table beside him summarising the changes in the deed, formally and without any kind of apology. As though he, Ramsay, had been in the wrong and it hadn't been her who'd made a nonsense of everything. And now he wasn't on equal terms with her any longer. She had a slightly larger share, which gave her the upper hand in a way, or he felt it did. Legally it didn't make a lot of difference and it certainly didn't mean that she could play fast and loose, have a hidden agenda. Then he remembered the medallion – that he had been burdened with a secret project of his own, by James McAllen. Sauce for the goose . . . ? No, that wasn't the same thing at all, and it wouldn't stay secret for long, anyway. You had to set limits and he knew where they were. How could he ensure that she did? He couldn't, he realised in that moment.

He said with more conviction than he felt, 'Just watch it, Julia, my darling girl, will you?'

He expected her to snap back on that but she didn't seem to hear him, sitting at his side, observing the fields going past them in the sun. A startled rabbit scurried along the offside verge and disappeared into the hedge. She didn't remark on it, though. Instead she caught him by surprise, asking bleakly, 'What do you mean by that?'

'Mean by what?'

'That condescending statement about watching it. At this moment in time I don't feel much like your darling girl.'

'I was simply trying to say...'

'What?' she demanded.

'You may get involved with him if you must—'

'I shall. Any time I want to.'

'Just don't forget that you are my partner. Not his.'

'No. I haven't forgotten and nor should you. Don't forget that you—' Are the junior partner was what she was about to say but she thought better of it, since it was her incompetence that had nearly wrecked their finances in the first place. She didn't want to touch off a conflagration in the seat beside her so she changed tack. 'I am well aware...' She stopped again, then said, 'You're thinking about the Canaletto, aren't you? Mind that rabbit.'

Another suicidal flop-eared runner was racing alongside them, about to veer under the wheels of the car. Avoiding it, he replied, with dignity, he felt, 'That's all finished. About the Canaletto. Forgotten. I said.'

'It's not. Because you're thinking about it. That bloody painting and the partnership deed. Don't you ever stop?'

'Stop what?'

'Thinking about things that can't be changed.'

She had managed to dodge the issue again. It would be a waste of time trying to retrace his steps so he concentrated on the road again.

They came over the hill and there was Carrucate lying below them with its monstrous green-roofed barn beside it, and beyond the sandy denuded expanse of the firth, deserted by the sea. Further out there was still enough water left behind by the tide in pools here and there to catch the sunlight and flash it back at them.

He stopped the car and they got out. Gazing down at the farmhouse he remembered how once before he had stepped out of a car on a coastal road and looked out towards the horizon. In the South of France. Just after Margaret Johnson had walked out on him. He closed his eyes for a moment, flinching as the memory of her hit him. Of her and his anger – and despair. She had been very different from Julia; nervy and vulnerable where Julia was well organised, composed. Her voice though, her voice had been ... memorable. A wonderful voice with harmonics and overtones in it that had caressed him. Uneasily he asked himself, suppose she hadn't walked out on him, would he be standing next to Julia now?

Just then Julia spoke, and he was not required to find an answer to his question, which was a relief. She said, 'The person I'm sorry for is the girlfriend Ian Lennox left behind. It must have been a dreadful shock for her to bear on her own – I bet she didn't get much sympathy from the locals. Think of it. Tam Forsyth, her former boyfriend, had been killed in action. He was the neighbourhood hero. He scarcely buried and she's shacked up with this drunken artist. So drunk he manages to get himself stuck in the quicksand and drowned. Jane, she was called. Isn't that what James said?'

'I think so,' he replied, only half listening because his mind was still on Margaret.

'Hey, you. What are you thinking about?' she enquired.

Unable to tell her, he feigned indignation, 'First I'm accused of still having the Canaletto on my mind, now this. Who do you think you are?' he asked, 'the thought police?'

She gave him a hug, which made him feel worse, and then said, as though she really could read his thoughts, 'You know, I think my school chum Cal may have a thing going with the guy who lives in that house.'

'Malcolm Forsyth? You can't be serious. She hates him. She and James both do.'

'Caroline may be impulsive, but you don't expect her to announce at her own dinner table that she's having it away with his pet enemy, do you?'

'They seem so devoted,' he protested.

She told him about the scene at the rehearsal. He

shook his head and scoffed until he recalled Caroline's approach to him on the first evening.

'I was there. I saw it all,' Julia insisted.

Maybe she was right, maybe not. One thing he was sure of – Caroline McAllen's behaviour overall was more than odd, it was erratic. The incident at the Steilbow Castle on the previous day seemed to fit a pattern. But so what? It was her business.

'Actually, Malcolm Forsyth is quite a hunk. Has a dangerous feel to him. I quite fancied testing him out,' she added mischievously.

Ramsay knew what he was expected to say so he said it. 'Do that and I'll break your neck.' He hoped the sagging cliché reassured her. For himself, he wasn't sure. He was the kind of man who liked a quiet life and that was one of the reasons why Margaret Johnson had attracted him. One of the reasons. Margaret.

Julia began to walk down towards Carrucate and he followed a few yards behind, watching her grace. Somehow the memory of Margaret Johnson had diminished his pleasure in it.

She beckoned him impatiently with a sweep of her arm. 'Come on, darling. Catch up.'

He did as he was told. Julia took his arm and said, 'You must take life as it comes, you know. Just relax, Charles.' Not darling, but Charles, and she had spoken to him in a tone of calm authority. Solicitous, but as though she was in charge and felt comfortable with that. Her new role.

She had been cleverer than he ever imagined she was.

* * *

David Forsyth is leading out the big Clydesdale from
the stable into the cobbled yard. Distrusting the farmboy
to do the job, he inspects its hooves. These days it's
difficult to find a smith who knows how to shoe them
properly. It's an operation now that has to be thought of
well in advance, planned for – a simple thing like
getting a horse shod. The boy stands beside him trying
to look as though he is contributing to the decision.

'Away with you, man. Get about your business,' the
farmer hectors him.

Instead of taking himself off the booby stands his
ground. Forsyth looks up at him and barks again, 'Get
away, will you? Away and feed the sheep.' The boy
still doesn't move; when Forsyth resumes his inspection
of the fore hoof, he plucks at his sleeve to get his
attention.

She is coming up the track, Tam's girl that was. She is
wearing a man's mackintosh with the sleeves turned
back – it must be an old one of Lennox's. Even so she
looks well in it, striding out against a wind which
carries rain on it.

Forsyth and the boy stand and watch her as she
swings the farm gate open, closes it behind her, and
comes across the yard. The Clydesdale jerks its head
back as though impatient at this interruption. Forsyth
glances at the boy and knows what is on his mind –
her naked shape in the painting – and feels a surge of
anger. For all that she betrayed him, this woman had
been his brother's once. Not for farm boys to drool
over.

148

'Get off now,' he snaps at the youth who goes sluggishly to pick up his worn khaki haversack lying against the wall. Slinging it over his shoulder he takes himself off. Forsyth moves round the horse to examine another hoof without offering a word to the woman behind him.

She says, bringing the sentence out after a delay, as if knowing it was going to cause her pain, 'I've come for his things.'

Forsyth continues to ignore her, fixing all his attention on the huge feathered cone of a hoof which he is gripping between his knees.

'I know you've got them. He told me.' She jerks her head in the direction of the departed boy. 'And somebody else.'

He makes no comment on that either. Instead, satisfied that the horse does not need the attention of a blacksmith for the time being he leads it back into its stable. Jane follows him and the horse plunges its head and lifts its back legs nervously in disapproval.

'Watch yourself, woman,' David Forsyth shouts as he grabs the halter, then looks back to see her fully for the first time. She looks thicker in the waist than he remembered, but of course he has scarcely seen her for months. Once or twice, perhaps, since Tam's funeral, fleetingly in the village street, passing her by in his Land Rover, catching sight of her face in his driving mirror.

She repeats, 'I've come for Ian's things. I know you've got them. Mr McAllen told me.'

'I don't care who told you,' he says, but she can hear

from his voice that the laird's name has had the effect she had hoped for. Now Forsyth is going to have to take her seriously. 'You'd better come inside,' he says.

She sees that the farmhouse is as much of a mess as ever it was. Dark and untidy – a place for sleeping and eating and that is all, she thinks, remembering her visits with Tam, when he was on leave and she was respectable because she was walking out with a paratrooper. She follows his brother into the kitchen. The unforgiving chairs are still the same, the blue linoleum with its pre-war pattern, the stone sink with the green-painted plywood cupboard set in the wall above it, a brass knob for a handle. Not a welcoming place at all, and it could have been; the Forsyths weren't short of money – Carrucate was one of the best farms on the estate. No, he and his wife simply didn't care how they lived.

She and Ian had lived in a muddle, but she had some excuse for that. There was never any money because of his other needs – she cannot even bring herself to think the word 'drinking'. She glances round. No sign of the wife, thank goodness. Jane knows how she would have been, the bitch: ready to condole with her in a sanctimonious way while censuring her with her eyes for being weaker than herself – less upright.

He turns to tackle her, speaking roughly, anxious to get her out of the house quickly. 'I have work to do.'

That is a transparent excuse – there is more to it than that. There are other reasons why he wants rid of her. Perhaps his wife is a suspicious woman and he's afraid that if she comes back and finds her there she'll make a row. Is that why there is a guilt in his eye? No, Jane decides, that can't be the reason. He's not the sort to let himself be henpecked over that.

She says, 'Mr McAllen said you had taken away Ian's things. That he had with him when he...' She pauses because she doesn't want to say the words in front of this man who everybody says did his best to save her man but didn't, didn't do enough. She feels tears coming and has to hold them back, suddenly choking. Why does she have to come up here to beg for Ian's bits and pieces? Forsyth should have brought them down to her. She is damned if she is going to cry in front of him.

'So what is it you think he had with him?'

She is hesitant because she isn't sure, not about all the things, but since she has been expecting this she has taken the precaution of scribbling down a list. She takes it from her raincoat pocket and consults it.

'There was his bicycle,' she says, 'and his big umbrella and his painting gear – his watercolour box, and a big leather holdall, a kind of portfolio that he used for keeping his work in.' She hates having to expose the pitiful inventory to him but it has to be done if she wants them back. Memories.

'Give it here.' Forsyth puts out his hand for the list but before he can take it she has folded it and put it back in her pocket. Safe from him.

'No bottles, I suppose. No, they would all have been emptied,' he says, eyeing her, and she looks back stoically, telling herself that her Ian was twenty times more worthwhile than the man in front of her, who hasn't even asked her to sit down although he must know that she needs to. He can see surely how it is with her. Her legs are tired but she isn't going to give up.

'There was a picture as well,' she asserts.

'Supposing I do have this stuff. What makes you think that you have any right to it? You weren't his wife, were you?' His eyes take in her shape under the drab mackintosh and he realises for the first time that she is pregnant. For a moment the knowledge throws him, before a quick reckoning tells him it cannot be Tam's child. She's not that far gone with it.

'Robert McAllen thinks I should have them and so does the village.'

Forsyth isn't prepared to argue about it. He has to balance his wish to damage her against the risk of antagonising the laird, and he is hard-headed enough to know which way the decision has to go. He's prepared to get on the wrong side of the laird if his own interests are at stake, but not for these remnants of Lennox. They aren't worth it. That isn't to say that he has to make it easy for her.

He leads her to a disused outbuilding, and drags open the door. She pushes past him into the interior, smelling of damp. There is no window, just a small iron skylight, and it takes a moment for her eyes to adjust to the half darkness. Then she becomes aware of the layers of lime crumbling from the walls, rafters honeycombed by worm, lengths of baler twine in a bunch hanging from a nail in the cross beam. As she moves forward in the twilight something else hanging from the roof brushes her face and makes her jump – a piece of cobwebbed harness, black with age. Grinning, Forsyth comes inside and stands too close to her. For a moment she thinks he might attack her and she panics. She is on her own with him – his wife is away, doing her messages. When she edges away he doesn't follow her, keeping his distance now. She is thankful although she knows that it is probably because he despises her. There is Ian's bicycle, on its side with the paintbox underneath it. The bulky holdall is in the far corner, covered in flakes of lime. Everything must have been thrown in there like that – by him and the half-witted boy in the hour after Ian died.

She picks up the holdall, brushing the specks of white off it. Lugging it open she looks inside then back at Forsyth, staring at him through the half light. 'The painting, *Mystery Four*. Where is it?'

Glaring back at her he hesitates, and that moment of hesitation tells her that the painting has been there – he has seen it.

He picks that up and realises he has lost that move. Before his next he has to work out what to tell her. 'The picture. Aye,' he sighs, distaste in his voice.

'It isn't here,' she accuses him. Forsyth comes a step closer and looks down at the empty bag in her hands. She picks up the smells which hang around his unwashed working clothes – sweat and sheep dung, cheap tobacco. He brushes the back of his hand against the peak of his cap, tipping it onto the back of his head at an insolent angle.

'No, and it shouldn't be. We're clean people here at Carrucate.'

'What do you mean?' But she has an inkling of what is coming next.

'It was dirty, that picture. You naked like that – showing everything.'

She sees his eyes look her up and down, pausing pointedly at her breasts, her womb, where she is heavy, and she doesn't give a damn. She protests, 'Robert McAllen didn't think so.'

'We may be his tenants but we don't need the laird to tell us what is right or wrong. Some things he is entitled to tell us but not that, so we burnt it. That was what we did with it.'

'Burnt it?'

'Aye. I broke it up and put it on the range. That's what I did.'

He is lying – she knows he is. He probably has it stashed away, hidden from his wife, somewhere secret but convenient where he can take it out from time to time and savour it. Perhaps he keeps it in the shed where the boy sleeps, under the bed. Perhaps they share it. Whatever they do there is no way she can prove that they have it or that it has ever been there. He knows that and so does she. There is no point in arguing with him or allowing him to humiliate her further.

'I'll take everything,' she says, picking up the bicycle and leaning it against the wall. Now that he has her beaten he thaws a little. Pulls down a couple of pieces of baler twine from the roof to help her tie the bag, the box of paints, to the carrier behind the bike saddle. The sooner that job is done the sooner he will be rid of her.

She wheels it bumping over the cobbles to the gate

and holds it steady there, forcing him to open the gate for her. Then she pushes past him without a word down the track to the road; still pushing it because the track is too pitted with holes to ride it comfortably.

Closing the gate he doesn't bother to watch her go. He enjoyed that interlude but now he has other tasks to get on with.

Julia clutched Ramsay by the arm. Her fingers dug into his flesh. 'I've had enough of this place. It's time we moved on to Dundrennan,' she said and started back to the car. This seemed to be one of her sentimental phases. Had he been cruel he might have said that she seemed to care more for the two unfortunates from the past, the woman Jane and Mary Stuart, than for those they saw each day in London – grey shapes in shop doorways or shifting in their sleep by the river. He amended that – those that he saw, because she never seemed to see them, certainly never commented on them nor gave them any money. She had not outgrown the eighties; if society was a meaningful concept to other people, then they could see to it themselves, not expect her to get involved.

At that moment a small flock of sheep came pouring through a well-used gap in a drystone dyke on his left. He noted a mixture of breeds – mostly blackface, with some Suffolk cross and a few Cheviots. They baaed to each other as they came. One or two stared at the incomers, expecting to be fed though it wasn't that time of year.

Sheep. The sight of them raised a doubt in Ramsay's

mind. He turned and, walking backwards for a moment, took another look at the farmhouse and the land surrounding it. A lot of it – several hundred acres, no doubt – thin grazing, though.

Glancing back, Julia tried to hurry him up. 'Charles, *do* get mobile.'

As he trudged after her, reached the car and swung into the driving seat the doubt that had planted itself in his mind grew into a simple question.

After dinner that night he asked James if he might make a telephone call.

'Help yourself. There's a phone in the library. Use that if you like.' In case he needed privacy.

Ramsay made a point of phoning his father every couple of days, keeping in touch, because he wasn't able to get to Bressemer often. Ernest Ramsay lived on his own there, had done for years. Imperceptibly his world was becoming smaller, the scope of his life shrinking, and not only because his physical capacities were failing. He was growing less venturesome too, losing the taste for it, Ramsay thought with regret. Since he had discovered his father's losses at Lloyd's, and had had to go to such lengths to deal with them, the old man had treated him with an unnerving deference which he hadn't sought and didn't enjoy. Before that they had spoken to one another as equals. Now it was as if the balance of power had swung over on to Charles's side and he hated it. What his father needed was to regain confidence in himself. He would give him a small job to do. It might help.

The telephone rang a dozen times before it was answered. How was Scotland? the old man enquired, listened dutifully for a while to what Charles had to say about it. And Julia? Julia was fine. Then his father talked as only the lonely know how. About the small events of his life – a lunch with neighbours, a visit to Ipswich. Next, the latest political scandal; he was invariably shocked by what he saw as a deterioration in standards in public life. His son had given up trying to convince him that politicians had always been sinners – the only difference being that in his father's day they had enjoyed the luxury of sinning in private.

Charles let him have his head for a while. Eventually when Ernest paused to find another topic, anxious to prevent his son from ringing off, he put in, 'Are you still on good terms with Williamsons?'

This was a local firm of agricultural auctioneers who had been doing business with Bressemer for decades – selling its wheat or cattle, carrying out valuations, buying acreage on its behalf. Charles had no reason to suppose that his father had fallen out with them, but he had grown less predictable latterly, sometimes difficult to please. Certainly the old man didn't rush to claim friendship with them.

'Reasonable,' he replied. 'Why, shouldn't I be? What've they been up to now? Have you heard something?'

'No. Nothing at all. I wondered if you would do something for me.'

'Depends what it is.'

'Ask them if they've ever heard of a man called Malcolm Forsyth.'

157

'Why?'

'I need to check up on him.' Charles could have pretended that he was selling Forsyth something and needed a credit reference, but he never told unnecessary lies – not to anybody, least of all his father.

'So what's he been up to, this man Forsyth?' his father enquired.

'He's a farmer up here. That is, he is now. Before that he was operating somewhere in East Anglia. Claims to have made a pile out of arable farming, using lots of rented land. You know the type.'

Ernest Ramsay did. Such people were no favourites of his. 'They'll have knowledge of him if anybody does,' he said as though he relished the task – if it meant getting even with one of them. 'What do I say, to Williamson?'

'Just ask if they've heard of him. Malcolm Forsyth. You'd better write the name down, don't you think?' Ernest Ramsay's short-term memory was no longer reliable.

'Don't need to,' he replied promptly.

'Malcolm Forsyth,' Charles insisted. 'And if they don't know him, ask around, would you?'

Chapter Eleven

At the other end of the line Anny sounded out of breath, as she did always, and petulant with it. 'Why the hurry all of a sudden, Mr Lewis?'

When she Mr Lewissed him it meant that she was put out, really and truly. He waited for her to speak her mind – expel her grievance. Get it all out of your system, Anny.

Her smoker's voice complained, 'I asked you to ring me Tuesday. Did you? You didn't.'

Excuses would only waste time so Ethelred plunged on, 'What I need is a cannon, just as I told you. Like a field gun, with big wheels.' Silence at the other end. 'You do know what I mean, Anny? A gun. That can be pulled along – by no more than five men. No heavier than that. That's important. Have you got that? Anny, are you with me?'

Was that a grunt of assent? He wasn't sure. 'Are you still there?'

'Yeh, course I am,' she assured him without commitment.

'Anything that looks pre-1850 will do. It doesn't have to be fancy but it must—'

'Be able to fire blanks. You said already,' she grumbled. 'You should've rung me Tuesday. Then O'Leary would've had two days extra. Two whole days to—'

'I had to check it out. I couldn't afford to get it wrong.'

She chuckled and coughed volcanically. 'You got to live dangerously, my boy. Take risks, like us. We're always taking risks, we are. As you well know, Mr Lewis. Talking of that, how much?'

'We agreed...' and he repeated the figure she had quoted when he'd asked her first.

'That's history. You can forget that. Put it right out of your mind,' she advised him. 'We need to talk more than that because there's the time factor now that's got to be considered. And if O'Leary's going to fit this in he's going to have to rearrange his schedule.'

'How much more?'

There was a pause, then he heard her speaking aside, a client in the shop by the sound of it. 'They're all a hundred and fifty, love. Each. All them in that case. Take your pick.'

'Well?' demanded Ethelred and waited while she brought her attention slowly back to bear on him.

'Five extra, Mr Lewis.'

Five hundred pounds more. That was heavy, but hadn't he already covered himself in his price to Forsyth? Naturally he had – because he had foresight, Ethelred.

'Done,' he cried, a man of quick decision too, 'provided you pick up that cellphone of yours and get on to O'Leary this instant.'

'In advance,' warned Anny.

He'd expected that. Had already made provision, too, for the long drive down to London and back. 'Half before, half after,' he shot back and was surprised that she swallowed it. 'Mind you, it's all off if the gun is delivered late.'

'I said you should have rung me Tuesday,' she replied morosely.

'You're a real professional,' said Ethelred. 'Bye.'

It was after he emerged from the telephone box that he got the shock. There, turning past the bank at the end of the street. It had to be her – that bright helmet of golden hair, the way she held herself – he couldn't be mistaken. He bustled after the figure, began almost to run, pushing past shoppers, women with pushchairs, almost cannoned into a huge white-haired farmer in a peaked cap who gripped his arm. 'Here, lad, what's your problem?'

Ethelred wrenched himself away, pressed on. She was crossing the car park now. He had to pause to let a car go past and that lost him several yards. It was her, he was sure of it. Then she stopped and hesitated as though she had suddenly remembered something she ought to have done.

He called out, 'Mrs Johnson. Margaret.' When she turned her face he saw that it was her – definitely. At the same moment she recognised him and walked away swiftly and decisively – not running, but obviously trying to avoid him.

He felt his heart pounding now, a pulse beating in his ears as he hurried on. 'Please, Mrs Johnson,' he called out.

161

A passer-by looked at him with suspicion, but was unready to intervene of course. People never interfered, thank goodness, Ethelred thought. He managed to get ahead of her and spun round to stop her in her tracks. 'I thought it was you,' he panted.

She made no fuss, didn't attempt to push past him. Just waited, arms hanging easily at her sides – waited for him to state his business.

'What's gone wrong? Couldn't you get Ian to leave?'

'We discussed it.'

'I suppose he took no notice. Would you like me to speak to him?'

'I am quite capable of communicating with my husband, thank you. I don't need help from anyone.' And her look said, *certainly not from somebody like you who knows nothing of men and women*.

He was used to that and shrugged the look away. 'Don't take it like that. You know that isn't what I meant. I explained to you. It's important, doesn't he understand that? This is a small place. Ramsay could appear anywhere at any time.' He looked down the Victorian terraced street uneasily, as though Ramsay might be lurking in the gloom behind one of those square plate-glass windows.

'I told Ian,' she said and opened her hands in a false gesture which said it had been an impossible case. Ethelred felt a surge of sympathy for her. That husband of hers.

'I wish you'd let me speak to him. This is very tricky, you know. Tricky.'

'Very well, why don't you?' she relented. 'You know

where we are. He's indoors much of the day at the moment.' Ever since she had taken charge of his secret and disloyal hoard she had kept him on a very close rein for money. With money she could control him – a tug here, a pull there – just as he had controlled her not so long before, kept her on the rein.

She allowed him just enough for his gambling each day to make sure that he stayed more or less on her side and didn't sulk too much or offer her nuisance. But the allowance didn't keep him in the betting shop for long. One thing was certain, though – unless he had a large win he wouldn't leave the town without her consent and these days it wasn't a winning time for him. The allowance she gave him simply dripped away each day. She kept him topped up – for him it was better than nothing. A small daily transfusion to keep him functioning; his life-support system.

Another sure thing was that she wasn't going to leave as long as there was a chance of encountering Charles Ramsay. She had already worked out when and where.

'Well? Do you want to come with me now and talk to Ian?' she demanded.

Ethelred thought about it. It wasn't going to help, was it? Intruding into that ordinary little flat of theirs and manufacturing a drama in their living room. They would gang up on him, dig in their heels. It would only make everything worse.

'Look, why don't you talk to him again and see what you can do to get him to change his mind? I'll phone him myself later on. Or maybe I'll come by.'

'That would be better,' she agreed gravely, then looking briskly at her watch she said, 'I must get on. I've a million things to do.' She smiled, fluttered her fingers in a friendly farewell and made off lithely down the street. Such a civilised woman, he thought as he watched her go. That wretched man Ian Johnson didn't deserve her.

The Earl of Auchenbrach spent as little time as he could at his place in Scotland. Scotland was damp and full of wild life – deer, rabbits and pheasants – which people shot at. Not him; he deplored field sports, considered them barbaric, but of course he kept his distaste to himself since there was no point in upsetting his neighbours. The best way to avoid that, he reflected, as he shook open his *Financial Times* on the terrace of his charming house near Carpentras, was to go near the place as little as possible. A glance across the valley, embellished with conifers and vineyards, smiling in the sun, confirmed his view that Provence was the place to be.

He poured himself another cup from the cafetière and settled down to a rather good article on the French government's strong franc policy. Then, over the pink horizon of the *FT*, he stole another glance at the view. There was a haze over the valley like the bloom on a peach and in the distance a small red tractor was crawling lazily down a road, sending up a cloud of yellow dust. It pleased the Earl to see things happening.

Something touched his cheek, something warm. It was the palm of his wife's hand.

'I've been through the mail, Adrian,' she said, and the tone of her voice told him that he wouldn't welcome what she was going to say. That was why she had stroked his cheek. It was a sweet, to prepare him for a spoonful of nasty medicine.

He pretended not to know what was coming next.

'Anything urgent?' he enquired.

'One or two invitations. And they're doing a pageant thing at Steilbow Castle. We've been asked to grace it with our presence. Arabella Knight has got it up and several people we know are in it. The McAllens and so on. It should be fun.'

'If it doesn't rain,' he replied, watching the red tractor in the shimmering distance. To hell with Scotland. It was eternal and he was in thrall to it, unable to escape from four hundred years of history – Drumpagan with its towers and expensive roof, his son's inheritance. All that had to be looked after. The Earl had a vivid sense of property and the need to preserve it, and he was clear-sighted enough to know that it was what enabled him to do whatever he liked with his life.

For most of the time.

'There is a long letter from the factor too,' his countess said. 'Lots of things to see to – and it's time we showed our faces for a bit, don't you think?'

He looked up at her, thought of asking, 'Do I have to?' No. Noblesse oblige. If noblesse obliged him to return to his own country, it wasn't going to be for more than three weeks, though. He was going to be absolutely firm about that.

He folded his newspaper – somehow it had lost its savour.

'Tell me the dates and I'll go to Avignon tomorrow and get the aeroplane tickets,' he promised.

The sooner they went the sooner they could return. He watched a mosquito land on his wrist and settle down for a leisurely feed. A smart slap with the folded pink newspaper and it was flattened. He rubbed away the black smudge of its corpse and felt better. Nothing wrong with his reflexes. That was one form of blood sport that he did enjoy.

O'Leary stretched out his legs in his big landcruiser. Rugged, high off the ground and plenty of room, it had cost him a stack and he couldn't set it off against tax because he didn't pay any. What else was money for, though, but spending? It had been high time he'd had a new motor, he mused, as it roared up the M6 on a clear evening. Phil was in the driving seat because O'Leary had reached an age and a girth which made driving a chore. O'Leary smiled with approval as the youth cut up a holidaymaker lugging his family caravan north, pushing him into the slow lane where the dozy bugger belonged.

O'Leary was getting lazy and he knew it, too old and slow for this kind of action – and a small voice in his head warned him that if he didn't sharpen up he risked a catastrophe. The police had too much going on to do more than go through the motions when any of his work was drawn to their attention, but he'd got so careless the last time that they'd nearly had him. The woman had been done for stolen goods and her silence had cost him a grand. More than that – it was no use pretending, was it?

He ought to get in shape, that was what. He glanced down at the bulk spilling over his broad leather belt, considered the problem, decided that any action on it would have to be put off, and pulled his donkey jacket round himself to cover it up.

He needed to get in shape mentally at least. His mind was getting so sluggish. He'd spent some time on this one – or Jamie had. The party was abroad, that was known for sure, and while the house was fully covered by alarms and that, there was nothing outside. No infra red or anything. O'Leary shuddered inwardly, because it was all getting so electronic these days. Jamie understood that stuff, though, and had gone up to the place and tested it – seen nobody, heard nothing. Taken a risk there and O'Leary was grateful. And he'd fixed up the van and a shed for them to use. He was a real asset, Jamie was.

Phil turned to him and asked, 'Which turnoff?'

'There isn't no turnoff. You carry straight on to the end.' He'd told the boy that three times. Suddenly O'Leary was hit by a burst of no confidence in himself. Here he was, not as fast on his feet as he had been, and with only this boy to help. Strong enough but not a brain in his head, as far as O'Leary could judge, which left all the planning to him, with Scotland not being his territory. He'd be glad when they met up with Jamie; he'd be a reinforcement. He saw things others didn't see.

And O'Leary had just seen a police car. 'Watch it,' he snapped. 'Get your speed down, will you?' The only drawback with a vehicle like this was that it was conspicuous. He glanced at his watch. Plenty of time to meet up with Jamie and get over to this house he'd found. A great discoverer of stuff, was Jamie. What was the house called? Drumpagan.

He reached behind him for the road atlas because he was going to have to give Phil directions in a minute and the boy'd need telling more than the once.

'Man, we'll skate it,' Jamie said cockily as he handed O'Leary the mug of tea when they'd been through the briefing session. As an afterthought he unscrewed the cap of a bottle of clear liquid and poured a slug into each cup. 'Here, have a drop of voddy in it. You've come a long way.' It was all clear as daylight. O'Leary envied him his efficiency, the planning – all like it had been before with him ten years younger.

'Where's the van?' he enquired, to try and assert himself as Jamie's equal. He felt the bite of the spirit as it passed his gums and warmed his belly; and then as he drew in his breath there was a pang in one of his back teeth. Age again.

'The van?' Jamie slipped the bottle back in the fridge. 'In the shed. You take me there. I pick up the van. Nae probs,' he announced, slamming the fridge door for emphasis. 'It gets light about four so we'd better be away as soon as you've had your tea.'

They travelled for a while on the Glasgow road then

turned east, Jamie in front, leading the way, the landcruiser behind, keeping in touch with its tail lights. O'Leary had taken the wheel now, his big hands at ten past two.

The road got narrower, down to a single lane with passing places. No traffic, though – nothing. Oak trees on either side now, looming up palely in the headlights – then they passed a whitewashed cottage with blank, unlit windows.

A mile further on Jamie switched off his headlights and drove on his sidelights only. O'Leary closed up to maintain contact with him. When he got to the crest of the hill he cut his engine and began to coast downhill. O'Leary did the same, keeping no more than twenty yards behind him. The two vehicles slowed to a stop.

Jamie descended from the cab of the van, the tiny torch in his hand throwing no more than a pinpoint of light on the ground. O'Leary and the boy joined up with him, their eyes already used to the darkness.

'The house is down the way a bit,' muttered Jamie, flicking the spot of light towards it. O'Leary could just make out its dark outline. Silent, no lights at all.

'The cannons are round the front. There are two of them. You'll see when we get there.'

Jamie had the steel hawser with the noose in it looped over his shoulder. He unhitched it and swung into the front seat beside O'Leary, who started the engine, switched the headlights full on and immediately saw a couple of roe deer there ahead, looking towards him, startled, frozen in the light. As the landcruiser moved forward they leapt out of its way and went turning and bouncing away to the safety of the woods. It accelerated past the side of the house and on to the broad stretch of turf in front of it. There was a stone balustrade with steps down to an ornamental lake. At the top of the steps were the two cannon, one on either side. Swinging the wheel over, O'Leary brought the vehicle round, crashed the gears into reverse and backed it up to the nearer of them. It seemed as though Jamie and Phil were out of the vehicle before it stopped, haring towards the cannon, attaching the hawser to it then to the tow bar of the landcruiser. It took no more than fifteen seconds and then O'Leary was dragging the gun back to the van as fast as possible. Once there they had the doors open, the planks in place and the cannon hitched to the winch inside in seconds. There was no sign of life from the house as the winch whined and laboured, dragging the gun up the planks and into the back of the van, a man on either side to hold it steady. The noise, though! O'Leary slammed the doors shut and banged on them to signal to Jamie to drive away. Phil was already at the wheel of the landcruiser when O'Leary got in and was off after the van. Panting, O'Leary looked at his watch and saw that no more than three minutes had elapsed from start to finish. There was life in the old dog yet.

Chapter Twelve

James McAllen had decided to hold the meeting in the library and he seemed to think that an extra formality was needed, because he was wearing a jacket and tie. Perhaps, thought Ramsay, it was simply out of deference to the feelings of Cameron Rae, clothed in a dark grey suit as befitted a solicitor on a working day – dark grey with a faint red stripe, Ramsay noticed. It would be just like James to avoid underlining the fact that he was a man of leisure who could dress as informally as he pleased, whereas Cameron was not.

The three of them stood in the spacious entrance hall at Glengarrick, waiting for the final member of the party to arrive. It was two minutes to eleven. For once James McAllen seemed to be on edge. It was understandable. It was a day of decisions.

'Andover will be on time,' Ramsay assured him and grinned as he remembered the man. 'He told me once that punctuality is the politeness of princes.' That was how he, Sir Anthony Andover, seemed to think of himself: a prince of commerce – a Renaissance magnate dealing in gold and jewels. Sir Anthony was the head of Golver's private client department – that was what they

171

called it now. Once it had been no more than an offshoot, a toy which his fellow directors had given him to keep him quiet. They had to put up with him because he had inherited a substantial block of Golver's shares and he was clever enough to make damn sure that he never ran the risk of having to sell them. So, however insufferable, he was also immovable. And he was getting worse now that the chairman had decided to give more weight to the private side, as he put it. However they dressed up the figures, the other directors couldn't gainsay it. Andover's sideshow was bringing in a much healthier return than much of the company's mainstream business. The unpalatable fact which their chairman was forcing them to take on board was that, however much they disliked him, within his own small empire Andover knew what he was doing. He had to be given his head.

And that was why, when Ramsay had tried to contact him, he had played hard to get. He was never in his office, always in conference with the chairman or at a departmental communication exercise. He had always been pompous – now he was absolutely regal. Eventually he had returned the call, as Ramsay knew he would, because the story would appeal to him: a Scottish landowner selling an historic medallion commemorating the doomed and romantic Mary Stuart; a private sale requiring all the qualities which Andover saw himself possessing – discretion, subtlety, flair. Once he had made a few enquiries on 'the other side of the pond' he would come up to Scotland himself, he said; adding, with a sigh, that he deserved a break...

They heard the taxi coming up the drive and went out to meet him.

He came up the steps cheerfully towards James, a chic and slender briefcase swinging at his side, hand out-stretched, moving quickly for such a bulky man.

'Anthony Andover. So pleased,' he said. A rosy, well-fed man, impeccable in cavalry twills and a nicely cut hacking jacket. In a world he understood, meeting his sort of people – in his element. The introductions over, James led him inside and marshalled the four of them around the neo-Gothic oak table in the centre of the library. What Ramsay liked about the room was that it was meant for working in, not just for looking at – there were no shelves of unread calf bindings put there merely for show; no ostentatious sets of books on British birds or African mammals which hadn't been opened since the reign of George V.

The setup on the table was businesslike too – pads, pencils, even bottles of Perrier water and glasses. Andover obviously liked the look of that – it meant he was being taken seriously. But the most important item on the table was the brown leather case stamped with fleurs de lys which McAllen had placed, open, exactly in the centre, on a soft oblong of dark green baize. Beside it was a powerful magnifying glass on a plastic stand. James ushered Andover to his seat and the others sat down after him.

Andover swivelled his heavy body round to speak to James McAllen. 'May I compliment you on these arrange-ments? I wish all my clients were as perceptive as you have been. As you have foreseen, the first thing I have to do is to satisfy myself that the article is what I have been led to expect. That is not to impugn the expertise of Mr Ramsay. Not at all. I have the greatest faith in his judgement. But there is always the possibility of a difference of opinion between experts.'

It was gracefully done, Ramsay thought – perhaps Andover wasn't as bad as he remembered him.

'Before we do anything else,' he continued, 'I should like you to see this.' He delved into the briefcase beside him, drew out a glossy dark blue booklet and proffered it to James, who thanked him while looking at it doubtfully, uncertain what it was.

'The catalogue of our last auction sale of medals,' Andover explained.

But why? Why should it be necessary? He knew who Golvers were. He didn't need to have their credentials confirmed to him. James opened it. From beside him Ramsay glanced down at the title page.

GOLVER PLC
PRIVATE CLIENT DEPARTMENT

Auction of Commemorative and Historical Medals

A Collection of European medals relating to the
Napoleonic Wars
The Benjamin Braden Collection of early
Renaissance medals
Highly important English medals of the 16th to
19th centuries including many portrait pieces of
the Stuart monarchs...

Why was he being shown this? Charles could see that McAllen was still at a loss.

Andover said, 'Before we start I wanted to put our discussion into context. Would you turn to page thirty-five.' James did so.

'I'd like to direct your attention to lots 349 to 353,' Andover went on.

Now Charles understood what he was about. He was going to knock the client down, or soften him up, or whatever. Andover was going to lower McAllen's expectations now to make him more willing to accept the deal he intended to lay on the table later: *if* the Mary Medallion came up to the mark – that was always the proviso.

'You will see beside each lot our estimate of what we expected to make at auction and I've pencilled in next to it the figure we actually achieved. I've chosen these particular lots because they are relevant to the one we are considering. These medals are silver, of course, and they are not particularly rare, but I think it would be helpful to look over the figures.'

Andover had another copy of the catalogue in his hand. 'Now here we have,' he looked down at it and began to read, '1588. The Defeat of the Spanish Armada. Pope with kings and bishops. Reverse – Spanish fleet driven against rocks. 50mm in diameter. 24.15 grams. Good to fine.'

He smiled mischievously at his audience. 'That doesn't quite mean what it says. In fact it tells us that this is not a particularly desirable example. You'll see that our estimate was £600 and the lot actually made £850. If you look down the list you will see that several medals of a better condition – what we in the trade call 'Very fine' or 'Extremely fine' – could be had for less than two thousand pounds, which you must admit is, these days, not a great deal of money.'

'So are you trying to tell us that the Mary Medallion is not going to be worth much?' It was Cameron Rae's voice, as direct as usual. 'You haven't come such a distance to tell us that, have you?'

'I haven't seen it yet so I couldn't possibly say that.' Taking care not to make the words sound like a reproof, Sir Anthony eyed the ancient leather case. 'All I wanted to get across is the need to be realistic. I want your client, Mr McAllen, to be aware at the outset that in this market quite important pieces in tip-top condition can be had for what I consider to be small money. From what I have heard from Mr Ramsay I believe this medallion to be intriguing, even exceptional, with much greater potential. Obviously, however, I cannot tell you what I believe that potential to be until I have inspected it. So let's get straight to it, shall we?' Pompous perhaps, but he'd made his point smoothly enough.

He took a silk handkerchief from his briefcase, folded it twice and placed it on the table in front of him, then drew the open case towards him and took out the medallion, placing it on the smooth bed he had prepared for it. The room was light enough. Sunshine streamed through the high windows and was reflected from the white shutters on either side of them. A pool of sunlight was creeping across the Turkey carpet, making it blaze with reds and greens, but had not yet reached the table. Andover picked up the magnifying glass, placed it over the medallion and bent his head to look at it, almost as though in prayer. Nobody spoke. Cameron Rae shifted in his chair.

The shadow of an uncertainty lurked at the back of Ramsay's mind, something which had bothered him ever since he had first seen the medallion. He had clear sight, and when it came to assessing objects he was unemotional. He hoped that in a minute or two this irritating little doubt of his was going to be squashed for good. Andover had lost his egotism, his grandeur; he was a sober professional now, dedicated to establishing the truth. With deliberation, he put the magnifier to one side, turned the medallion over, and replaced it. His lips moved, Ramsay noticed. What was he whispering to himself? Very fine? Extremely fine? It did make a difference. Next he took the moulds, obverse and reverse, out of the ancient leather case. Finally, he inspected the case itself.

He looked up and said to James, 'I understand that the medallion has been in your family's possession since it was cast, a year or two after the Queen's execution. Is that correct?'

McAllen nodded.

'What do you have in the way of documentary evidence which supports this provenance?'

Ramsay put in, 'I mentioned to Sir Anthony the inventory of 1595, and the account of the story of the medallion which was written by your great-great-grandfather, in 1824 I think you said.'

James had papers ready on a side table. He got up and gave them to Andover. He said, 'The inventory is in the language and calligraphy of the time. The typescript attached is a transliteration which my father had done thirty years ago. I have taken photocopies of everything for you to keep.'

Andover's gaze flickered from the originals to the photocopies to verify the latter. Then he slumped back in his chair and began to read the first page with fierce concentration.

Cameron Rae leant forward. 'If you need—'

A gesture from Sir Anthony silenced him. He was a judge absorbing a crucial document and was not to be interrupted by a provincial solicitor. Cameron Rae seemed nervy, Ramsay thought; understandably anxious for his client's interests. There was no need. Ramsay had gone over the documents with James the night before. The provenance was as good as you could get. Rae should keep quiet – this wasn't his moment.

When he had finished reading, Andover didn't speak for a moment; sat instead with his head down as though burdened with thought – probably savouring the moment of suspense, Ramsay guessed. Then he threw the photocopies down on the table with a theatrical gesture and said, 'Well, that's fine. Excellent. Just what I was hoping for.'

Ramsay watched the other two relax. This was when it got interesting.

Sir Anthony went on, 'Before I came up here I got our people in New York to put out one or two feelers and they have come up with something quite promising, I think.'

'A buyer?' Cameron Rae asked. What did he think? Sir Anthony ignored the redundant question and looked across at McAllen.

'Have you ever heard of the Walter Malling Museum?' When James shook his head Andover transferred his gaze to Ramsay.

'Sure,' he replied. 'It's in Washington, isn't it? It specialises in sculpture, bas reliefs, medals. Set up in about 1955, I think.'

Andover gave an encouraging nod. 'Not bad,' he conceded grandly. 'The background is interesting. Malling was a speculator who made a fortune selling stocks short during the Wall Street Crash; made more money than he knew what to do with, so he became a collector. Not an omnivorous collector like Hearst or Burrell; Malling collected the sculpted portraits of the famous. Why he went for that I don't know. Perhaps he was conscious of being something of a fraud himself...'

Cameron Rae shifted in his chair impatiently and Ramsay wondered why McAllen had asked him to this meeting at all. He hadn't proved much of an asset so far. He didn't seem to understand how fortunate they were that Sir Anthony was taking a personal interest in the medallion. He had come a long way to inspect it for himself; the least they could do was to let him tell the story in his own way. But it didn't matter, for Andover was above all that.

He sailed on, 'At any rate he became an avid collector of medals, coins, and miniature sculpted portraits of the famous. When he died in the fifties he left a fortune to endow a museum to house his huge collection and to extend it. That brought its own problems, though. Which were?' Like a benign schoolteacher he turned to Charles as his star pupil, knowing he would provide the answer.

'Tax problems,' Ramsay said.

'Exactly. The trustees have to make regular acquisitions in order to maintain its charitable status. It's a major difficulty for them.'

'Why?' James McAllen asked. 'If they have the money.'

'They have too much. Malling's fund was well and conservatively invested and has grown enormously in value since his death. Also, as I have explained, these objects are still relatively cheap. Besides which, the will laid down stringent conditions on what items were acceptable. They have to be portrait medals, and absolutely authentic. He still has hungry heirs who would benefit if they failed to meet its terms, and to make matters worse there isn't much around left to buy. When he was alive he laid his hands on much of what was available himself. There is a lot held in other museums who aren't going to sell...' His voice trailed away as he left the other three to absorb the implications.

The obvious question lay waiting for James McAllen to ask it, but he seemed reluctant, as though he knew he was about to commit himself and was hesitating at the last moment. At length he said, 'You think they will want to acquire the Mary Medallion?'

'Yes, there's a good chance they will. It's very much

their thing. I would have thought they can't afford not to.'

'Will they accept your assessment of it?' Ramsay asked.

'I should think so. They might want someone of their own to look it over, but that could be arranged, couldn't it?' Andover glanced at its owner.

'Of course,' James agreed.

'I understand you want a private sale,' Andover said.

'If possible.'

'That would suit them.'

Cameron Rae broke in harshly, 'I've told James, I'm against that. I think it should go to auction.'

His client was about to speak but was forestalled by Andover who asked, 'Why?'

'That's obvious, surely,' Rae replied shortly. 'Putting it on sale in the open market is the only way to make sure James gets the right price for it.'

'If only it were as simple as that,' Andover said. 'Now let's be clear. These people operate in a small and specialised world where everybody knows everybody else. To begin with they'll have a good idea of who is likely to be bidding and who is not – who can afford to bid against them and who cannot. They would most likely bid through a leading dealer, and the dealers are all like that.' He interleaved his manicured fingers.

Rae wasn't prepared to give up: a solicitor, a friend of McAllen's determined to do the job he was paid for – looking after his principal's interest, ready to worry at the argument until it turned his way. He shot back, 'They are all acting for different clients. They have no common interest.'

Andover gave out a worldly-wise chuckle. 'Of course they have a common interest – to make money. Have you ever heard of a ring? You know what it is?'

'Aye, and I know it's illegal,' Rae rasped.

'Of course it is, and Mr Ramsay will confirm that there is likely to be a ring of some kind operating at half the auction sales held in Britain this week. And if there's one going at every country antique auction, you don't imagine that for an item as important as this the dealers won't gang up, do you? They'll fix their maximum, which will be far below what the item would make if there were a free-for-all among them. Then there will be a private auction afterwards.'

'Come on!' Rae burst out triumphantly. 'Their clients will know what was paid for the lot. They won't stand for it.'

'Most probably they will know exactly what is happening and will benefit too, one way or another,' Andover replied.

That, Ramsay felt, was going too far. Andover was exaggerating. He put in, 'You may have a point, Cameron. But there are other considerations. When we first discussed the medallion, James told me he preferred to have no publicity. I proceeded on that basis and that was why I consulted Sir Anthony. If you are now saying you want to go to auction you have put me in a false position. I might be prepared to waive my fee, at least in part, but Golvers can scarcely be expected to do so. The auctioneer would require a commission from James and probably from the buyer as well. All that is going to take a hell of a bite out of the price they get for the medallion.'

'Yes, yes, you proceeded on that basis,' Rae said sardonically glancing from Ramsay to Andover and back again. You have stitched up my client, the glance said – and it said something else. You two have something in common – that was the other message, and Ramsay realised that it wasn't simply that they were both involved in the antique business. There was a deeper distrust there which went much further back. What else had he and Andover in common? They were both from over the Border, weren't they. English. It looked as if Cameron Rae hadn't forgotten Bruce, the execution of Wallace ... the Rough Wooing ... Culloden ... He probably recited the names of the dead at Flodden to himself at night before he went to sleep...

Sir Anthony was far too diplomatic, too adept at this kind of discussion, to show any irritation. He said easily, 'It was our understanding that Mr McAllen wanted a private sale, but of course if...?'

He looked for confirmation to James, who put in tactfully, 'Look, Cameron, it's already been decided. I want this kept as quiet as possible. You know why as well as I do.'

Rae grunted and shifted angrily in his seat. The man seemed to be a bundle of neuroses and looked almost ready to get up and leave. One of those awkward Scots with a permanent chip on the shoulder.

There was a silence. Andover said, 'There is a danger here of losing sight of our objective. What is it, Charles?'

'To get the best price,' Ramsay replied dutifully.

'Thank you. Now, gentlemen, in my judgement the Malling situation presents a window of opportunity. Why? Because they have surplus money they have to find a home for, and they need something like this medallion to spend it on. It exactly fits the guidelines laid down for them and they need a private sale. Why do you think that is?' he challenged Rae, who knew the answer very well. He wasn't a fool and he didn't want to look like one.

'Because if it doesn't go to auction they can pay as much as they like for it – within reason, I suppose.'

'Exactly. It's unique, so nobody can say they paid too much. If it's auctioned the price is going to be set by the market and that could be a hell of a lot less, ring or no ring.

'When we started this meeting I took pains to point out the kind of price level which obtains in the market. OK, this piece is very special. It's gold, it has a history, Hilliard designed it – but the open market won't produce the kind of money that we are looking for.'

'Which is?' James put in. He was getting impatient with so much talk.

They'd come to it at last. There was silence for a moment. The shaft of sunlight, Ramsay noticed, had reached the legs of the table, would soon be glinting on the medallion itself.

'Where does all this put us?' James asked again brusquely.

Andover wasn't going to let himself be cheated of his moment, though. He took his time before he said, 'I think we should indicate that you would be prepared to consider an offer of three hundred thousand pounds; let's call it four hundred and fifty thousand American dollars. That would be not just for the medallion but for everything we see here. The case and the moulds as well. They add enormously to the interest of the object.'

'Not the papers, though,' James stipulated quickly.

'No. Not the papers. Although I am sure they would wish to have copies.'

Rae exhaled while Ramsay watched McAllen's face for his reaction. Was he satisfied? Was it enough to compensate him for parting with the items on the table?

Suddenly, as he spoke, James McAllen's voice cracked. He was under more stress than he wanted to admit. 'How long would it take?' He was seized with a coughing fit, almost as though the words had caught in his throat. He poured himself a glass of water to settle it. After a moment, when he had got his composure back, he asked again, 'To complete the sale, I mean. How long would it take? I don't want to hang about on this.'

That surprised Ramsay. He hadn't expected him to be in a hurry for the money, imagining that he would be better organised than that. He couldn't possibly be under pressure from his bank, could he? The whole setup here seemed so solid.

Andover took the question in his stride. He was used to dealing with that kind of question from people who found themselves not as rich as they thought they were. He wasn't going to make any concessions, however.

'This can't be rushed. The people who run the Foundation aren't unworldly innocents. If you press them they will immediately assume that you are short of cash.' He raised a hand to fend off a denial from McAllen. 'And to put it bluntly you will get screwed. They will simply take their time and make you sweat. Your stance has to be that you are totally relaxed about the whole thing, happy to dispose of this family trinket if, and only if, they are prepared to make it worth your while. So I'm afraid you must possess your soul in patience.'

Signalling that he accepted the advice McAllen looked round at the others. 'Right. That concludes our business, I think. Time for a gin,' he said.

At that moment the door opened. It was Julia.

'Charles, can you come to the phone? It's your father. Nothing serious, he says. In the drawing room.'

Ramsay went there.

'I haven't caught you at a bad moment, have I?' Because he had become less sure of himself it was the kind of question his father asked these days.

'Your man called Malcolm Forsyth. You wanted to know if I could find out anything about him.'

'Sure. What did Williamsons say?'

'They've never heard of him.'

'Are you certain?'

'Of course I am. I spoke to the old man – Ted Williamson himself.'

'Did he have anything else to say?'

'No, just that. He didn't know any Malcolm Forsyth – full stop. And to do me a favour he made one or two enquiries while I was there in his office. Rang round, you know. Gave me one or two names to try in Ipswich as well. I don't know why he should want to get on the right side of me. Perhaps it's ...'

'And nobody had heard of Forsyth?'

'No, nobody at all. And I was talking to people who ought to know. It's their job to know who the big people are – their living depends on it.'

Charles was silent for a moment. His father chuckled. It was an unusual, welcome sound.

'Is it what you wanted to hear?' he enquired.

'What I expected, rather. The chap's into sheep up here and not in a large way so it seemed odd, you see. He's got plenty of money, that's obvious ...'

'If so, it doesn't look as though he's made it out of farming round here,' his father interrupted, sounding pleased with himself.

'It doesn't, does it?' Charles agreed. If not, why had Forsyth said that he had? And if he was trying to conceal the source of his wealth, where had it come from?

When Charles got back to the library, Julia and Caroline were socialising before leading the guests off to the lunch they had prepared.

Julia asked, 'Any problems at Bressemer?'

'No problems.'

'He sounded on top of things.' She meant that his father hadn't sounded ... confused, that was the euphemism, wasn't it. He felt a twinge of resentment at her presumption. The old man wasn't in bad shape. She was too brisk with him on the rare occasions when they met, and she exaggerated his lapses of memory.

'Why did he ring?'

'Tell you later.'

Over the cold beef and salad, the walnut chutney, beer in pewter mugs again, nothing was said about the morning's meeting. It seemed to be accepted by everybody that it was up to James to broach the subject if he wanted to and it was obvious that he didn't. Ramsay hadn't expected him to celebrate the outcome but there didn't seem to be much evidence of even the quietest satisfaction. He managed to make conversation with Andover about the history of the house, the shooting – it emerged that Sir Anthony was an enthusiast and ran an annual shooting weekend for Golver's clients – but it was more of a duty than a pleasure.

After Andover left – Cameron Rae had at last managed to make himself useful by giving him a lift to the station to catch his train south – and the four of them sat over coffee in the kitchen, James was monosyllabic and for once Caroline wasn't hyperactive – she seemed to be overtaken by lethargy, though the meal they had just eaten couldn't have taxed her stamina much. Despite the brightness of the day there was a feeling of anti-climax in the air. Ramsay felt too sated after a third mug of beer, which he should have refused. He would have liked to take a brisk walk by himself. It wasn't going to be possible, though, was it? A fly buzzed against the window in the sun. The man had gone, Rae had gone, the meal was finished, and nobody else felt like moving.

It was then that Julia began to probe. She surprised
Ramsay by asking McAllen directly, 'Did you all have a
successful meeting with arrogant Sir Anthony?'

Hadn't she taken on board that James didn't want to
talk about it? They'd all been tiptoeing round the topic
for a couple of hours.

James deflected the question. 'I didn't find him
arrogant at all. Urbane, I thought – a bit self-important
perhaps. He certainly got through the business effec-
tively enough.'

'Was he optimistic?'

She had no business asking that kind of question
Ramsay thought. He put in, 'All in good time.'

James didn't seem to mind responding, though. 'The
outcome was OK. As good as we could have expected.'
But he wasn't going to submit to any more cross-ques-
tioning. He got up abruptly, put out his arm to beckon
Caroline from her chair and ushered her out of the room.
'We'll take ourselves off for a while.'

When they had gone there was a silence until Julia
said defensively, 'He didn't mind. You do realise that,
don't you? He didn't give a damn.'

Ramsay shrugged – it wasn't worth making an issue
of it. She looked across the table at him. 'How did it go?'
Her eyes didn't leave his face.

'Well enough. Andover was happy with the medallion, the provenance . . . and he thinks he's got a buyer.'
He wasn't breaching any confidence and she had to
know, since this was a joint effort and she was his
partner. She shouldn't have asked McAllen, that was
all, not so directly. It was what? A sort of impertinence,

Ramsay thought. No one imagined the guy was keen to sell the medallion. Then he kicked himself for being over fastidious.

He at least saw his own faults. Perhaps that wasn't the thing, though. Perhaps it was rather that he was looking for faults in her. Why? He had an uncomfortable feeling that he knew why. Reluctantly he began to spell it out to himself. It was to justify the fact that she didn't excite him these days as much as she had when . . .

Fortunately her voice broke into the thought. 'So he's got a buyer?'

For a moment he was absent. 'Who?' he said.

'Andover, of course. You weren't listening.'

Nor was he. He said quickly, 'The Malling Foundation in Washington, he thinks.'

'How much?'

Why was she so persistent? Oh, because of the commission.

'Three hundred K.'

She considered for a moment before she said, 'That's not bad.' She didn't need to spell out how much he was going to earn for the partnership. A comfortable sum for a straightforward task. It was who you knew that mattered.

'Maybe,' he warned. 'Maybe three hundred K.'

'It's nice to know where the figure lies though, isn't it. We had no idea.'

'We?' he queried. She hadn't been involved.

'Well we hadn't, had we? You could only guess.'

'It's unique,' he reminded her, as though he needed to defend himself.

She changed tack. 'And it went smoothly? No hiccups?'

'Not bad. That man Cameron Rae was a pain in the butt.'

'How?'

'Oh. Ignorant, and too solicitous for his client's welfare. Wanted it sold by auction.'

'Did he? Really?'

'Yes. There were undertones of resentment there. It was a pity James asked him. He was a waste of time. Just got in the way.'

'You know why that is, don't you?' She had the anticipatory look of someone eager to pass on a piece of gossip – something which exposed a flaw in an acquaintance.

He put down the last of his cold coffee and moved to the sink to rinse the cup.

'No idea,' he said.

'Guess what.'

He wasn't going to try – he didn't care for the sound of the voice behind him.

'Go on. Caroline told me. Bet you can't guess.'

'About what?'

'Why Cameron Rae has a chip.'

'How on earth should I know? I've only met the man twice. He's just bloody awkward. Some people are, I find.'

'He's Ian Lennox's son.'

He had to think for a moment to remember who Ian Lennox was. The drowned artist. Out in the firth.

'He's what? Come on,' he protested.

'It's absolutely true. Caroline said. She only found out

a couple of years ago. His mother was Jane Rae, Lennox's girlfriend. After he was drowned she went to Edinburgh to get away from the gossip and had Cameron there. He did well. Made it to university – law school ... But he doesn't want it spread around here, for obvious reasons.'

'Then why are you telling me?'

'You need to know,' she replied promptly because it was the kind of question she expected from him.

Was it odd that he had said nothing at the dinner party the night of their arrival, when James had been describing his father's death – as an anecdote? Was that odd? Of course not – on a formal occasion in front of strangers. What was bizarre, he said to Julia, was that James had calmly sat there at the table telling the story with Lennox's son practically sitting next to him.

'Not bizarre at all,' Julia replied. 'James doesn't know.'

'You're joking.'

'Not at all. He knew about Jane, of course, but Rae's a common enough name. He wrote it off as a coincidence.'

'And she let him go on with the tale knowing what it might be doing to Cameron Rae? Screwing him up?'

'Yes, sure. She thought it was a hell of a laugh. Do admit, he's not much fun. Come on – you don't like him. You said as much.'

'What's the matter with that girl?' he asked.

'Nothing,' she said sharply, 'she's a perfectly straightforward person who likes a joke.'

Straightforward? That approach to him on the first

night of their stay. Those swings in her mood. And any normal wife would have told her husband about Cameron Rae's parentage just to warn him off the topic.

Julia put out her hand and took his.

'Sorry, OK? Didn't mean that.'

He gave the hand a formal squeeze. 'I'll tell you one thing,' she went on. 'That picture, *Mystery Four*. I bet Rae thinks he has a better claim to it than either James or Malcolm Forsyth.'

'Could be,' he said. 'Could be.'

Chapter Thirteen

The little car nosed its way up the unmade track towards Carrucate, negotiating the potholes worn into it by the combined effect of traffic and standing water. As it came round a curve in the gathering darkness the headlights picked out a huddle of sheep which had long since given up grazing and now seemed scarcely conscious – too dazed, at any rate, to react to the burst of unexpected light.

Caroline McAllen looked towards the farmhouse higher up the hill. In its dim wall an oblong window was suddenly alight and the sight seemed to put new energy into her. She put a firm foot on the accelerator and forced the car forward, bumping and squeaking over the rough ground. The whole chassis juddered as the back axle bounced against a half submerged boulder, but she didn't care – she gave the car no mercy.

When she came to a halt in the yard she got quickly out of the car banging the door hard behind her and ran down the slope to the kitchen door. She beat on it with the flat of her hand and heard the dog bark indoors – it had been taken in for the night. Nobody came, so she tried again. The light in the kitchen was switched on. Then Malcolm Forsyth stood in the doorway.

'I thought perhaps you'd gone out. Then I saw the light. You must have been sitting in the dark,' she said teasingly as though it was worth remarking on.

'Yes, that's right,' he said, as though it wasn't, putting out a hand to usher her in. The dog was behind him and sidled past them both, escaping into the yard.

'You. Come back here,' he ordered, his voice peremptory. It slipped back into the house like a shadow and lost itself somewhere inside.

Forsyth followed Caroline into the drawing room, turning on the lights as he went. The curtains were undrawn leaving the picture window gaping – it turned dusk into darkness as the light went on; a black oblong hole that made her feel uncomfortable because it was incomplete. The curtains ought to be drawn, she felt; but she wasn't going to touch them.

Looking back at him she said, 'I was worried.' Her gaze moved around the room as though seeking reassurance from the flamboyant white leather of the furniture, the pictorial rug with its barbaric messages lying like a circular blot on the pale carpet, the brash gilt and glass. They all told her something about the man beside her: that he was hard, modern, a man of his time. Somebody whom she needed. She felt the need dragging at her, in the region of her waist, below her waist. And beside her, to her left, those undrawn curtains still nagged at her.

'Worried. About what?' He spoke quietly – but not

gently, and because they both knew the answer to it they both knew it was a cruel question. He knew the answer very well; of course he did.

'I thought you might not be here. Then I would have had a wasted journey,' she replied, as if that would have mattered, was relevant.

'You shouldn't get so worked up, woman,' he chided her. 'I'm usually somewhere about, you know that. You only have to wait.'

Wait. He spoke as though that was an easy thing to do, as though it was nothing. With a longing in her eyes, she looked at him standing in front of her — lithe, balanced. Relaxed, yet ready to move in an instant. There was no doubt who was in control of the situation, where the balance of power lay.

'What did you tell him?' he asked.

'I said I had to go and see Arabella — about some last minute script changes for the pageant. I think.' All at once she was vague, then she nodded as if remembering, reassured.

'Get it straight,' he said. 'Next time you'd better write it down.'

She was wearing dark trousers, a bright, candy-striped cotton shirt under a blouson. He stepped forward and pulled down its zip, busied himself unlocking it at the bottom.

It was only then that she seemed to hang back. 'This isn't the way it should happen,' she protested. 'It's too—'

'It's the way it's going to be today.'

'Please,' she said, glancing at the blank black window

which threatened her with exposure though she was not yet naked. She stared at her own image which the glass reflected at her against the dim landscape outside. She turned her face towards him.

'There's nobody there,' he said scornfully. 'There's never anybody here at Carrucate.' She couldn't tell whether, for him, that was a good thing or a bad one.

'Not here – and not yet,' she said.

'It's the way I want it,' he insisted. 'You've got to pay attention to that. You know your problem?'

She didn't reply. She didn't want to be forced to tell him what it was. She didn't want to be told, either, so she stood irresolute, submissive, waiting for the blow.

'You're not hungry enough, that's your problem. If you were you'd do what I tell you.'

'I am hungry, really really hungry ... Malcolm.'

'Who calls the shots?' he enquired, without raising his voice.

She seemed easier, as though what he had said was not what she had expected to hear. 'You do. Of course you do. I've always said. But you haven't even offered me a drink yet. You know? You can't expect me just to ... I'm not...' She didn't dare finish her protest.

'I can expect it. Because I call the shots. That's what it's all about.'

She watched him, the lean figure in the worn blue denims drawn tight across the narrow waist, hugging his buttocks like a second skin.

She said with an assumed courage, 'A drink. It's not much to ask.'

He had installed a bar in the corner – a semicircle of

glitzy laminate, a couple of bar stools, a shelf of glasses against a mirror. Anywhere else its vulgarity would have made her purse her lips. Here it was appropriate, acceptable. He picked up a glass, groped behind the bar for a bottle at random. Without looking at the label he poured a treble measure into the glass and gave it to her. Then poured one for himself. 'There you are.'

She took the glass from him and drank deeply, both hands round it. 'Thanks.' Despite his brusqueness she seemed grateful. It would make it easier.

The dog pushed open the door and peered into the room, not willing to risk entry until he knew he wasn't going to be ejected. As soon as he saw it Forsyth shouted, 'Out,' and went to slam the door. The dog had withdrawn long before he reached it.

'Poor dog,' she said. Forsyth did not reply. Instead he approached her again, hand outstretched. She pushed it away with a gesture which said, leave it to me. Another glance at the window and her reflection. A hesitation. She took off her blouson and laid it on the sofa. Forsyth sat down beside it and began a slow hand clap as though at a strip show – taunting her.

'Come on, woman – or you won't get what you're waiting for.'

She looked at him quickly. 'You promised me. You said you would.'

'Then hurry it up or you're bombed out.'

She still hesitated and that provoked him. He stood up, picked up her blouson and brandished it at her. 'All right, away with you then. Away back to Glengarrick and your husband. You're bombed out, woman.'

Bombed out? She had no idea what it meant. He repeated, 'You're bombed out. You're no bloody use to me.'

'No,' she said with sudden defiance. 'No, I won't. I'm not going.'

Keeping his eyes on her he sat down again.

Her crisp shirt was removed, the trousers. She glanced again at her reflection. He began the deliberate hand clap again.

Compliant at last she lay down on the dark circular rug. He had said nothing but she guessed that was where he wanted her. Finally he began to undress – quickly but not completely because he didn't need to obey the rules he imposed on her. Beneath the thin pile of the rug, beneath the carpet and its rubber underlay she could feel the unyielding flagstones of the old farmhouse floor. They made a hard bed but she knew that she would not have much longer to wait. That was a consolation.

The dog began to bark – sharp, defiant barks which resounded in the hall and up the staircase. They heard it hurl itself against the door of the room, yelping.

He rolled over on to his back, then sat up in a single movement. Eyes open, half dazzled by the light from the chandelier above her, she watched him – as though he had a steel spring in his spine. In a single movement.

He pulled on his jeans, groped for his shoes beneath the sofa and shuffled them on to his feet. Holding up his jeans with his right hand he wrenched open the door and yelled at the dog, 'What is it with you?'

It took no notice of him, but began barking again, louder than ever, then hurled itself down the passage towards the kitchen. She heard it yammering at the kitchen door as Forsyth followed it, shouting at it, 'Hold your row, will you.'

Caroline went to the door and turned off the light, feeling the balm of darkness. Her eyes became accustomed to it. She went to the window, a dim, grey oblong now and looked down the hill.

Something moved there – she had seen something move. She strained to see what it was, then called out, 'Malcolm,' but he couldn't hear her, of course, above the noise the dog was making. She searched for her clothes in the dark, trying to identify them. Nothing would persuade her to switch on the light now, not until she was dressed; and he had forbidden her to close the curtains. She dare not go as far as that.

There had been somebody outside, she was convinced of it. A piece of clothing slid from the slippery leather of the sofa onto the floor and she felt for it – that must be her tights, and this? Her shirt, was it?

She had seen a silhouette moving against the sky, above the silver ribbon of the sea, for a moment. Where were her underclothes? There they were – where she had thrown them in a mood close to desperation only a few minutes earlier. When he returned she was only half dressed – fumbling in the dark for sleeves, buttons.

'What the—?' He turned on the light.

'Don't,' she said. 'There's somebody out there.'

He went straight to the window. 'The bugger. He'll be away now. Half a mile, easy.'

'I saw him.'

The dog agreed with her. It was still barking; she heard the sound coming round the outside of the house – underneath the window now.

'I saw a shape. A head against the sky. A man.'

She looked down at herself, realised she had put her shirt on inside out and began to take it off again.

'Get yourself straight, woman.'

That made her lose patience with him at last. 'Don't stand there staring. There's an intruder. Go and find him.'

It was urgent. She had to know who had seen them together. She had finished dressing now and was pushing her feet into her shoes. Walking over to him she pulled at his arm. 'Move,' she ordered. 'Please. It'll be too late.'

She followed him out to the yard. He went into one of the buildings and came out with a halogen lamp which he had already plugged in to the power supply. As he carried it to the centre of the yard to set it down, dragging the cable behind him, the shadows bounced and flickered under the eaves of the buildings, in the open doorway. Had somebody been there?

He retrieved the torch he had brought with him and beckoned to her with it to follow him into the building. The dog had stopped barking.

The torchbeam travelled across the whitewashed walls, skirting the brass bedsteads. Forsyth bounced into the corner of the dusty table and swore. He bent down to peer underneath it with the torch, gave a small grunt of disappointment and stood up again. He went to the huge wardrobe and pulled open the door of each hanging cupboard – both empty.

'Here.' He handed her the torch. 'Hold it up,' he ordered. She did as she was told. He reached up and put his hand over the moulding that surrounded the top, feeling for something. Whatever it was he couldn't find it there. He dragged one of the dining chairs away from the table with a clatter and set it beside the wardrobe.

'Get up there and look,' he said.

She stood on the chair, and peered over the top of the wardrobe, poking the torch ahead of her. 'What am I supposed to be looking for?' she asked. 'There's nothing here.'

'The picture.'

'Picture? What sort of picture?'

'A canvas,' he said. It was then that she understood. '*Mystery Four*. This was where you hid it.'

'Give the torch here,' he demanded, pulling her down off the chair and taking her place.

'I told you,' she said, 'it's not there.' Suddenly she began to laugh.

'Away to hell,' he said, climbing down.

'It's such a bizarre place to keep it.'

'Bizarre place,' he repeated, mimicking her accent.

'Well it is.' He lifted up his hand to strike her and she cried out, 'Don't hit me. Don't. It'll leave a mark. He'll see it.' His arm fell to his side, reluctantly.

There was a sudden renewed storm of barking, from the yard now. Forsyth bent his head to look out of the window and saw a shape at the gate. He gave a shout of anger and made for the door, the latch caught and he had to wrench at it a second time to get it open. He ran across the yard torch in hand.

Caroline fell limply into the chair. The hunger inside her was unabated. It would take an age now to calm him down, bring him round. This business about the picture was going to take hours. Why had he kept it in an outhouse? He had some wild idea that it would be safer there, she supposed. She shook her head as though to get rid of the thought, because the picture wasn't important. James, with his inbred instinct for his family's rights, might care who owned it – or Cameron, who did have a claim on it arguably – but she didn't give a damn. Oh damn the bloody picture – damn it damn it. After what she had just endured. And Malcolm, damn him, too, for failing her.

Desolation and the pain of her longing overwhelmed her as she leaned against the back of the chair, forcing herself against it so that its edge bit into her shoulderblades through her thin coat, trying to use the physical pain to cancel out the inner ache, and to prevent herself from crying. Whatever happened she had to avoid weeping. If she cried she might not have a chance to wash her face and repair her makeup before she returned to Glengarrick. James would probably guess anyway. Time was running out too. Time, time, time.

Forsyth strode out of the white glare of the halogen lamp into the blackness beyond, the dog behind him, keeping its distance. He stared down the lane. Even when his eyes had adjusted to the darkness he could see nothing. He needed light. The only way to get it was to drive one of the vehicles down to the main road with its headlights full on. Would it be another waste of effort? He had a distaste for making himself look a fool in the eyes of Caroline McAllen – more than he had done already. He hesitated, then turned towards the garage searching in his pocket for his keys. At that moment he heard an engine starting in the lane. He ran through the gateway and a few yards down the lane, trying to make out what kind of vehicle it was. He could see the rear lights and the curve of its roof silhouetted by the headlights for a moment before it was obscured by the overhanging branches of a beech tree. It could have been anything. He couldn't even be sure whether it was a car or a van.

In a couple of minutes it would reach the main road and he had no way of knowing which way it would turn when it did so. There was no point now in trying to pursue it so he went back to the outbuilding to find her.

Still slumped in the chair she saw him move into the slab of bluish white light thrown through the small window by the lamp outside. It lit no more than his torso – his head remained in shadow.

'We knew you still had *Mystery Four*.'

'Since when?'

Realising that she had said too much already she said nothing more. In a moment he had made the connection. 'That fat poofter Lewis. The dealer. He told you, didn't he?'

'Not me.'

'That friend of yours then. Julia. He must have told her and she told you.'

Her silence was confirmation enough. He said, 'The wee blackguard – he's had that picture. That was him, wasn't it? Just now?' His voice rasped at her out of the dark. 'What do you know about it?' Had the alarm she had raised about an intruder in the garden been a diversion? No, he rejected the idea – she hadn't been acting. She had been in real distress.

For her, time was pressing – pressing down on her, pressing life out of her like a burden of the heaviest of stones. She felt them crushing her and she had to speak. 'Malcolm ... Please.'

His face was still engulfed in shadow. She had no way of telling the effect of her appeal. Did he want her to be more abject? Would she have to undergo another humiliation? If so, she would go through the ritual – any punishment that he imposed on her – there was scarcely any time left. She felt as if another stone had been added to the weight on top of her.

She repeated the single word, 'Please.'

'Come into the house,' he said. For the first time that evening he spoke to her as though she were an ally, a friend. At least it seemed like that to her. She rose from the chair so quickly that she bumped into him without intending to.

'Whoa,' he said, clutching her by the elbows, holding her against him.

With something like desperation she kissed him, moving her head as though trying to impress her lips on his, to convince him that she meant it. Then she followed him into the house filled with relief that her agony was going to be relieved. Soon.

Caroline pushed in through the kitchen door at Glengarrick and called out, 'Where are you?'

No response. She walked through into the hall, feeling as though she was walking on a cushion of air, floating in a golden mist. Smoothly through this wonderful, hallowed mist. She would have to be careful to keep herself tethered to the earth, to hide her happiness.

'James?' It felt as if she was singing his name with seamless tone to a rapt audience in an opera house. Row on row of crimson seats ... diamonds, exotic scents, white shirt fronts ... 'James,' she called again and listened as the harmonics echoed and died away.

She floated all loosey-goosey to the library on a wave – and there was nobody there. They must be in the drawing room then. Limp-wristed she sashayed back to it and pushed the door open decisively – wham. Nope, that was empty too. She shrugged and relaxed; it didn't matter a bit. Nothing at all mattered.

'James. Where are you?' She heard his muffled voice upstairs somewhere. Too far away to hear what he was saying.

She heard his feet on the floor above – saw him appear at the head of the staircase. 'I was just checking the alarms,' he said. She was too preoccupied with the joy inside her to remember that she had never known him do such a thing before. A man came and checked them every twelve months. It wasn't a job James had to do.

She asked, 'Where are the others?' She inspected him – he seemed to be a long way away. Still his usual big, calm self.

'Julia and Charles went out. Don't know where. Needed a break, I expect.'

That was a relief. It was easier to cope with the problem of appearing normal with only him there. One to one.

She had just got used to that idea when the front door opened and they came in. Julia with a silk scarf over her hair. Not really her style, Caroline thought. Ramsay behind her, dark-haired and diplomatic as ever; watchful. It would be much more difficult to pull the wool over his eyes than the others'. What was it with that man, she wondered. He was the kind who behaved as though he was thirty-five when he was twenty and stayed the same age for the rest of his life. He was the one who made the partnership's money, Julia had told her, and that was just the kind of thing that made Julia green-eyed jealous. She remembered how Julia had been at school: completely destroyed when she lost her place among the top three in the form. Never for long, though. She was an achiever, Julia, one who sometimes cut corners to get what she wanted – who sometimes cut people up.

Caroline felt the thoughts racing through her head. Her survival of the events at Carrucate earlier in the evening, their satisfying conclusion, had released new insights in her, given her a fresh vision. Be careful, a little voice warned her. Be normal, normal. It was important.

'Good rehearsal with Arabella?' Julia asked, pulling off the scarf. That scarf! Caroline managed to avoid a giggle, pulling in her diaphragm firmly. Oh Lord it was difficult to keep the giggle in.

'It was just the moves, running through them again. To get them absolutely right. The choreography, Arabella calls it. She wants to go through the big crowd moves with everybody there before the dress rehearsal tomorrow.' Caroline turned to her husband. 'You haven't forgotten, James, have you? The dress rehearsal – three o'clock?'

'It's been in my diary for weeks,' he said shortly.

He shepherded them to the drawing room for a drink before bedtime.

'Arabella. She's very professional,' Julia observed to James as she sipped her whisky. He didn't reply, seeming not to have heard. He had his back towards her, busy with his bottles. He wasn't normally intolerant of small talk. Was he snubbing her? She ran over the events of the day in her mind to try and pick up an omission on her part, some small failure of hers or Charles's that might account for his ignoring her. Nothing she could think of. Something wrong there, though. He was in a mood. They must have had a row, Julia decided. She and Charles had interrupted a small domestic tiff between James and his wife and he hadn't yet emerged from it; that was what it was. Feeling the need to cover the gap she turned quickly towards Caroline, hoping that she would fill in for him, and she did.

'Sure. She's a manager – she can make things happen.

Do you know she's got Cameron Rae to help with coordinating the lighting?'

'Brilliant,' said Julia.

The telephone rang. James got to it ahead of his wife.

'McAllen.'

A voice said, 'Where's my bloody picture?'

'Who's this?' James said.

'Who d'ye think?' Malcolm Forsyth asked.

'I have no idea, I assure you,' James McAllen said and replaced the handset.

He turned to the others who, naturally, had been listening. 'Wrong number,' he said. 'It's all these BT changes. They have reduced the system to total confusion and chaos – the telephone system is getting almost as hit-and-miss as our electricity supply.'

Just as he sat down and picked up his tumbler of whisky the telephone rang again.

'Damn.' He answered it again.

'Don't you hang up on me, laddie,' Forsyth warned.

McAllen didn't slam down the receiver. If there was an issue it was better to settle it immediately. 'What is it?' he asked impatiently.

'Somebody's made off with my picture.'

'Picture? What do you mean?'

'Away to hell. You know fine well the one I mean. The Lennox picture.'

'Lennox?'

Charles Ramsay glanced across at the other two. Hearing the word 'Lennox' Julia raised her eyebrows and pulled down the sides of her mouth as if to say, this is an interesting development. She turned to Caroline for her reaction, and there was none; her pale face was immobile as she set her glass down on the rosewood games table beside her, on one of the inlaid squares of the chequerboard top. Tentatively. As though she was placing a piece at a game of chess, Ramsay thought, and wasn't sure of the strength of her opponent's position, or the weakness of her own. Something was going very wrong. He could sense it.

James looked triumphant. 'The Lennox picture. *Mystery Four*. So you admit you had it.'

There was silence at the other end of the line. Forsyth hadn't expected that. Then he shot back, 'Somebody's made off with it from the old byre.'

'Good luck to him. You were a damn fool for keeping it there. Should've had it in the house. I'll tell you why you didn't, though. It was because you knew you had no right to the picture. You knew that so you kept it hidden.'

'Away—' Forsyth rasped and then recovered himself. 'That picture, it's always been ours. I had it in the shed because it was safer there than in the house. I had every right. It belonged to us. My dad told me. It was your father, Robert McAllen, who said he could keep it and then left Lennox there to drown, the poor wee bugger. Mr McAllen, I want it back and I'm going to get it back. I don't know for certain who has it – whether it's you or that dealer Lewis. So I'm going after you both. Just to make sure.'

The others couldn't hear what he said – could only sense that the conversation was getting out of hand. It was becoming an embarrassment for them. Except for Caroline, who didn't seem to have taken in what was going on.

James said deliberately, 'I believe your story to be cock. And even if the picture has gone you can't accuse me of stealing it because it didn't belong to you in the first place. I've no idea why you've come to me with this nonsense.'

'Why should I lie?'

James McAllen's voice had an edge to it now. 'I've no idea, Forsyth. Your motives are a mystery to me. I've no idea what makes you tick and I don't care much. One thing, however, that my father did say, that I know about, was that he never trusted any of you at Carrucate. Neither your father nor your mother, nor that uncle of yours.'

'My uncle Tam was a hero. He died for his country, McAllen.' That clearly was part of Forsyth's family mythology. A raw and private spot which couldn't be touched.

'Just because he got himself killed? Never believe it,' James retorted. 'It takes more than that to make a hero.' He had lost control of himself and was becoming reckless. It was a side of him that Ramsay hadn't seen before, and not attractive either. However unpleasant Forsyth was managing to be, abusing his family wasn't going to help matters. There was a pause at the other end of the line. Even Forsyth sometimes thought of the consequences of his words before he spoke them.

He said, 'If you don't believe me ask your wife. She was there.'

They saw James colour up but had no idea what he had been told. He replaced the handset without another word. Having got himself under control he turned to them, keeping his eyes away from Caroline. 'Sorry about that. As you may have gathered, it was Forsyth. He did have *Mystery Four* up at Carrucate. He admitted it to me. But somebody's lifted it. The bloody fool accused me of doing it. I shouldn't have gone over the top. It makes an unpleasant ending to the day.'

Julia asked, 'Who did take it do you think?'

It was a moment before James understood the question. 'The other candidate Forsyth produced was your antique dealer friend.'

'Ethelred,' she laughed. 'He hasn't got the bottle.'

'Not now,' Charles insisted. 'Let's talk in the morning.' Better to leave James alone for now. He couldn't see Lewis as the thief; receiving was more his line. There was another obvious candidate of course. 'In the morning,' he repeated.

Julia glanced at James and his wife and agreed, 'Yes. Time for bed, I think.' She got to her feet quickly and finished her drink. There was no dividend in hanging around trying to make small talk in the aftermath of that little spat.

The first thing she said to Charles when they reached the privacy of their room was, 'Why do you think James cut the conversation short like that?'

'Obvious. He was pissed off with Forsyth.'

'The second time, I mean.'

'I know. That's what I meant.'

'Forsyth said something that stopped him as if he'd

been shot. Did you see his face? Perhaps he's got evidence that James did take it.'

'So what. It didn't belong to Forsyth anyway.'

'Rae's the other candidate.'

'Sure.' Whoever it was they had no means of working it out that night, and he had another question in mind. He began to undress, opened the wardrobe and took out a hanger for his corduroys. With his back towards her he said, 'There's something about your friend Caroline that you didn't tell me, isn't there?'

'There are lots and lots of things I haven't told you about Caroline. That she wouldn't want me to. She's my very best friend,' Julia replied, trying to warn him off. He wasn't going to be diverted, though. It was too important, and anyway it was obvious.

'Cal's into drugs, isn't she?'

'Oh, come on,' Julia protested. 'Look, I've told you, she's a friend of mine. You haven't any friends so it may be difficult for you to grasp. Just try to understand.'

He ignored that and pressed on. 'What's she using?'

'Nothing as far as I know.'

'What is it?' he insisted. It couldn't just be hash. 'Speed? Ecstasy? She had already started when you were at school, hadn't she?' he speculated.

'Don't be stupid,' she said. 'You're just making things up.'

'Her behaviour's erratic. Up and down all the time.'

'She's always been like that, ever since I've known her.'

'One thing I didn't tell you. On the first night, when the power failed, remember?'

Julia was sitting at the dressing table, patting cream into her skin. She turned her head. 'Yes. Why?'

'When the lights went out, she made a pass at me. A really heavy one.'

'A pass? You're so old fashioned. What did she do? Put her hand on your arm?'

'Not far off,' said Charles. 'I'll skip the detail. You know me. You know her. I am telling you that no more than three hours after we met she was trying to grope me.'

Julia patted her face some more in silence, reached for a tissue. Best friends in the fifth form didn't do that to each other. He'd made her take him seriously.

She said with less conviction, 'It's nothing to do with you. She's a real friend of mine.'

He surprised her by saying, 'OK, I believe you. A friend wouldn't do that. So there has to be some other cause. Maybe she's had a breakdown or something. But after her performance this evening, I reckon it's drugs.'

'Performance? What do you mean?'

'She was stoned. High as a kite. Not with us at all. Something's gone wrong, hasn't it? What is it? What's she taking?'

'There was a man she knew ... He was grown up, rich. It looked as if he was rich. It wasn't like the schoolboys who bothered her. He treated her as an adult. He took her around.'

'What did he get her on to?' Ramsay demanded.

'Keep your voice down,' Julia said. Even in a solid old house like this you never knew what could be overheard.

'What was it? Look, now that we've got this deal going with the medallion I need to know. It's not simply the money . . .' He wanted to say, I'm not happy with this and I want to know what's going on – we've our good name to consider. The partnership. She'd scoff at that, though, so he left it out.

'That's sheer bull,' she replied, 'and you know it is. That's no reason. This is a private thing which is none of your business. I'm not telling you and that's that.'

He got on with brushing his teeth. She had told him what he needed to know.

Chapter Fourteen

'It ain't here,' Anny said, her fingers moving the needles busily. It was a quiet day in the market so she was catching up on her knitting. She stopped and held up the garment like a buxom sail for him to admire – it billowed. It was going to be an ample garment, Ethelred could see that – huge enough to fit her or O'Leary, but he couldn't visualise her partner being willing to wear lime green so he guessed it was going to be for her. She tucked one of the needles into her left armpit and resumed her rhythm.

'It'll keep me warm, this will. It gets cold round here you know,' she confided. 'Especially when you're sitting about because there ain't much doing like today and . . .' She lifted her beady gaze to the open door, as if challenging the hazy open air market to produce a clutch of punters and prove her wrong. She had forgotten what she was going to say.

'The cannon,' Ethelred reminded her sharply. 'I know it isn't here. I can see that.'

'Makes two of us,' she riposted and chuckled, wobbling here and there.

Ethelred wasn't pleased. He had other concerns

beside this, doubts that niggled in the back of his mind. When he had phoned Ian Johnson he had laughed at him – refused point blank to leave Galloway, even though it was in everybody's interest that he should, his own most of all. The perverse little jeweller was holding out for an inducement. Though a year or two back they had collaborated over a deal, they had no love for each other at all. He had no right to a payoff, and Ethelred's resources were stretched thinly at the moment. More than ever, what with this cannon, wherever it was. He demanded sharply, 'Where is it, Anny? In the yard?'

Her needles clacked with deliberation. Thick needles, because she liked a loose weave. It was quicker and she had a lot of ground to cover. 'Where d'you think? You know your way, don't you?'

'Thanks.'

O'Leary was in the yard. He led Ethelred past a stack of cast iron railings, Victorian chimneypieces spotted with fresh orange rust, past a complete spiral staircase and balustrade – it might even be Regency, Ethelred thought but he hadn't a customer for it – to a group of stone urns in various states of disintegration. Behind them was a big irregular shape covered in a sheet of black polythene weighted down at the corners with ancient, eroded bricks. O'Leary kicked two of them aside and pulled on the sheet. As he did so the wind caught it and blew it back in their faces. Only when they had grabbed hold of it and bundled it up did O'Leary stand back to announce breathily, 'There you are. One cannon. As per instructions. From us to you.'

Ethelred took a step backwards and knocked his heel

on a brick. There wasn't much room, but enough for him to see that it was exactly what he had envisaged. He wasn't sure whether you should call it a cannon or a field gun. It was old enough to be a cannon. A big iron barrel slung low on the axle between two big wheels, an antique carriage. He patted its back end – you couldn't call it the breech since it was a muzzle loader. Then tried to lift it – not a chance. It was reassuringly immovable.

'It's genuine,' he said.

'Right,' agreed O'Leary.

'Will it fire a blank shot?'

'What do you think?' That wasn't an answer but they both knew the question was a formality. You just had to look at the solidity of it. Since his buyer seemed to have no other queries, O'Leary held out his hand palm uppermost, expecting Ethelred to slap it with his own in the ancient gesture which would seal the bargain. He didn't though. He shook his head.

'Wait a moment.'

O'Leary waited, quite relaxed. He could afford to be patient with Ethelred since he had paid a substantial amount up front. Besides – he looked his plump client up and down – he wasn't going to be any trouble; not that he and Phil couldn't handle between them. Dim as he was it was the type of situation Phil understood. You just had to point him in the right direction.

Ethelred said, 'Where did it come from?'

O'Leary replied, 'Up north.' He could have lied and said anywhere else – Wales, Devon ... Buckinghamshire – but what was the point? He wasn't going to be more specific, though – he had his sources to protect.

Ethelred glanced at him, trying to read his face. 'Up north? How far up north?'

O'Leary kept his lip buttoned because he'd made his mind up. There was Jamie to consider, a useful bloke to know ... he had to be looked after.

Ethelred repeated, 'How far up north? This didn't come from Scotland, did it?' He regarded the cannon again – it was already looking less attractive. The bloom had gone off it.

O'Leary's eyes flickered away, then he looked Ethelred straight in the eye, 'No, no, no, not as far as that,' he answered heartily ... falsely. Ethelred could hear it in his voice.

'It's no deal unless I know exactly where this came from.'

'You should've said before. It's too late now, me boyo,' O'Leary boomed in an avuncular way. He was a big man.

'It came from Scotland, didn't it?' Ethelred felt a spasm in the pit of his stomach, a feeling like cold water pouring down his back. He had laid out a lot of money already and getting it back from these two if he didn't go through with the deal was going to be awkward.

O'Leary stood as silent as a monument.

'I must talk to Anny about this,' Ethelred announced and bustled past him down the gangway flanked by O'Leary's stock.

There was Anny, tranquil, with a young man slouching against the side of her showcase with all the fake Chiparus figures in it. She said, without looking up from her knitting, 'Hullo, Mr Lewis. You found O'Leary all right? Done your business have you then? Have a cup of coffee. This is Phil, by the way.'

Phil was ignored.

'Anny,' Ethelred asked urgently, 'where did it come from?'

'What, dear?'

'The cannon?'

'Ooh, you got me there,' she temporised.

'It came from Scotland, didn't it?' he demanded.

Phil smirked.

'Where in Scotland? I need to know,' Ethelred insisted. She could see that it mattered to him. He was a useful client, Lewis, and he didn't usually make a fuss so it must be important.

'It's a funny name – Phil'll know. He helped bring it down. What was it, Phil? Drumpogle – something?'

Being asked made Phil feel important. 'Drumpagan it was called,' he said.

At that moment O'Leary loomed in the doorway. 'Who said that?'

'I did,' Phil said. He didn't think much to O'Leary – he was over the hill. Paunchy.

'Well you're wrong. It wasn't Drumpagan, that place. Not far away, I grant you.'

'I can't take it,' Ethelred said.

'What do you mean?'

'The cannon. It isn't for me.'

Anny thrust aside her knitting. 'What's wrong with it?' she asked sharply.

'It's impossible. Drumpagan's only forty miles from

Steilbow Castle. Where they're having this pageant. Where I've got to deliver it,' Ethelred said.

Anny closed her eyes in supplication and complained in a soft bellow, 'Oh for Chrissake. Lack of communication. You should've *told* us. Why didn't you com*mun*icate?' Phil began to laugh. 'Shut it,' Anny commanded and he did so.

'It's not just down to me,' Ethelred said, aggrieved. 'You didn't say where it was coming from either, did you?' He knew he was right, that the fault should be shared, and feared that the penalty wasn't going to be. He remembered clearly how much he had already paid them.

'A bit of a mix-up then,' O'Leary commented, glancing at his partner.

'Forty miles is a long way,' observed Anny.

'Besides it didn't come from Drumpagan, I told you. That boy got it wrong. The place we fetched it from was well on from there. How much would you say, Phil?'

'Ten, twelve miles easy,' Phil said, his face serious.

'Almost the other side of Scotland. It's a big country,' O'Leary suggested.

Lewis considered his choices. If he didn't take the cannon he could say goodbye to the money he had already paid – and all the effort would have been wasted. There was still a profit to be had in that piece of artillery, too. All he had to do was deliver it, collect his cheque and fade into the mist. There was a risk, a calculable risk. His eyes narrowed as he calculated it. If he didn't take it they would have to sell it on quickly. They wouldn't want it hanging around the yard.

'It's chancy,' he said. Anny resumed her knitting. 'I need a discount,' Ethelred added. Neither of the others made a move. 'Come on. You're looking at nothing but profit. Solid profit.'

'There were expenses,' O'Leary protested. Jamie, Phil, the petrol, his time.

'I need six hundred,' Ethelred essayed. Anny didn't look up from her knitting.

'Four,' said O'Leary, 'in the circumstances.'

'Done,' said Ethelred.

The grassy area beside the moat at Steilbow Castle was alive with people. Some of the men had strapped sword belts over their day clothes, were carrying round shields. The womenfolk were queuing up to have the hats they had made for themselves vetted by the costume mistress. The workmen had not yet finished erecting the scaffolding for the raked seating but Arabella didn't seem concerned. She sat with Cameron Rae, going through the lighting and audio plot.

'I wonder how she got him so cooperative. Strange man,' Julia commented. 'They're all odd, though, aren't they? Those sort of people.'

'What sort?' Caroline asked.

'Born the wrong side of the blanket. Illegits. They always have a chip.'

Caroline wasn't interested, waiting for her turn with the crowd, as Devorgilla announcing her decision to set up a new Cistercian community in Galloway to the cheers of its grateful population. Pious Gallovidians. She tried to remember her first line and couldn't. It wouldn't come. Arabella would get tight-lipped and schoolmistressy of course. Who cared? There were other things on her mind.

Julia asked, 'Something wrong?' There was no reply. She looked so moody that Julia felt she had to be reassuring. It must be awful not to be in control of one's life. Devastating.

'Darling, I'm sure when this deal comes off and James has the money you'll be able to find someone who can get you over this thing. All you need is some space and a really good specialist. Then you'll be able to kick it and everything will be hunky. Everything hunky dory, honey, you'll see.'

Caroline didn't react so Julia tried again. 'Look, don't be angry but I had a word with Mummy last night. I had to ring her anyway. Now you know what she's like – has the oddest friends, and one or two among her naughty old dowagers have been experimenting. You know – keep up with the times and ease their declining years. Of course the crumblies found out they'd got more than they bargained for and wanted out.' She eyed her friend and took a deep breath, 'Anyway, one of them's been absolutely cured, would you believe, by a wonderful man, a Dane who operates out of the Fynen Clinic. Flies over to Wimpole Street once a week. He costs, of course.'

Caroline looked at her with astonishment. 'Who wants to be cured?' she asked. 'I don't. You don't understand anything, do you? It's wonderful.'

Julia stared back, bewildered. Then, watching that beautiful wasted face, she felt nothing but anger. 'But you must,' she ordered.

Caroline shook her head, her hair flashing in the sunlight. Putting her face close to Julia's, invading her space, she whispered savagely, 'Don't lecture me.' Then she pulled back and eased off. 'It's nothing to do with that – not being cured. It's James.'

'James? I thought he knew? You can't mean that he doesn't?'

Caroline wagged her head. 'Yes of course he does. I couldn't have got this far if he didn't.'

'What is it then?' A big pause.

'I was at Carrucate last night.'

'Carrucate! With Forsyth! What on earth possessed you?'

'I needed to go. Had to.'

'Had to go? I don't understand. You must have been crazy.'

'Stop scolding.' It was what she had always said in this situation when they were at school. Caroline, charming and out of her depth, seeking help because she'd got herself into another scrape, not over some small infringement of school rules dreamt up by a spinster in the 1930s, but something much graver than that. Trouble with a man, or over money, grown-up trouble. Because she was clear-skinned, supple, beautiful, whatever it was it had never seemed as bad as if it had happened to one of those ordinary girls – the dairymaids, they had called them – pink-faced daughters of farmers enriched by CAP subsidies. Dairymaids – secretly hated species: bovine, incurious, strong at lacrosse, haunting the food counters of the department store in the town. Food, for goodness' sake! She and

Caroline had left that far behind – had other, womanly concerns.

And now that they were grown up here was real trouble again.

Caroline running to Julia for advice – sitting together in the darkly varnished pews at the back of the chapel after the evening study period. That was after Miss Renishaw, the principal, had tried to separate them, exiling Julia to Mrs Lawrence's house because of her undesirable influence on Caroline, she said. She had been a perceptive old bitch though, Renishaw. Julia remembered how she had always been the competent one – just as wayward, but much better at concealing her wrongdoing. For one thing, it had been she who had successfully cached their store of really serious substances. It was because she was capable of weighing up risks and looking forward – walking on water, if the occasion demanded it. Something Caroline had never been able to do. She simply subsided into it with a low moan and a gentle splash, like one of those pre-Raphaelite paintings of Ophelia – except that she lacked those massive auburn tresses they always had.

Still, Cal had achieved the only thing that mattered. She had seen James across the room at a drinks party in Holland Park, homed in on him and got herself engaged within a fortnight. A lucky girl, if you went for the land-owning type. Julia did, and she felt a twinge of jealousy like a small electric shock in her temple, but it faded straight away because you couldn't be jealous of beauty like Caroline's. It was a privilege to be near it – to be recognised by her, to be needed by her. Julia knew just how James had felt. A man of property would overlook a great deal to possess someone whose looks were so much admired by his peers. She went with the house. Its undoubted glamour needed somebody like Caroline to complement it; someone whose grace would still compel your attention in forty years' time.

If she were still above ground by then, Julia found herself thinking.

Caroline said, 'You've clammed up. What's wrong? You were ticking me off, you know.'

'Nothing's wrong... So you were there when somebody made off with *Mystery Four*. You must have been in a sweat when he rang James last night.'

She nodded towards Malcolm Forsyth, who was ignoring them both, nestling a cellular phone against his cheek, confiding into it, playing the organising genius, swollen with importance. With him, everything was part of a huge self-promotion exercise. He was probably talking to his feed merchant or booking in his car at the garage – the man who was supplying her dear friend Caroline with what? A snow-white powder which wasn't icing sugar.

'What's he like in the sack?' Julia asked casually.

Caroline looked blankly back at her and managed to reply, 'Quite vigorous.' How could she admit the truth – that he appalled her?

'He looks as though he would be,' Julia allowed judiciously, 'but one never knows. Sometimes they are a big, big disappointment. They come on strong and then fall off when it matters.' She didn't mean Charles.

'No, no,' Caroline said, shaking her head too hard

from side to side, so that it swam and an artery thudded in her ear. She forced herself to say lightly, 'Not him. No one could accuse him of being deficient down there. He's the original tough dick in jeans. Can't you see?'

Julia screwed up her eyes. 'Not from here. He's too far away. Believe you, though.'

Caroline didn't reply – a spasm of nausea provoked by her memories of him had grabbed at her solar plexus.

Arabella Knight had rearranged the extras for the Devorgilla sequence with Cameron Rae's help. They had been standing, bored and cold, trying to remember why they had let themselves in for all this. Now something was going to happen. They were going to hear Caroline deliver Devorgilla's big speech for the eleventh time. Rae summoned her with a sweep of his arm. 'Caroline! Apparently it's your big moment, luvvy,' he shouted, pretending that he hadn't put himself forward for this artistic endeavour, had been con- scripted. No enthusiast – more of a detached observer of events.

Caroline observed, 'Well, I'm on, I suppose. Ciao.'

'Ciao,' responded Julia, recalling the back seat of the chapel. It was what they had always said to each other when they parted to go back to their respective houses. Ciao. Everyone had said it at the time. People who didn't know another word of Italian. It was com- monplace, but to Julia it was precious, because Caroline went back a long way, to use another cliché – much further back than Charles did. Which, she supposed, must have been why she had taken her side against him. The trouble was that his moral sense was so – set in concrete. He was too blinkered to see, even when he stood right back from a problem, that it had a wider context. Right and wrong were much more complicated than he thought. However much holier than thou he was she had always recognised that his reputation for integrity was a real asset to the business. This time, though, it was going to be a liability if things went wrong. And they might do, because, looked at objectively, Ethelred really hadn't the nerve to do what needed to be done. He was shrewd, her former boss, but he was a marshmallow. He lacked grit.

A cheer went up from the cohort of extras. There was an excitement. A van was arriving – it must be the cannon. It came slowly through the gateway with Phil at the wheel and Ethelred beside him. The cannon had come. The great cannon. They looked bleary, having set out from North London at three that morning. They came to a halt beside the sandstone façade in the castle yard. Stiffly Ethelred climbed down and made his way over to Arabella.

'Here it is. We've got it for you, dear. You'd better have a look at it before it's unloaded.' Two or three of the extras standing nearby left their positions, drawn by the thought of real artillery. One or two others followed, all militaria buffs – that was why they were there, they remembered now. Others, who weren't quite certain what was going on but wanted to make sure they didn't miss any excitement, joined the group coagulating around the van. Arabella turned to a girl aide and said, 'Find Malcolm for me, would you?'

She waited at the back of the van for Phil to open it up so that she could inspect the piece.

After a minute or two inside she looked down at Ethelred who had bustled along to join her. 'Fine,' she said, 'just fine. You've done very well indeed. Where did you find it?'

Ethelred didn't seem to hear her question and she didn't bother to repeat it, because Malcolm Forsyth arrived. 'Give way. Let the man see it,' he demanded, pushing his way through what by now was a considerable crowd. How many of them, Ethelred wondered, came from the neighbourhood of Drumpagan? He waited, cringing inwardly, for somebody to let out a cry of recognition.

No. Malcolm Forsyth said, 'It'll do.' That was all. Then he commanded a few enthusiasts standing nearby, 'Will you give us some help to get it off the van.'

Space was made busily, a ramp of planks put in place and half a dozen volunteers eased the cannon slowly down it to the ground. There was the cannon and there was Forsyth, trapped by the crowd pressing round him. Ethelred needed the money and needed it fast. He seized the moment. From his inside pocket he produced a paper and presented it. Emboldened by the jostling crowd, he announced, slapping it lightly, 'One cannon, as ordered. Cash on delivery, as agreed.'

Malcolm Forsyth regarded Lewis with loathing. If he refused to pay in front of so many witnesses the whole benefit of the exercise in terms of PR would be lost, so he drew a chequebook from the back pocket of his jeans and glanced carelessly at the paper he had been given. Then resting on the muzzle of the cannon he made out his cheque and gave it to Ethelred. An ex-military voice from the back shouted, 'Well done, sir.' There was some clapping. Ethelred responded with a bow and opened wide his arms in acknowledgement, the new cheque fluttering in his hand. Next he folded it carefully and placed it in his wallet before pushing through the crowd towards his former assistant.

Julia saw him. 'Ethelred! Ethelred, over here.' She gestured with her arm, as if trying to drag him over to her.

With the cheque safely in his pocket he was expansive. 'Julia, my love. What can I do for you?'

She spoke quietly, urgently. 'Charles is coming to the first night tomorrow. Have you got rid of the Johnsons? Where are they?'

'Still here, my dear, as far as I know. I met her in the street the other day and I did remonstrate with her, I assure you. She's being reasonable. It's the man who won't budge. You know what a drag he is.'

'Oh no,' she cried out. One of Devorgilla's tame priests, a dim hooded figure with a rope around his waist, looked across at her, surprised. She lowered her voice again. 'Charles will certainly be in the audience tomorrow. He's threatening to come to the dress rehearsal tonight as well. You're lucky he hasn't turned up with James McAllen already.'

'Yes, I guessed that.' Of course Ramsay would be there. Both his hosts taking part and Julia there to act as Caroline's dresser; he wouldn't want to stay at Glengarrick on his own. And this was a small town where everybody knew each other. Margaret would have friends who were going, so it was more than possible that she would come to the first night – and if she did she would be bound to see him. The auditorium only held three hundred. Everyone would be milling about before the show started, anyway.

'Johnson may come too,' Julia insisted. 'You must find a way of keeping him away, at least.'

She was right. If Charles Ramsay caught sight of Ian Johnson he would know immediately what was going on. Ian Johnson, the talented worker in silver and gold who threw his money away on the horse, the wheel, and the pack of cards.

How to do it though? Separate them by force? Ethelred wasn't a physical person. Pressure? Blackmail? He didn't know anything about them that was to their discredit which didn't involve him as well. What else was there? Money? That was the only lever he had. Ethelred winced; he seemed always to be having to dip into his Golden Harvest building society account. Then he brightened, remembering the cheque in his pocket. That could be used to finance the bribe he would have to offer Johnson. He could give himself a bridging loan. But why shouldn't Julia make a contribution?

'Couldn't you entice Charles Ramsay away somehow? Hold him back at Glengarrick?' It would be so much cheaper.

Julia shook her head. 'With what? A tow rope? He does have a mind of his own.'

Ethelred pondered. Money might work with Johnson, but not with his wife. He would just have to work on it.

He had twelve hours. At least nobody had recognised the cannon yet. He trembled, feeling as though he was inching forward on a tightrope, every inch another risk. And the money; how little could he get away with? A thousand? It would be worth it for the peace of mind.

He said goodbye to Julia and made for the van. Phil started up the engine and they edged their way through the crowd of actors, leaving the black cannon in isolation on the grassy space next to the moat.

Watching them leave Malcolm Forsyth picked up his phone again and picked out a number. 'Hallo? Is that the Galloway Bank?'

'It is,' a Scottish woman's voice replied. 'How may I help you?'

'I have just issued a cheque which I wish to stop.'

'I see.' The voice sounded intrigued at such an exotic idea.

'Can you deal with that?'

'Oh no. That'll be the manager.'

'Then put me over to him.'

She did so, fast. In fact when the business was completed the van was still in sight. He could still see Lewis, turning to speak to the driver beside him. At his ease and smiling, Forsyth imagined.

Chapter Fifteen

That child was crying again, Ethelred noted, as he passed the door of the ground-floor flat. It was a sound he hated because it reminded him of his own childhood; tears of frustration at the injustice of life as much as the pain from the slap, the cane, the clip round the ear.

He knocked firmly on the Johnsons' door and was almost bowled over by Ian Johnson – hurrying out to the betting shop, Ethelred supposed. Face to face each feinted to get past the other, then hesitated until Johnson said, 'If it's Margaret you want she's not here.'

His tone was brusque and Ethelred wasn't standing for that from any unlucky penny punter. 'I have to speak to one of you, I'm not fussy which. You'll do.'

'I'm on my way out. You can't wait here.'

'Then you'll have to remove me by force,' Ethelred replied, planting his small feet wide, feeling quite brave. This man wasn't going to eat him, anyway – he had no appetite.

Ian Johnson avoided his eyes and capitulated. He'd had a slack week and his self-esteem had worn thin.

'Sit down,' Ethelred ordered. 'Let's run over today's news, shall we? Ramsay's over at Glengarrick and is certainly coming to the first night of the Galloway Pageant tomorrow.'

'What pageant?'

'At Steilbow Castle.'

Johnson shrugged.

'What I need to know is whether you or your wife intend to be in the audience.'

'We've never heard of it.' The lie was obvious.

'Ramsay's going to be there. Your wife ... Look, your private problems are of no concern to me and I'm not enquiring about them. But you know perfectly well that she may want to go there to see or be seen by him.'

Johnson didn't utter. Ethelred said angrily, trying to shake him out of his lethargy, 'Come on. I haven't got time for tact. It matters to both of us. Admit it.'

Eyes averted, Johnson grumbled, 'What am I expected to do about it?'

'Stop her, what do you think?'

No response from the supine man on the sofa.

'I've been through all this with her twice already,' Ethelred sighed. Then Johnson's apathy got to him and the words spilled out. 'You and I, all of us, know bloody well that what we're doing is in a decent cause. Others aren't going to see it like that, though, are they? People who are more conventional than us? Ramsay certainly won't – and if he sees your wife at Steilbow Castle the ordure is going to hit the punkah and you're going to get it on the rebound, my friend. Because when it does hit the fan, not only are we all going to lose comfy little commissions, but some tall Scotsmen in dark blue uniform are going to be out searching the hills and glens of Bonnie Gallowa'. And it's you, Johnson, that they'll have the dogs sniffing for. You did the deed after all; it's got your scent all over it, and they'll be coming for you. So if you want to protect your bedraggled person you'll persuade your wife as soon as she returns to get the next train out. If you'll take my advice you'll go into that bedroom now, chop chop, and get your bags packed.'

Ian Johnson turned the palms of his hands upwards in a gesture which said that the task was beyond him.

Ethelred bent down to speak sharply in his ear. 'Look, boyo. Get firing on one cylinder at least. Activate yourself. Function. Spark. Otherwise you're going to be busted.'

'What are we supposed to do for money?' Johnson asked, his eyes suddenly alive.

Ethelred exhaled with satisfaction. A breakthrough. He'd got through to the guy. 'How much do you need?' he asked briskly.

'Four hundred.'

Of course it was outrageous, but it was necessary. Ethelred had his Golden Harvest passbook in his pocket enfolding the cash he had withdrawn on his way there. Turning his back on the jeweller he counted out the amount and gave it to him. Less than he had feared — quite a bit less, in fact.

'And you'll be able to persuade your good lady to come with you?'

'No problem.'

Ethelred took his word for it, since there was no other option, and went to the door, wanting to duck out before Margaret Johnson returned and found him bribing the character she had been misguided enough to marry. Fingers crossed. He was getting fed up with the complexities of doing business in Scotland, he grumbled to himself. All this toing and froing. Back to that cosy hotel he'd found for a hot shower and a gossip over a cup of tea with the owner who was really quite sympathique. He'd be able to look everyone in the eye again after that restorative break.

Ramsay had insisted on driving them to Steilbow Castle in his own car. McAllen sat beside him, already changed into his Scottish Captain costume. Over it he was wearing a heavy white mackintosh, greying now, and abraded where the belt had pulled it into the seams. 'Since I am to be a military man for the next few days I thought I ought to bring out my father's old trenchcoat,' he grunted to Charles. 'I found it in a bedroom on the third floor. I am always astonished at what junk I find in the house.'

Ramsay said, 'Comforting though, don't you think?'

'What?'

'To have things around you that have been there for ages.' It was why he always enjoyed returning to Bressemer. Something else that he and McAllen had in common. Roots. The security that they gave, and the price you paid because they pinned you down.

Making a huge effort, McAllen managed to say, 'Yes, I daresay.' A fascinating contribution to the conversation. Ramsay could see that the need to wear his costume was irking him. Arabella had told him he would have to wear a wig, too, but he drew the line at that. The one he had been offered stank, he said. He wasn't having that on his head. Arabella hadn't insisted. She knew him too well.

Ramsay kept his mouth shut, having made his attempt at small talk. It was heavy weather after the row over the picture with Forsyth last night, and Julia and Caroline in the back weren't trying either. There was a morning-after feeling in the car, without the jollity which ought to have gone before.

Then Caroline shouted, 'Look out!'

There was a hedgehog in the road – trundling along, bang in the middle. Ramsay hadn't seen it, hadn't been paying attention. Too late to brake. The car passed over it and he heard no sound. A hedgehog is a small animal.

Caroline turned to look back, dislodging her mediaeval head covering, a sausage of material bent in a triangle and dressed with braided cord and veiling. Toppled over her ear it made even her look ridiculous.

'You've killed it,' she screamed. Julia fussed at first, tried to adjust the headdress, then turned to look behind herself, but it was too far away now. Just a small grey bundle in the road. Perhaps alive, perhaps not.

'I'm sure he's killed it,' Caroline muttered petulantly.

'Cal, darling, you can't see – and anyway Charles didn't have time to brake or anything. Really and truly,' Julia remonstrated.

Caroline blazed back, 'Don't call me Cal. I've told you so often before. I hate it.' Because it reminded her of the days when she had been innocent? Ramsay wondered.

At last James came to his defence. 'Charles didn't have a hope of stopping. He didn't see the bloody thing until it was too late. Light of my life, we all know that you're strung up, but do save your emotional energy for the performance, there's a good girl.'

He might as well have poured neat petrol on the flames. For the next five minutes she indulged herself shamelessly in an outburst of anger, at his chauvinism, at the brutality of the pair in the front seat, their callousness. As if by mutual agreement they stayed silent leaving the storm to blow itself out. How long would it take to repair the social damage it had inflicted? Hopefully she would have recovered enough by the time her turn came to perform not to make a complete fool of herself.

Ramsay thought she must have been like this for some time; sinking into addiction, sometimes hyper-active, sometimes torpid, her mood swings becoming more and more extreme, more difficult for her husband to control and keep hidden from his neighbours, tenants, from these two guests. He would have taken the best advice he could find – he was a competent man. She would have been touted round consulting rooms in Edinburgh, London, abroad even. There were all sorts of aids to deal with the symptoms of withdrawal these days. Not just the old standby methadone but blockers, therapy, even acupuncture had been found to help some addicts. Ramsay knew that, and he wasn't into drugs at all – had never even dragged on somebody else's joint as a teenager. Julia said it would have made a more interesting man of him if he had, which was nonsense –

McAllen could have told her that. He would have gone into it methodically, found the very best care. But none of it was any use if she didn't have the will to try to give it up – whatever it was. Something heavy, obviously. A killer in the end. In which case the pain of kicking her addiction would be outrageous and she hadn't the strength to do it. She didn't have the willpower to endure the agony of withdrawal, cold turkey they called it. James McAllen could have done it, but what was the good of that? It was a rough ironical old world.

There was silence still in the car. Sitting there looking shabby in the mackintosh that had belonged to his father before most people had heard of heroin, cocaine, Ecstasy, amphetamines, crack, McAllen broke into it with two words – all that was needed: 'I tried.'

Ramsay glanced sideways at him, going out of his way to exonerate himself when there was no need – and replied, 'It's not over yet. It's never over.' He spoke quietly so that the unhappy women in the back couldn't hear. He didn't want to touch off another outburst from Caroline. It's never over – it was easily said, and as far as Ramsay could judge it was no more than a lie which might bring a moment's relief. He owed it to McAllen, though, however transitory it was, however false they both knew the words to be.

Caroline, the beautiful and wayward Caroline, would be better off dead – that was Ramsay's regretful opinion – and James McAllen would be better off if she were.

There was a sudden wail from the back of the car. 'I can't remember my words.'

'When you get started it'll be all right,' Julia consoled

her. 'You'll remember them then. You always did at school, in the house play.'

'Fingers crossed,' Ramsay offered, not caring whether she did or not.

McAllen said nothing.

The small rain spattered against the windscreen of Ethelred's car. He activated the wiper a single time to clear it so that he could see the front door of the house where the Johnsons lived. The child from the ground-floor flat came bouncing out into the street liberated from that awful mother. Ethelred watched it double purposefully off down the street and congratulated it silently on its escape. He shifted in his seat and yawned. He'd seen the husband off safely to Carlisle from Dumfries station. That was the major part of the problem solved. He would have liked to see Margaret off the premises as well. To get to Ian Johnson was simple. If you gave him enough to feed his habit for a few days he went off like a lamb to gamble it away and that was that. With her, it was different. She was quixotic, unpredictable – and if she was hankering after Ramsay she would feel it her duty to tell him what was going on. Not at all desirable in Ethelred's view. She had to be saved from herself if he could manage it.

There were other places he would rather be right now, he reflected. Back at his hotel, in the dining room, at the table, with the generous Scottish menu in his hand. That was where he would like to be – not in this car. They had some quite drinkable wines too...

She was coming out of the front door, the evening sun

glinting on her hair as she set off down the street. He wasn't going to approach her yet – merely shadow her, like in those film noir movies he remembered; though he was no Philip Marlowe, no Sam Spade. All he had to do was watch her and, if she showed signs of wanting to sample the Galloway Pageant, to prevent her from doing so. He wasn't sure how yet – Marlowe would have known.

He let her reach the end of the street and turn right towards the station. It was a good sign. Gently he put the car into first gear and followed her.

Arabella Knight looked down from the lighting box at the back of the stand at the empty arena and felt reassured by what she saw. The seats were filling up nicely – few tickets had been returned. In one corner the cannon crouched blackly, pregnant with dramatic possibilities. It was raining spottily, but thanks to Forsyth the audience at least was under cover. The bank of rostrums arranged beneath the rose-pink façade of the castle's inner courtyard looked fine now, standing solid and professional-looking under the spotlights, which were just beginning to be visible against the fading daylight, bringing a growing excitement with them. She had been right to insist that the set should be completely repainted after the dress rehearsal last night, despite the protests of her volunteer painters. Beside her, close to her, Cameron Rae sat, clipboard in hand ready for any last-minute instructions before he took his place behind the scenes. Arabella was strung up to concert pitch and her anxiety infected him, the sceptic, whom she had dragged in at the last minute. She glanced at him wondering why he had agreed to take on the job of her assistant and hoping that she had guessed the reason. He had given her not the hint of a clue though, infuriating man. A deliberate solicitor, methodical at tying up loose ends, adept at remembering all the detail of moves, business and timing, and ensuring that none of it was lost, that there was no slippage. An invaluable ally, but an enigma all the same, because his profession had taught him also to keep his feelings under wraps. Which was not at all what she wanted.

'I have checked on the turnout. All the principals are here, made up and ready. One or two extras haven't arrived yet, or have decided to stay at home, but the turnout has been excellent on the whole.'

'I allowed for that. Besides, we can do with the extra space behind,' she said absently, watching the pair she had met at Glengarrick making their way up to their seats. She turned to Cameron, pointing at the man. 'I can remember her name,' she said, 'but not his. What is it?'

'Charles Ramsay,' he replied and she nodded, and felt a twinge of misgiving because that had reminded her about Caroline.

'Caroline was in form when you saw her?'

'In reasonably good shape,' he said. That didn't sound too promising.

'She complained that she still wasn't sure of her words.'

'I know,' he agreed. 'I got the props people to make up

a parchment sheet with her speech on it. She'll carry it on and if she gets stuck she can just read it.'

'Bless you,' she said with satisfaction; the man was a godsend.

Cameron shrugged off the benediction and she hoped that there were some feelings of a human sort hidden under that tight exterior.

The cellphone on the folding chair beside her gave an urgent buzz. In her ear the voice of one of the girls warned, 'Arabella darling, it's me, Consuela. He's here.'

'Coming,' murmured Arabella, looking sideways to note that the rain had begun to fall more heavily. Then she said to Cameron, 'Cameron, darling, he's arrived. I have to go down and welcome him. I think you ought to be getting backstage, don't you? Good luck.'

The word darling had slipped out before she could catch it. The girl had used the word and she had copied it without thinking. It was a theatrical word – used just as often by luvvies as by lovers. Anyway it couldn't do any harm. It might have penetrated his serious world of deeds and tribunals, rents and conveyances. It wasn't a crime to use the word? Not yet, please. As she trod lightly down the plank steps of the stand, catching each cold scaffolding pole to steady herself as it came past, she wondered what his straitened childhood in Edinburgh must have been like and whether it had left anything warm inside that hard and polished carapace. She knew there was something worth rescuing. Darling. It was a gentle word to use to Cameron Rae.

* * *

In the grassy parking area close to the castle Ethelred put on the handbrake and skirted the crowd of latecomers moving towards the castle gate. Margaret Johnson, he'd lost her. No he hadn't. There she was with the others, swinging along with a purpose, looking formidable, unstoppable, but he had to try. He caught up with her, smart in her cream linen jacket with a Van Cleef and Arpels brooch pinned to the lapel, and a pine-green, pencil-thin skirt. She looked, he had to admit, like a million. His eyes became small as he eyed instinctively the brooch – worth several hundred of anybody's money. Probably concealed from their creditors, saved from one of the shipwrecks her husband engineered so regularly, he thought, with a tiny drop of spite. Looking at her, slim and superb, he couldn't imagine her stooping to hide it from some bailiff in a blue suit smelling of cheap aftershave. Pride. Perhaps that was the line he should take.

'Mrs Johnson. I am surprised to see you here. Really.' She didn't reply. 'Running after a man who, shall we say, is already spoken for.' He made a doubtful face and opened his arms in a baffled gesture. She still said nothing. 'You are, after all, married.'

'My marriage is my business,' she countered and strode off. He stopped to try to remonstrate with her but she carried on and he almost lost her. 'Please, Mrs Johnson. Please—'

They had almost reached the gateway, the stout wooden bridge where once a drawbridge had been. And there were the Earl and Countess making small talk with Consuela until Arabella Knight arrived to conduct them into the castle. In his brown sinewy hand the Earl held above his lady a large red, white and blue golf umbrella against the drizzle which was worsening by the minute. Margaret Johnson skirted them and then came Ethelred, legs active, trying to keep up with her, throwing an ingratiating smile at the Earl but too preoccupied to realise who he was.

'Please, Mrs Johnson, you really shouldn't be here. We did agree, you remember. It isn't at all wise. There's a risk of...' He broke down, unable to think of a safe word to describe what there was a risk of.

The Earl pretended to ignore this unexpected diversion and held fast to his duties. He caught sight of Arabella and called out gallantly, 'My dear, you ought not to have bothered in this fearful wet,' knowing very well that her bothering, damp or not, was part of the performance.

She led the way into the castle as though they were royalty – the nearest available thing. As they came over the bridge a spotlight picked them up and a voice announced over the loudspeaker: 'Ladies and gentlemen, will you please welcome the Earl and Countess of Auchenbrach, who have cut short a holiday in the South of France to be with us on the first night of our Galloway Pageant.'

This provoked a burst of enthusiastic clapping which was reinforced by recorded baroque trumpets. The Earl looked out benevolently from beneath his huge umbrella and ushered his wife to her seat at the front.

In the aisle to the side of them Ethelred was crowding

Margaret Johnson, whispering in her ear, 'Surely I don't have to tell you again what is involved here for all of us. Mrs Johnson, you are being very very selfish. There's no other word.'

Nonchalantly she pushed past him towards the lighting box, her eyes scanning the audience, looking no doubt for Ramsay.

It was then that Ethelred heard a voice behind him say in a commanding accent, 'Good of the Auchenbrachs, don't you think, to come all the way from Drumpagan to support it like this.'

Drumpagan. The name clicked up a warning light in his head. His gaze shot to the Earl whose own eyes were on the cannon. Drumpagan. The cannon ... a jumble of images and ideas flashed through his mind. O'Leary and the boy. Anny knitting her lime green jumper. The boy, that strapping great lying boy – so well muscled too. The cannon. He remembered slapping its solid iron. The cannon belonged to the Earl of Auchenbrach who lived at Drumpagan. Oh confusion! Confusion indeed.

In consternation his mind flew to Reading Jail. That's where he would be sent. He, Ethelred, would go the way of his beloved Oscar Wilde. Martyred. In chains to Reading Jail or somewhere like that – imprisoned for a mere misdemeanour – a tiny trespass. Receiving a cannon? Nothing at all – but all his Brighton clients would find out. That awful woman Blennerhasset would read about it in the *Telegraph* and tell them and they'd all come into his shop and sneer at him. At his stock. *She* would sneer at him. He would have to up sticks again, start again as a mere pedlar with a market stall (holding bits of china up and saying, 'It *is* rather pretty, isn't it?').

With a final despairing glance towards Margaret Johnson's slim back as she made her way to a vacant seat, as close as she could get to Ramsay – he could see that – Ethelred made a fresh decision. To retreat.

Ramsay was amazed. Sitting next to Julia he determined that he would not fail her in loyalty as she had failed him in the past and was, he suspected, failing him at this moment. Amazed because he had seen Margaret, he was sure he had. Down there to his left – that was her hair, glinting in the light spilling from the acting area.

'What is it?' Julia asked. 'Why are you pulling such a face? You look as though you have eaten a curate's egg.'

'Nothing. Nothing at all,' he replied, his mind busily putting the pieces together. First piece: the fact that when he had last seen Margaret Johnson – it *was* her; the elegant carriage of the head was unmistakable – when he had last seen her she had been in the company of her husband, walking out of the breakfast room of the Hôtel de Rome in Monte Carlo. Arm in arm, if he remembered correctly, and a heartbreaking sight it had been for him. The details were as clear as a Dürer woodcut, the waiter offering *jambon d'Ardennes* cut from a whole joint on the sidetable, the view through the big plate glass window of the croupiers leaving the white iced-cake casino after the graveyard shift. The scent of strong French coffee, the other chic people in the room looking up from their morning croissants to glance idly at the couple who were just leaving: Margaret Johnson and her husband Ian, who had been on an upward roll then; full of bounce, self-confidence.

She wasn't with her husband now, though. There were plenty of possible explanations for that, but Ramsay's mind jumped immediately to the most extreme, and the most attractive. That either her husband had left her or, better, that he had been found out and she had left him. No, Ramsay decided regretfully, it wouldn't be that. If Ian Johnson was in financial trouble again that would only make her stick more closely to him. Loyalty was her middle name; something he couldn't claim for the woman beside him, leaning forward to get the benefit of Arabella's no doubt creative opening for this piece. No, Margaret, having thrown in her lot with Ian, was much too loyal and much too proud to admit that she had made a mistake. His eyes on Julia, it seemed to him that he himself was cast in the same mould – too loyal and proud for his own good.

But something had changed. There had been a shift inside – a once-for-all change in his view of things. Because Ian Johnson was the best goldsmith that he had ever come across; and when he considered the links between them all – the woman seated over there, the woman beside him, the one who was shortly to appear on stage in the part of Devorgilla, and her husband, it was quite clear to Charles Ramsay what was going on.

What was going on was not clear, however, to the Earl of Auchenbrach in his place of honour. He inclined his head towards his wife and murmured something in her ear to draw her attention away from the worthy man on her left.

'Yes,' she said briskly, 'what is it?'

'Over there,' he murmured, nodding towards the piece of ordnance in the corner of the acting area.

'Yes, my dear, it's a cannon,' she said tolerantly, 'very exciting. But we've one already; two in fact, very like it.' They had arrived late from Heathrow that day and in the rush to get over to this pageant they had promised to attend they hadn't had time to inspect the grounds at Drumpagan.

'Yes,' he said firmly, 'a pair. And that, I'm convinced, is one of them.'

'Nonsense, it can't be.'

'Do you think I don't know my own cannon?' he demanded indignantly. 'I know every scratch, every mark, the sign of the founder who cast it. I'll bloody soon identify it if it's mine.'

'They must have borrowed it while we were away and forgotten to ask us. But for goodness' sake don't make a fuss about it now. You can't.'

'I have no intention of doing so,' he returned. 'But I shall certainly speak to Arabella about it afterwards.'

'Do that,' she said, returning her attention to the man on her other side. Nice wee man. Knew a lot about sheep.

Arabella settled herself in the lighting box and surveyed the audience for last-minute arrivals straggling to their seats. No, they were all in place. Reaching forward she slowly dimmed the lights down to full blackout before turning to her assistant in charge of sound, holding up an arm to bring in his opening fanfare at precisely the same moment as her spotlight. There were speakers all round the castle, set up on the walls, in the towers . . . She dropped her arm and the trumpets blared from everywhere as she threw the switch and a beam of light cut through the darkness to light up the herald. Well done, she breathed to herself. He was there, where he should be; he had found his mark exactly in the darkness. A tall man with a good round Scottish voice who waited calmly, just as she had taught him to do, until the fanfare was over. Then he spoke.

'After a series of strange vicissitudes and alterations of fortune. After difficulties almost incredible and invincible, this noble brave warrior, Robert the Bruce, made his entry to the throne and began his reign in the year of our Lord 1306, in the year of the world 5276, and in the 1636th year after the foundation of the monarchy of Scotland. Robert, by right of blood . . .' As the phrases rolled on she settled back with satisfaction in her canvas chair. Her pageant was up and running.

Out of sight in the inner courtyard of the castle, away from the acting area, the actors for the next scene were gathering. Robert Bruce, an anorak draped over his bonneted head because the rain was getting heavier, waited to enact the slaying of the Red Comyn in Greyfriars in Dumfries. The Red Comyn, round shield in hand, was stamping his feet to keep warm.

Behind them the first abbot of Sweetheart Abbey broke a generous section off his chocolate bar and put it in his mouth. It was a comfort. His benefactress Devor-gilla looked nervous, he thought – taut under her makeup. He decided against offering her a piece of chocolate since she was what his mother, who had always known her place, would have called a landed lady.

Caroline said, 'I wish this bloody rain would stop,' and turned away from him sharply, as though she couldn't bear the sight of his moving mouth. Then she laughed and exclaimed, glancing up towards the sky, 'This bloody rain.'

'It'll be all right. You'll be grand. You'll see,' the abbot said in a low voice. All those in the inner courtyard had to keep their voices low. Miss Knight had given them strict instructions.

'But I'm not grand now, am I?' she demanded sharply. He put his finger to his lips. 'Am I?' she asked again, taking no notice at all.

'Will you hold your noise, woman,' he whispered back without thinking, and then she had gone off in a huff. Should he have kept his mouth shut? He hoped she was coming back. There was no way he could set up Sweetheart Abbey on his own. She'll be back, he decided, and gave himself another square of chocolate. Cameron Rae came past in the gloom, pencil torch in hand, making a quick check that at least the principal characters appearing in the next couple of scenes were present and correct. He knew, of course, that it was the job of one of the girl assistants, but he wasn't prepared to delegate it yet.

Caroline had disappeared to find Malcolm Forsyth. Dressed in plaid and wig in the part of Prince Charles

Stuart, he was standing in the dim light opposite a semi-circle of younger men. They all knew who he was – a notorious character with the whiff of sin about him and the rewards of sin as well. There were stories of drug-pushing – in the schools, among the young on the estates – but nothing had been proved, no charges laid against him. It was curiosity that had drawn them to him. One or two were almost respectful because they knew how rich he had made himself, what a generous patron of this event he had been. They had seen him sign a cheque for the cannon. The lights and sound equipment were down to him too. And the stand.

'Aye. When the pageant is over I shall set it at the front of the house at Carrucate,' he was boasting. 'That's where yon cannon will end up. I—' Feeling Caroline's hand on his arm, he turned his head and said, 'What can I do for you, my lady?' One of the boys grinned at such familiarity with the gentry.

'Malcolm, I'm not feeling well. Have you got something you could give me?'

Dismayed, they fell silent. Her voice became more urgent. 'You said you might be bringing something.'

Forsyth made a gesture to the group as if to say, I'm a sucker for a pretty face, and found that it drew no reaction from them.

'I've an aspirin maybe somewhere.'

Obediently she followed him into the castle's gatehouse set aside as the dressing room for the leading men; a room with bare, sandstone walls with the names and initials of vandals of the past scratched on them. T McINNERY 1807 here; over there were the initials VL in an elegant, bold Roman script and the date AD 1823. In the corner above the opening for the fireplace a wit who hadn't been brave enough to reveal his name had ploughed deeply the words THE IRON DUKE and below that THE LONG NOSED B.

They could hear the Herald telling his audience the story of Bruce and the Comyn as his murder was re-enacted.

'Robert having now full proof of Comyn's vile practices, and his design to cut him off...'

The room had been fitted out with simple lamps, which had been switched off now to avoid spillage of light towards the audience and was in semi-darkness. It had folding chairs, a couple of trestle tables, and long, heavy metal coat-racks to carry the clothes of the cast.

The disembodied voice went on, '... rode straightway to Dumfries, and found Comyn in the Franciscan's church where he confronted him with his own letters, which Comyn denying impudently, Robert in high rage, ran him through the body with his dagger, and left him there; so Comyn justly fell a victim to his own perfidy.'

Forsyth went over to one of the coat-racks and, rummaging in the pocket of his leather jacket, brought out a package wrapped up roughly in metal foil which he handed to her. 'There you are. Buy now, pay later.'

She couldn't bring herself to reply. She took the packet slowly, with as much dignity as she could manage, and was beginning to unwrap it when Cameron Rae appeared in the doorway behind her.

'Caroline, are you there?' He flashed his little torch at her – the disc of light floated over her pale face, caught her eyes, making her blink, then, as it moved lower, glinted on the package in her hand. It flicked around the room and rested for a moment on Forsyth's dim figure before it went out.

Rae's voice came out of the gloom, making no judgements and betraying no opinion. 'You're on in five minutes, Caroline. You do have the parchment I gave you as a prompt, don't you?' She didn't reply. 'The one with your words on it, remember? I gave it you. Caroline, you—'

James McAllen's voice interrupted him. His shape appeared in the doorway. 'Is my wife here? Caroline, is that you?' She was still silent. 'Who is it in here?' he went on. 'Is it you, Caroline?' Cameron Rae switched on his torch and sent the beam moving round to pick out her face. Then he had it, and Malcolm Forsyth at her shoulder.

James took two paces forward and took the packet from her hand before she could resist. 'If you must,' he said, 'but not now, you bloody fool. Not yet.'

She let out a long moan and tried to get the package back. She needed it and he was leaving her no time.

Forsyth said contemptuously, 'Give it to your wife, you spoilsport. Let her have her sweetie.' The petal of light from the torch was still on his face, quivering, jumping about. He was smiling because he didn't give a damn for any of them.

James McAllen turned and smashed his right fist into that image, felling him with the single blow. Cameron Rae caught him by the arm, the beam of the torch bouncing round the room as he did so; caught both arms, pulling him back. McAllen let fly with a full-powered kick at the shape on the ground and was rewarded with a yelp of pain. But then Rae had him securely and was manhandling him, pulling him off-balance, dragging him backwards towards the door.

'Caroline,' he managed to say in a harsh whisper, 'get out there and take your place. You have two minutes. Do it.'

In the dark she hesitated. For months her husband had managed to maintain the pretence that there was nothing wrong in their house, that her changeable moods were down to her temperament, her lack of a child, any explanation that would serve. It was important to her and vital to him. If she didn't go on stage and at least say her words with some touch of intelligence and conviction the whole pretence, which had cost so much effort over the months, would be blown apart. She put her hands up to her face and felt a renewal of the craving. It came in bursts, wrenching at her stomach and her diaphragm. Heavily, as though weights were attached to her limbs, she moved towards the acting area. Her husband, who was calmer now, walked beside her, his face immobile.

The first abbot of Sweetheart welcomed the sight of her with relief. 'Madam Devorgilla, I'm real glad you're back,' he whispered to her. Uncertain what to say next he added nervously, 'Here, have a bit of chocolate.' He proffered the remains of his bar and was ignored. He wasn't at all offended, since she was a landed lady who behaved as a landed lady should. He would have been disappointed if she had accepted.

Cameron Rae muttered into his mobile phone to Arabella, far away in her lighting box: 'Everyone in place for the Sweetheart Abbey sequence.'

'Go now,' she replied. He signalled them on with a wide sweep of his arm and they moved into the warm light which bathed the acting area.

Someone had to find Forsyth, calm him down and make sure he wasn't going to walk out, thought Rae. Not him, though. He would do much for Arabella Knight, but not that. One of the girls could do it; Janet perhaps. He'd overheard her once chatting about the man with approval during a rehearsal coffee break. Rae was sure she would be more than ready to soothe his wounded pride. It would be a chance for her to get to know him better. He plunged off into the darkness to find her.

Charles Ramsay watched Caroline McAllen move centre stage with a grace that he hadn't expected, lift her eyes to the audience behind the glare of the lights in front of her and begin her speech. Her voice was steady, her delivery forthright and lively. She didn't have to refer to the parchment in her hand more than twice.

Charles Ramsay whispered in Julia's ear, 'I didn't expect this.' Her stamina, her ability to put a bold face on things in the face of enormous stress was extraordinary – something she shared with her husband. Not to be admired though, given the story as he understood it now, as he had understood it since the moment Margaret Johnson had arrived in the auditorium. The McAllens had forfeited his respect.

Julia said, 'I told you that she would perform,' as though that mattered. He supposed it did to her, and certainly it did to them. For his part he wasn't bothered either way, considering the fix he'd been landed in. It would have been so much easier if he hadn't developed so quickly a real concern for them both, a concern which they had betrayed. Of course Julia must have foreseen that he would have so much in common with those two that his judgement would be blunted and his eyes blinded to what was going on. Worse than that, she must have calculated, as she watched his friendship for them growing, that if anything went wrong and his eyes were opened it would be difficult for him to cut himself out of the web and make the decisions which had to be made. Decisions which with anyone else he could have taken without a second thought. *Probitas*. It was an easy word to say, but it pointed to a difficult road. He had enough experience to know that life had a habit of presenting one with problems that did not have an ideal solution – just a least bad one. Sometimes people had to be hurt; nice people too. But you had to be bloody sure of your ground before you put the knife in, because a knife thrust was often terminal.

He didn't blame the McAllens, either. They had been walking a tightrope for long enough. He had the grace to recognise that in that situation he might have been tempted to do the same thing; and he was open-minded enough too to concede that Julia owed her friend a loyalty. But he was her partner, for goodness' sake; something she had forgotten. And a question which begged to be answered was, why had she chosen to use him? Ethelred Lewis would have done the job without a qualm – but then Lewis hadn't the same clout with Sir Anthony. In any case the podgy little guy was probably part of the scheme; might even have provoked her into choosing him, Charles Ramsay, as the fall guy. No doubt she had been persuaded that her partner, in business and in bed, was an easier option than anybody else the two of them could dream up.

Probitas. It had never been an idea that she accepted. Which thought prompted him to survey the audience below him and to his left, trying to make out the shining blonde head of Margaret Johnson among so many ordinary ones. She would know the story, of course, and that was not to her credit. He was prepared to stretch a point where she was concerned, and he knew that was unfair in a way to his partner and he didn't care. He had to make contact with Margaret straight after the pageant was over, he told himself. Otherwise he was going to be in for a very frustrating time indeed: face to face with the McAllens, up against their toughness, their talent for pretence, trying to penetrate the masks they had put on. He had to talk to her.

The rain stopped shimmering down on the cast. Steilbow Castle was besieged; the Scottish Captain impersonated by James McAllen defended the ramparts valiantly against the oncoming English in a swirl of action with broadsword and shield, and was overwhelmed by unequal odds. Having surrendered against a promise of quarter, he was taken away in chains to be hanged along with the other Scottish prisoners. To celebrate this successful stroke of realpolitik the English knights paraded with shields emblazoned with their coats of arms and long banners which swirled in an antique amber light, highlighting Arabella's choreography in a way which made her catch her breath at the absolute beauty of her own creation. She was so choked with pride that now and then she found it difficult to whisper her instructions into her mobile phone, sitting high above the audience in her lighting box, a queen directing her unfolding story.

The audience saw it differently. They had begun to take much of what they saw for granted. Those with the most limited attention span were beginning to get bored with the earnest ceremony, and the ancient language which was being dinned into their ears from the loudspeakers. The seats were hard; they could only hope for something novel. The cannon was promising. They could see that it was heavy – the real thing. Surely it hadn't been put there simply as a prop, part of the decor. Too much trouble had been spent on getting it there for that. At some point it was going to go off, and the discharge would be a most satisfactory event. By now the question in the mind of many spectators was, in one word – When?

Even Ramsay caught himself asking that question. He wondered, too, where Ethelred Lewis had run the item to earth, as his gaze strayed again over the audience, failing to find Margaret. Was she still there? He hadn't seen her leave and he couldn't let her escape him when these proceedings were over.

He glanced at Julia's profile, her attention still caught by the performance, and felt a certain guilt.

She turned to him and asked, 'Enjoying yourself?'

'Completely,' he replied untruthfully. She made a little kiss in the air at him. It was a habit of hers – the kind of thing lovers do when they are satisfied.

They had reached the scene where the Jacobites came to Dumfries during the rising of '45. Arabella and the committee which had co-written the piece had perceived that having highlanders simply marching about lacked dramatic impact so liberties had been taken with history and the facts reconstructed. The sequence now consisted of Prince Charlie's speech to his troops at the Midsteeple followed by a skirmish with the Redcoats – so the programme said.

Five highlanders in kilts appeared in a pool of light in the centre of the acting area, proceeded into the semi-darkness in its corner and at last collected the cannon. Then they busied themselves with it in a theatrical way, intent, it seemed, on priming it for firing. Other bonneted warriors carrying targes and broadswords gathered round and approved of this activity with enthusiasm. The audience, alerted to the explosive potential of the scene, waited for Prince Charles Stuart to appear.

In her lighting box Arabella was tense, waiting, her ear to the phone, for Cameron Rae to tell her that Forsyth in the part of the Prince had reached his position high up in one of the window openings of the sandstone inner façade. She heard Cameron's steady voice say, 'Ready . . . *now*—'

Every light went out. In the box, on the stage, everywhere. There was a surge of disappointment from the audience, a sigh, a low moan of frustration.

'Power failure,' Julia said. 'It must be.'

Ramsay was high enough up in the stand to see over the moat towards some cottages nearby. Their lights were still on. It must be simply a quirk of the supply arrangements.

He turned to look up towards the lighting box and saw a small light appear in the darkness. Someone had switched on a torch.

Arabella issued a crisp order into her cellphone. 'Cameron, try and see that nobody moves or speaks in the acting area, will you?' The device crackled but there was no reply. She tried again.

She turned to her assistant, 'Make an announcement, love, would you?' He picked up the microphone and blew into it experimentally. It was dead.

Blundering against her with the torch he pulled open the flimsy door of the box and went outside. 'Ladies and gentlemen,' he bellowed experimentally and heard his voice hit the façade of the castle and echo back to him.

One of the highlanders on stage said, 'There's nae need to shout,' and provoked a laugh.

Someone else said, 'Cut it out.'

Arabella's assistant repeated less loudly, 'Ladies and gentlemen, as you can see—'

'But we can't see,' a smart English voice in the audience pointed out. This was well received too.

Doggedly he tried again. 'As you are aware, the main

power supply has failed. If you would be kind enough to stay in your seats, we shall do everything we can to restore it as quickly as possible.'

The Countess of Auchenbrach's hand sought that of her lord in the dark, and she moved her head closer to her husband's. 'Are you really going to complain to Arabella about the cannon?'

'Might do,' he muttered, though he wasn't altogether sure. The truth was, now that he thought about it, visualised Drumpagan without them, he wasn't convinced the cannons embellished the place. A little vulgar, perhaps? That possibility made him grimace. A touch too imperial for this day and age? Still, they did belong to him, and the idea of possession was important. It was what had got the Auchenbrachs where they were today. In the front row.

The lights went on – all the lights, everywhere. At the back there was clapping. The Earl smiled courteously at his nearest neighbours and made an encouraging gesture towards the stage where the highlanders had been discovered, dazed by the light, standing about in various states of unreadiness. Showing presence of mind their leader roared fresh orders to the gun team who went back to their efforts with the cannon.

Malcolm Forsyth in his plaids had climbed the stone staircase behind the façade towards the topmost row of dark window openings and his big moment. A spotlight picked him out and he delivered his set speech in a stiff, uninflected voice.

'And so, my highlanders, on to England to topple

George of Hanover off his throne,' he roared and was left in darkness as the spotlight went off in search of the English redcoats entering stage right. A skirmish ensued, some of the highlanders holding the enemy away from the cannon while the gunner brought down his flaming linstock.

It went off with a tongue of fire and an enormous noise, far louder than the audience had expected. It had grabbed their attention – all eyes were focused on it. 'Well done,' breathed the Earl, and again there was a burst of applause from the back. It must have been just then, when no one was looking, that Malcolm Forsyth fell from the dark window opening at the top of the façade to the paved floor beneath it. As he fell he gave a long and hopeless cry.

The lights went out again.

'Defenestrated, by God,' the Earl exclaimed to himself with delight. 'I wonder how they did that?' This was exciting. For the first time since he'd been told he had to attend, he was glad that he'd come to this show – if only they could sort out their electricity supply.

It wasn't authentic though, surely. Sitting there in the dark, he reran his memory of the '45 – what he knew of it: a fair amount, since one of his forebears had changed sides at a crucial moment, a fact his descendants were grateful for but did not publicise. No, he couldn't remember any story that had Charles Edward Stuart thrown down from a window; certainly not from the Midsteeple in Dumfries.

He leaned over to his wife and whispered, 'Arabella's been taking liberties with the facts, don't you think?'

In the same moment the lights came back. He watched the highlanders rush over to the fallen figure and pick him up. Someone shouted in alarm, 'Don't touch him! Leave him alone.' Too late. Hands under his armpits they had already started to drag him upright.

'I think not,' answered the Countess, nodding towards the body of Malcolm Forsyth held sagging between two highlanders. 'I think someone has been taking liberties with him.'

Dead, the Earl judged; he'd seen dead men before. Dead as mutton, and that thought provoked a decision. He would not after all lay claim to the cannon. It meant publicity, police enquiries, involvement, and delay in returning to his beloved Provence. He would turn a blind eye to its removal. That was best. They would have to rub along at Drumpagan with a single cannon in the policies. Anyway it was an anachronism; it didn't go with the house. Perhaps they could persuade someone to take the other one too.

In the stand behind them, Charles Ramsay watched as they laid Forsyth down again, and stood shading their eyes from the spotlight, uncertain what to do next.

Had Forsyth fallen, or had he been shoved? Shoved was most likely, Ramsay thought, and the implications were not comfortable. There were three people behind the scenes who might have given him a push at the psychological moment: James, Caroline and Cameron Rae.

An alternative explanation for his death was that someone had tampered with the cannon. The shot had certainly sounded too loud to be a mere blank. That made it no easier, though; those three were still solidly in the frame. Opportunity, motive and everything. What a pity. What a mess it all was.

The lights went up on the acting area, in the stand, everywhere. There was a cough from the loudspeakers, then a voice said, 'Ladies and gentlemen, as you have seen there has been an accident. A serious accident...' Two men in everyday clothes came on to the stage and one of them knelt beside Forsyth, checked his pulse, his breathing. The other began clearing the actors out of the way, gesturing towards stage right. There was a long and uncomfortable pause before the voice spoke again. 'In the circumstances it would be wrong to continue with the pageant. Would you please stay in your seats for the time being.'

A hubbub of comment and speculation had begun in the audience. Julia said, 'Caroline will be in a state. I can't stay here. I must go down and see to her. Are you coming? She will want to get home.'

'In that case you'd better take her,' he said, handing her the car keys. 'I'm going to do what I'm told and stay here.' His eyes were still seeking for Margaret Johnson down there among those talking heads.

'How will you get back? You may be stranded here,' she warned.

'A taxi,' he replied.

'Please yourself,' she answered curtly, pushing past him out on to the raked aisle and striding down it without looking back.

A voice nearby said, 'Well, this is too much for me. I don't care what they say, I'm going home.'

Another voice said petulantly, 'I really don't see the point of keeping us here.'

Ramsay made for the section of the stand where he thought he had seen Margaret. People were already clattering down the stand and leaving, each trying to avoid looking at the shape, covered with a tartan plaid, on the stage, almost as though Forsyth had done something indecent by dying and they didn't want to embarrass him by inspecting what was left of him too closely.

She was there; it was her. Margaret. Her pale golden hair glinted in the flat, overpowering working lights.

She said, 'I thought you might be here,' and the thin promise of the words gave him a kind of hope. He remembered the last painful sight he had been given of her in that hotel in the south, when he had failed to speak and she had taken his silence as proof of something he hadn't meant – of a lack of concern, perhaps; certainly of his desire to be free from responsibility.

'I'm glad I caught you. I thought it was you. I need to talk to you.'

'We might as well get it over with now,' she said wearily. Because the story wasn't going to reflect well on her or her husband – because she knew him and his overdeveloped sense of right and wrong, the whole burden labelled *Probitas* that he carried everywhere he went and that threatened, by the time she had finished the story, to destroy any warmth for her which he might still have left. For days she had been planning for this meeting, moving towards it in hope, towards touching him again, eager to revive the relationship they had once had. Now she saw with bleak certainty that the meeting itself was going to burn away that purpose of hers slowly like a fuse, leaving nothing but a worm of ash behind. Once he knew the whole truth about the medallion and her part in the deception he would be away, gone after a few stiff words of farewell. The ritual had to be endured nonetheless. 'You'd better come home to the flat.'

He watched her face and couldn't make out what he saw in it. If he didn't go with her now, he decided, there wouldn't be another chance to get her story, to renew his contact with her. She would simply disappear into the darkness for good. He stepped heavily after her down to ground level and once there took her arm. She wrapped his round it with her other hand and marched past the appalled group standing close to Forsyth's corpse without a tremor.

Chapter Sixteen

The flat was much as he had expected it would be. Brittle, sun-faded curtains, saleroom furniture and worn carpet all confirmed the verdict. Failure, they said.

Glancing at his face she agreed unemotionally, 'Yes, it's a cesspit.'

He had no time to waste on polite denials. 'Where has your husband got to?'

'He was here. He's gone now.' His absence didn't seem to bother her.

'Would you like a drink?' she asked. 'There's sherry somewhere and he may have left some whisky. I think he bought a bottle at the weekend.'

'A whisky, thanks. It's been a rough day.' Watching her, always highly strung, her composure ready to crack, he felt as though he was walking alongside a precipice.

'Sit down, will you, and I'll see if I can lay my hands on something.' He did so, finding that chair of hers in the corner. He recognised it, remembering it from the sitting room of their house near Bressemer. He had sat on it before – the day she had told him, months before the Monte Carlo episode, that she and her husband were bankrupt. That was the first time Ian had vanished, and left her, alone and vulnerable, to face the bailiffs: the officious men in reach-me-down suits, taking charge of the keys, ordering her about. He, Charles Ramsay, wouldn't have deserted her – and it was he who had picked up the pieces on that occasion, so she'd been fully aware of the kind of man he was, and her husband was, when she'd made that miserable choice over breakfast at the Hôtel de Rome.

The thought made him resentful. OK, he was a young fogey, if you like, taking pride in his standards of conduct and contemptuous of those, like Ian Johnson, who didn't match them; but how could she have preferred that little man to him? Come on, don't be childish, Ramsay, he told himself. It's a question of body chemistry, that's all it is, and you have to live with the fact. He forced himself to think about something else. The chair, that would block the fact out. A walnut side chair – mid-Victorian, 1870 say, and incisively carved. Before he sat down his hand caressed the back. A beautiful chair. He'd always liked it. It gave the room a touch of distinction it sorely needed.

She brought the drinks in cheap glasses; neat whisky for him, for herself something red and nondescript – grape juice, perhaps, masquerading as wine. Because she hadn't been able to find the sherry – or the bottle had been empty. Such makeshifts must have been an habitual part of her life.

'So what's been happening to you?' she asked, sipping whatever it was.

Julia had happened. He skipped that. The partnership had happened — which involved Julia too, so he missed that out as well. It didn't leave much to say.

'Nothing altogether new,' he lied, feeling somehow cheated of the chance to tell her of his successes, such as they were. At the moment they didn't seem important. 'I've been up here on holiday staying at Glengarrick. A friend of a friend.'

He still didn't mention Julia, and then found that he didn't need to, because she said, 'Caroline McAllen. I know.'

'And you?' he asked. 'How is life treating you?' It was easier to speak in clichés; there was less risk of doing damage with the wrong word.

'Look around you,' she answered. Her surroundings said everything that he needed, or was going to be allowed, to know.

'You know why I'm here, don't you?' He could see that she thought she did but wasn't going to try to force him into the open.

'I haven't the slightest idea. Not a ghost,' she replied, lying in her turn, leaving it to him to decide which path to take, emotional or otherwise. The old flame bit or business — which was it to be? Business, he decided.

'It'll be less painful in the end if I say it quickly and get it over with,' he said. Like pulling a sticking plaster off. One tug, a flash of pain and there you were. 'James McAllen of Glengarrick has asked me to handle the sale of a rare item which belongs to him.'

She had turned away and was looking out of the window at the ordinary-looking street with the yellow glare of its lamps and the occasional car purring past. 'What rare item?'

'Stop pretending you don't know. A gold medallion bearing the image of Mary Stuart. He calls it the Mary Medallion.'

She didn't move. Her back was towards him as straight and immobile as a guardsman's.

'It's a copy, isn't it?'

Unready to admit that yet, she took another sip from her glass.

He tried again. 'A reproduction, if you prefer the word. That's why you're here, isn't it? You're here because Ian was here, which was because he was commissioned to make a new casting in gold from the original intaglio moulds which McAllen still has. Yes, he had them in that leather case of his, but not the medallion, probably because some ancestor sold it long ago when times were hard.

'Then James needed money himself, didn't he? He was financing his wife's drug habit: crack, I daresay. What does it cost? Four, five hundred a day? He paid because it was the only way he could keep it secret. Am I right so far? Does all this ring some bells?'

She whipped round and stood now with her back to the window though her gaze was fixed on the floor to avoid the verdict she expected in his eyes. Her arm came awkwardly out from her side in a gesture of pleading. Pleading was difficult – it embarrassed her, which didn't in the least surprise him after the hammering she had given him a couple of years back – the rejection. She hadn't forgotten that any more than he had.

'Couldn't you leave me alone, please? Look – use your imagination – I'm feeling gruesome. All the guilt over this medal thing ... and I've had enough humiliation for today, thank you.' Tears came to her eyes.

Humiliation – why? Oh, because she had made the wrong decision before, had ditched Charles Ramsay and gone back to her loser of a husband. Why had she done it? Because just then he had looked like a winner, that was why, Charles Ramsay told himself. Johnson had been on an upswing with tens of thousands in his pocket. It had looked like the right thing to do, to try again with the man she had married. But after a few days she had realised that he was sliding down the roller-coaster again, and had found herself back in the familiar marshy acreage of evasion and broken promises. Now he had vanished once more and she was left out on a limb in a strange town, staring the Social Security department in the face. With a former lover sitting there ready to wave her rejection of him at her – after he had shown that she and Ian had been involved in a fraud. She had thrown Charles over and he'd come to claim his small revenge. That was her humiliation.

Charles said, 'OK, it's difficult, but I have to know. It's important to me because I've been brought into it now. And I can't—'

'Your bloody reputation again. There are other things that matter.'

'It's not my reputation I'm concerned about. I'm not sitting here being holier than thou. It's the partnership's reputation that's on the line. I'm being absolutely practical. It's a business thing. We simply can't afford the damage.' His tone was matter-of-fact and that carried weight with her.

She said, 'Your new girlfriend Julia told them that they needed a clever goldsmith and she and Lewis got in touch with us. Ian had done small jobs for him – repairs on bits and pieces of Georgian jewellery.'

Ramsay sipped his whisky and nodded. Gold scarcely showed its age so it would be almost impossible to detect a facsimile if they had used the right sort – Johnson would know where to find it and how to make it look right – and the story was that the medallion was in mint condition anyway. He would also know precisely how to take the wax impressions, make the mould, do the delicate casting, and of course he'd have made a good job of it. It was the one area where he was absolutely competent. The chance of it being detected was negligible.

They were in the same business, on the same wavelength, and she read his thoughts. 'No, it couldn't be distinguished from the real thing. It was magnificent – he did a superb piece of work – and what difference does it make?' she demanded fiercely.

That was disingenuous. She knew quite well that, at the level where the Malling trustees were operating, the idea of the medallion was as important as the thing itself. Take a painting accepted as the work of Rembrandt for hundreds of years. Experts prove that it isn't and its value is immediately cut by three-quarters. It's the same picture – it hasn't changed but the idea has.

'What difference?' he shot back. 'You know as well as I

do. If the medallion was the original its value would be in the low hundreds of thousands. A facsimile is worth what? The price of the gold plus the cost of his work. Five, six hundred?'

'It isn't sensible,' she said.

'It doesn't have to be. You know the golden rule.'

'What's that?'

'Don't argue with the market.'

Knowing her position was hopeless she still wouldn't surrender. 'Charles,' she protested, 'as long as the trustees don't know, they're losing nothing.' She had used his forename and he took the opportunity to use hers.

'Nonsense, Margaret, of course they are. Suppose somebody tells them. Or suppose someone doesn't tell them and they only find out when they decide to sell later on? You know how eager the Americans are to go to law. They'd sue us bloodless.'

'Who do you mean?'

'Julia – my partner – and myself.'

'She can live with that; she told me so herself. It's you who are out of step with the rest of us.'

It was because he didn't bother to reply that she capitulated. 'Why are you always right?' she asked petulantly, and because he knew that wasn't true either he remained silent. They had renewed their relationship, he felt, but they were toiling uphill.

'Charles. I'm sorry.' Her voice had recovered the splendid musical tone which he had remembered whenever he had thought about her. And that had been too often for comfort, often in Julia's presence. It had been one of the things which had got in the way. But all that was in the past now.

Then she tested him a little. She said, 'I daresay you won't be staying for long. Soon you'll finish your drink and leave. Close the door on all this.' She gestured at the sad room. 'Me.'

He caught a light in her eye and smiled because she was being disingenuous again. Of course she didn't believe that – not for a minute. Her face changed as she went on. 'There's something I should have told you before, and I suppose it would have made a difference if I had. My only excuse is that it didn't seem so at the time. It's all over now, but you ought to be told.'

'What's that?'

'When we split up I was pregnant.' It was something that had never crossed his mind when he had tried to work out what had happened and why. Why hadn't she told him? He stifled his question since she had to tell it in her own way. After a moment, avoiding his eyes again, she managed to bring out the words – the voice as mellow and melodious as ever.

'It was yours and it miscarried.'

'When?'

'Later on.'

When the statement hit him he closed his eyes for a moment, drew a deep breath and tried to absorb the information in easy stages, to work through its implications step by step.

If that had been the situation at the Hôtel de Rome, that she was pregnant, the whole thing made more sense. Security was what a person like her would have needed above everything else – security for herself and the child. It was the one thing he hadn't thought to offer her, and at that moment it had looked as though her husband would be able, at last, to provide it.

A child. Given and taken away in the same instant. He felt a pain in his head like a rogue charge of electricity, where the loss had struck him. He would have to try and cope with the grief later; it wasn't something he could deal with now.

He said very deliberately, trying to control his voice as he pronounced each word, 'What were you going to call it?' Him, or her, he should have said, not *it*. It. He'd used the wrong pronoun and it made him wince, though Margaret appeared not to notice.

'Charles, if it was a boy,' she replied and shrugged as though the choice was obvious. It was something worth keeping although it didn't signify now, of course.

She was hugging herself now, her arms folded across her chest, trying to keep the grief from bursting out because she didn't want a scene. 'Would it have made a difference if I had told you?' she asked, and looking into his face saw the answer.

He had never been a demonstrative man. This he knew and regretted. Now, though, he came quickly to his feet and opening his arms he said, 'Will you put down that glass of redcurrant juice or whatever it is you favour and come over here?'

She did as he asked and held him against her to bring back the warmth.

Chapter Seventeen

His taxi crunched up the drive at Glengarrick at two in the morning. He paid the fare and it left, its rear light retreating past the banks of rhododendrons that lined the pale ribbon of gravel, leaving him in total darkness with the huge grey house waiting for him. The front door opened, flinging out a flare of light, with Julia in silhouette in the centre of it, beckoning to him – Julia at her most uncompromising, overestimating her own importance as she was prone to do.

As soon as he reached the top step she clutched him by the arm and whispered fiercely, 'Why didn't you say you were going to be this late?'

'I did. I rang James.'

'And said as late as this?'

'Of course I did. I'm not a child.'

'I'm not at all sure about that,' she said presumptuously. He was glad of her antagonism, because it made his guilt a little easier to bear. He felt like an errant husband coming home in the small hours after deceiving his wife, which was what she was in all but name. He was grateful to her for not kissing him – otherwise she might have smelt Margaret's perfume on his cheek.

No, that was a mistake, he wasn't her husband. He was her business partner with a special claim on her loyalty and that would have to be gone into when there was time.

He followed her into the sitting room, which was cold; the central heating had turned itself off. She seemed confused, angry – angrier than would be warranted just by his late arrival.

'Have they gone to bed?'

'I wish you'd been here. Where were you, for Chrissake? I've had to try and cope on my own.' She'd had more than one drink – he could smell it from where he stood. No doubt there'd been nightcaps – James acting the host as usual, the edge of his collar stained with pale brown makeup.

How Julia's voice croaked – as though she had been smoking. It couldn't be that, because she didn't use tobacco. It was stress that was causing it. What did she mean? Why the hassle? What was going on?

'Cope with what?'

'Those two. That pair up there.' She spoke as though they were a brace of pheasants, a couple of hounds, a pair of people you didn't care for. She had jerked her chin towards the floors above. Then he heard a shriek from upstairs.

'What the hell is that? Is he murdering her?' It seemed a possibility. He took a pace towards the door and she intercepted him – barred his way. He cannoned into her without meaning to, which didn't help.

She was tense, aggrieved. She burst out, 'They are both raving mad.'

'What's going on for goodness' sake? Talk English. Say what it is.' He wanted to shake her but that wouldn't help either.

'It's James. When he got home tonight there was a serious row about Malcolm Forsyth. She accused him of murdering him by pushing him out of that window. He shouted that he'd been cuckolded, that he'd seen them the other night at Carrucate: Caroline and Forsyth on the floor of the living room, rutting – in the missionary position, she hugging him with her legs – you know? James was quite explicit, he can't have been making it up. Then he dragged her upstairs and swore he was going to punish her. Do you know what he's doing, the bastard?'

Although he thought he had guessed, Charles shook his head.

'He's putting her through cold turkey. The bad bit started just fifteen minutes ago. He's locked her up in the tower room where he keeps the medallion and all that bric-à-brac his great-grandfather collected. The treasure room. He's gone crazy.'

He'd better go and see. He pushed past her and took the stairs two at a time.

James McAllen was sitting in the corridor with his back against the big mahogany door and a heavy tumbler of whisky by his side. Behind the door, thick as it was, Ramsay could hear his wife, not sobbing, but making an occasional burst of noise, a kind of yelping. She was close to the other side of the door. Then there was a moan which grew into another scream. As though to fortify himself, James McAllen took a swig from his glass.

'You're back then.' He patted the carpet in an invitation to join him at his post. Charles remained standing.

'What's up?'

'She is. My wife. She's going through a period of re-education and not liking it much, as you can hear.'

There was a banging behind him. McAllen stood up and placed his ear against the door. It seemed that she had asked who was out there, because he shouted at the door, 'Just Charles Ramsay, my honey love, come back from an evening out.'

There was an indistinct mumbling from inside and a moment later something heavy crashed against the door – and again. The second time it splintered one of the upper panels. The third blow splayed it outwards so that a piece of the wood was leaning into the passageway. The lights were on inside the room. Ramsay saw Caroline's face appear for a moment, blotched, smeared with tears. Something shot through the opening and fell on the carpet. It was one of the miniatures painted on ivory which McAllen had shown him not long after his arrival. The black frame with its tiny brass acorn was smashed, the fragments only just hanging together, the glass pulverised and the shards driven into the tiny picture. It was a total ruin. She must have stamped on it, then ground her heel into it again and again. McAllen picked it up and showed it to him, shrugging. Then her hand appeared through the opening holding some screwed-up pieces of paper which she released, her fingers stiffly extended, allowing them to fall to the floor.

'You can have these too from your bloody treasure,' she screamed at him through the hole in the door. McAllen picked those up too and smoothed them out against the wall, fitting them together. It was the remains of a Japanese print by the nineteenth-century master Kunisada – *Girl By the Seashore*. The pale face of the girl and the muted pinks and browns of her dress contrasted sharply with the deep blue of the waves behind her, each crisply headed with stylised foam. In the pain of her frustrated craving his wife had torn it and crumpled up the pieces.

'Pity,' he said rolling everything into a ball and throwing it down the corridor, as far from his sight as he could.

Caroline shouted, 'You have to let me out. I need to go to the toilet.'

'I have provided facilities in there,' James answered dismissively.

'A chamber pot! You really can't be serious. What is this, James? James, I need the loo. I'm going to be sick.' McAllen didn't move.

Her face appeared at the splintered aperture again. 'Look, this is private. Between husband and wife. Leave me some dignity for the love of ... and tell that brothel creeper Ramsay to go away. To get out—' She began to cough and retch.

Charles said, 'I'll go.'

McAllen didn't try to stop him, but as he turned to go downstairs he called after him, 'We need some water up here. Drinking water for her. Would you see if you can locate some bottled mineral water? There should be a crate in the kitchen. Otherwise could you fill some empty tonic bottles with water and bring those up? Plastic bottles, not glass, obviously.'

'Sure,' Charles called back. Where did he stand in all this, he asked himself, as another cry pursued him down the stairs.

Julia had no such doubts when he reached the kitchen. 'He's torturing her, and you've got to stop it. She's in agony and she needs medical help.' He didn't need to be told. A doctor he knew had once said it was like the organs being dragged from your body, like the flesh being dragged from your bones. How long did it take before you were through it? Thirty-six, forty-eight hours?

He couldn't find the mineral water so he filled bottles at the tap. By the time he reached the third of them he had made up his mind whose side he was on.

'She's ill, you know. If you don't do something I'm going to call the police.'

'Make sure you think it through before you do,' he replied as he stowed the bottles in a cardboard box he'd found. Then he asked deliberately, 'What happened after I left? Were the police called?'

That forced her to remember how much was at stake for everyone if she alerted the police to what was going on at Glengarrick; it made her stop and think.

'Yes, the police did come. They took statements from one or two people and collected a lot of names and addresses from members of the cast and the audience.

They took mine and James' and Caroline's too. They said they might want to interview us, to establish exactly what had happened I suppose, whether it had been an accident or whatever. Then an ambulance arrived and I heard somebody say they'd taken the body to the hospital mortuary, because there was going to be a post mortem.'

Leaving her to reflect on that, reflecting on it himself, he took his burden upstairs and handed over the bottles to James.

By the time he returned the screams from upstairs were coming less frequently. He reckoned that Caroline was getting tired out and would eventually fall asleep from sheer exhaustion, which was going to be a much-needed relief all round. Julia had made coffee for Caroline and James, and took it to them.

She was up there for some time and when she returned she said, 'He insists on sleeping up there in the passage in case she has a crisis in the night. I helped to make up a bed on the floor.'

It was clear that she had been having a serious chat with James as well, because she added reluctantly, spacing out her sentences, choosing her words, 'He made me stay and talk about it. He thinks it's the only chance of breaking Caroline's addiction. I don't agree, but he does seem to have tried everything else. Everything I could think of. Half the clinics in London.' She shrugged her acceptance of what was being done.

At last silence seemed to have returned to the house; there hadn't been a sound from Caroline for fully ten minutes. The hand of the clock on the kitchen wall flicked another minute away, moving towards three o'clock in the morning. The worst time.

Trying to warm his hands round his mug, Ramsay remarked, 'She doesn't want to be cured. She never did. That's his problem.' It was time to get some things straight at last. He went on, 'It's ruined him hasn't it? He's borrowed on the estate until there's nothing left to borrow on and the income's all swallowed up in interest.'

He had done everything he could to keep up appearances – to keep his plight from his friends, from everybody except the personal lending manager of his bank. The whole thing was a front. The cheerful farms, the snowy-white buildings, the well-kept woodland. James McAllen's inheritance had been hollowed out from within by his wife's addiction to crack cocaine as though it was an apple eaten from the inside by wasps until there was nothing left but a shell.

'The sale of that medallion was his last throw, wasn't it? The three hundred grand might just have enabled him to turn the whole thing round. If he'd felled a big area of timber, say, and caught the stock market at the right moment.'

He had used the past tense; that told her that he knew all about the medallion.

He spoke slowly, 'I'm your partner and you let me in for this.'

'Caroline and I go back a long way,' she answered. 'She's my oldest friend.'

'But you used me,' he insisted. 'You could have found somebody else to do it, somebody like Lewis. He wouldn't have minded.' He didn't say, that would have kept me out of it – but that was what he thought and he didn't like it.

For once she didn't leap to Ethelred's defence.

Ramsay said, 'We've been through a lot together, you and I. We were a good team.' The words might sound trite but they were accurate.

'Spare me the Rover Scout bit for goodness' sake,' she said. 'I don't need it.' He wasn't put off by the jibe.

'I don't know what makes you tick,' he said. 'We set up a business. We take the most horrendous financial risks – you were gambling with a significant chunk of your mother's capital. You worked like hell; just as hard as I did – you had to run everything on your own when I was in Sweden. We risked everything and it worked because we made it work. The partnership was going places. We'd just got it off the ground – established a clientele, a reputation. It was something I at least was proud of. And you were happy to throw the whole lot away – the work, the worry we went through, the future – by going into a ludicrous scam like this.'

'Caroline's my oldest friend,' she repeated. 'And James, you like him, you get on really well together. You know you do, Charles darling.'

The last word threw him because it wasn't what he wanted to hear.

'That isn't the thing.'

'Loyalty to one's friends. Isn't that the thing?' she shot back.

'Of course,' he said, 'loyalty to one's friends. You said it, not me.' And he remembered that two hours before he had been in Margaret's arms in the bedroom of that dim little flat and as happy as a king. A bloody disloyal one, though, who had cuckolded Julia. Deceived her. But it wasn't the same thing. Was it? Deal with that when you come to it, he thought. Stick to the point.

'You know the business we're in as well as I do. Trust has to be our stock in trade. In a world as full of rogues and vagabonds as ours they have to be able to trust us – our clients, the people we buy from. Sir Anthony Andover – he may be pompous and a pain but he understands that. In our trade trustworthiness isn't a luxury, it's an essential.'

'Nobody will ever find out,' she protested. She had heard and not heard and was determined not to understand.

'*Would* ever find out,' he insisted. 'And don't be so sure. You haven't thought it through. We live in an age of technology, and those trustees can certainly pay for the very best. Besides, they can't afford to put a foot wrong. I think you'd have come unstuck. It would have been detected and they'd have stopped the cheque or Golver would have ended up suing James for the money, or us. Our good name would have been destroyed. Nothing would have come of it but disaster.'

Her face troubled, thoughtful, she took his empty cup and walked to the sink. He watched her, knowing that he wasn't going to allow her to perform even a service as small as that for him for much longer. Yes, he'd betrayed her too, but she was a dangerous person to have around and now she was already part of his past.

* * *

He made no excuse for looking for a separate bedroom, collecting his things from the one they had shared – with some delight, he admitted to himself. It was a harsh decision but the sooner everything was clear the better. There was no point in pretending that nothing had changed. She watched him collecting everything up, and said nothing except, 'You'll need a towel,' draping it round his neck in an affectionate gesture; probably the last he could expect. She hadn't really understood yet what had happened. They were both too poleaxed by the events of the day to indulge in any more argument. Besides, they both knew they were going to need every ounce of strength they possessed to cope with the McAllens in the next few hours.

He managed to find some bedclothes in one of the linen cupboards on the top floor. Up there, where the chambermaids had slept, he was closer to the elements. A storm had arrived from the west, and rain was lashing at the small panes of the corridor windows. He could hear the wind roaring now and then in the roof. It was so cold suddenly that he decided to lie down half dressed. He finally got to sleep at four, and at five was woken up by Caroline again: a long full-throated scream of pain and indignation about once every five minutes, returning just as he thought that perhaps she had given up, and he would be able to drop off again.

James wouldn't be able to sleep either. Ramsay felt a rush of sympathy for the man whose hopes he was going to ruin in the morning. They had developed an empathy which was about to be destroyed. It was part of the price he had to pay.

He closed his eyes – at least that rested them – and a voice said, 'Charles.' A man's voice. 'Charles? Are you awake?' It was James. Of course it was.

He found himself whispering, although there was no need. He heard another wail from Caroline in full cry from the floor below.

McAllen was fully dressed, his face as white as chalk; he had a glass in his hand and stank of whisky. 'Charles, would you do something for me?'

'What?' He wasn't writing out any blank cheques in this situation.

'It's simple. It won't involve you. Not much, anyway.'

'OK. Try me.'

'The postman comes at about nine o'clock. He mustn't come up to the house or he'll hear Caroline yelling and start making a nuisance of himself. Can you go down the drive to head him off? Make as if you're having an early morning walk.'

'But it's pouring with rain, and it doesn't sound as if it's going to ease off.'

James burst out, 'For goodness' sake be serious. This is important. Take a gun, say you're out after rabbits. Use your bloody head.'

From below they heard Caroline cry out, 'James. Please. *Please.*'

'OK, I'll do it,' Ramsay replied. 'You'd better go and see to her.'

James hesitated. Was there another favour he wanted

to ask – to do with the Mary Medallion? If so he could forget it.

'Go on. Get down there. I'll do it,' Ramsay added brusquely, wanting to get this man who had become his friend out of the room before he asked him to do something else. Or rather not to do something else. Not to ring Andover in the morning and tell him the medallion was a fake.

Perhaps it was the smell of whisky, or a night without much sleep that had made him feel queasy – or perhaps it wasn't.

James lent him his old military mackintosh; the one he had put on the day before to cover up his Scottish Captain costume. It all seemed a hell of a long time ago. He lent him a shotgun, too, and gave him a handful of cartridges to go with it. Charles began the long walk down the drive, the gun hanging open over his arm.

He couldn't hear Caroline – that was something. The mail van didn't arrive at exactly the same time every day. What if it came early? He was about a hundred yards down the drive when Caroline started up again. And then he heard the van turning at the gate, beside the gatekeeper's cottage. He heard the driver change up and start the easy run up the drive. He could still hear Caroline, loud and clear. He wasn't going to get there in time. He broke into an awkward run, the gun bouncing at his left elbow. It didn't matter. He had to get as far from house as he could, as quickly as possible. The red van came round the bend and stopped as the postman caught sight of Ramsay, slowing to a walk, holding out his right hand to take the mail from him.

The engine was running, which meant that the man might not hear anything anyway. Another cry came from the house. If he hadn't known it was her, would he have been able to tell what that sound was? Ramsay asked himself. The man was sorting through his letters, his packages, finding the packet for the big house, held together with an elastic band.

He handed it to Ramsay and there was another scream; much louder this time.

'It's a rough day,' the postman observed. 'They say it'll be grand by lunchtime, though. Maybe. On the radio.' He showed no desire to go about his business. 'Out after rabbits?' he went on, nodding at the shotgun.

'Yes, yes. The laird asked me to have a walk round. Too many of them this year.'

'Aye, they don't know much but they know how to breed,' the postman said.

Ramsay knew that another cry was due from Caroline imprisoned in her tower at any moment. He loaded the gun and snapped the breech shut with a gesture of impatience. 'I'd better get on,' he said, 'or they'll have produced another litter.'

'Aye,' the postman grinned. 'Bye.' He put the van into gear, did a neat U-turn in the drive and roared away. Just as he did so another scream came from the house.

Ramsay turned towards it and marched back to the next task he had to face.

Outside the house he stopped beside his car, which

Julia had used to bring the three of them back in the night before. Unloading the gun again he leaned it carefully against the car, slipped into the driving seat, picked up the mobile phone and stabbed out Golver's number.

'Sir Anthony Andover, if you please. Charles Ramsay speaking.'

A girl's voice at the other end. He remembered her, a debby kind of girl – so many of them were – and supercilious with it, he had always thought. 'Sir Anthony's in conference, I'm afraid. I'll ask him to call you, shall I?'

Tomorrow. Next week. Next bloody month.

'No, I'm afraid I have to speak to him now.' There was enough of an edge in his voice to shake some politeness into her – attention at any rate.

'Please, Mr Ramsay. He is in a meeting. Really.' This isn't some gambit, that was what he heard her saying. So what?

'I'm short of time so I've got to be brutal. Your job's on the line if you don't put me through to him at once. Now. *Instanter.*' Had she understood? There was silence. 'Are you still there?' he asked the apparent vacuum at the other end.

'Yes, Mr Ramsay.'

He'd just made her dig in her pretty heels. 'There are plenty of decorative girls queuing up for your job. This is important and I'm in a hurry. Put me through now – or my next call is to your chairman.'

'He's in Hong Kong,' she answered automatically and then giggled uneasily.

'You have two seconds,' he said and that killed the laugh in her voice.

'I'm putting you over now,' she said, pretending that she hadn't heard the threat, and something buzzed at her end.

'Andover here.'

'Charles Ramsay. It's about the Mary Medallion.'

'Nothing new to report yet, I'm afraid, but our people over there—'

'It's not that. There's been a cock-up.' He spoke the word deliberately, with bitterness.

Silence at the other end. Then Andover said, 'What do you mean? What kind of a cock-up? Be more precise.'

'I shall be precise. The medallion is a reproduction. A facsimile.'

'There's more than one, then?'

The question threw Ramsay for a moment. He swerved and followed the new direction. 'Yes, there could be. At any rate this one wasn't cast under Nicholas Hilliard's supervision, nor at the end of the sixteenth century.'

'Are you sure? Who told you?' Andover's usual pomposity had dropped away from him – the voice was businesslike.

'Margaret Johnson. The wife of Ian Johnson. You must remember him?'

'Yes, I do. The man who buggered up the reliquary for us.' It was the right word, and Sir Anthony's fluting upper-class accent made it sound even acceptable. He continued, 'The bloody man. What did he do?'

'Took an impression from the intaglio moulds and

cast cire perdue from that. It's simple enough. No problem for him at all.'

'You need a furnace, though. I thought his workshop had been sold up? He did something tricky for us last year and we had to find him somewhere to work.' Sir Andrew dragged himself reluctantly back to the point. 'But...'

'There's a doubt,' Ramsay put in.

'Yes. There has to be. Kaput. Isn't it, really?'

'Yes,' Ramsay agreed, 'I'm afraid so.'

There was no way the sale could go ahead until it had been resolved one way or the other. And it couldn't be resolved with one hundred per cent certainty so that was that. No sale now, I'm afraid, or ever. Sir Anthony is sorry but ... good afternoon. A few thousand of commission up the chimney but it couldn't be helped.

Although it didn't matter now, Charles went back to the previous question. 'You're right, of course he needed a furnace. He has plenty of trade contacts though. He's respected.'

'For his craftsmanship,' Sir Anthony said. 'We wouldn't have gone anywhere near the man after that fiasco with the reliquary. Not under any circumstance except one, and that was it: a special job for a client in the Middle East. Johnson could do the work and nobody else could – nobody else in the world, as far as I know.' Sir Andrew sounded almost bewildered by the injustice of it.

Past history.

'So where does that leave us?' Ramsay asked after the briefest of pauses.

'No comment,' Andover said. He still sounded displeased by the idea of the inadequate Johnson with so much skill in his fingers.

Ramsay said, 'Look, I only found out last night. You met McAllen. I thought he was...' kosher; one of us, was what he meant, but it sounded too old fashioned.

Sir Anthony asked, 'Any idea what happened to the original?'

'None. Somebody in the family must have sold it. His grandfather possibly. I haven't discussed it with McAllen yet.'

'It's a damn shame,' Sir Anthony said reflectively.

'I owe you an apology,' Ramsay offered.

'Don't bother,' Sir Andrew replied, 'at least we caught it in time.'

'What shall you do about the Malling people?'

Sir Anthony said, as though dictating a sentence in a fax, 'The vendor has decided he cannot part with this piece after all because it is too important a part of his family's heritage.'

Ramsay had to admit that this conversation with Sir Anthony had been much easier than it might have been with a lesser man. Someone who might have tried to fudge it, blur the line, keep some kind of deal going. Sir Anthony had simply shot it dead. Bang – and the Mary Medallion was just a curiosity, worth its weight in gold – that and no more. When you got down to it, Andover was worth his weight in gold too. A type to be respected.

Ramsay picked up the shotgun and walked slowly back to the house. He was going to have to keep his wits about him today.

* * *

Julia was looking ragged. She had a tray in her hands with what had recently been Caroline's breakfast. The coffee had been poured into the cereal bowl, the toast had been broken up and fragments crammed into the milk jug. Then she had ladled marmalade over everything, smearing it generously across the neat little traycloth as well. Ramsay eyed her efforts.

'Not an easy patient,' he said.

As she scraped the debris into the bin Julia affected nonchalance. 'If it helps her through this crisis I'm willing to put up with much worse.'

She was trying to make him feel like a pimp and she wasn't succeeding because he suspected that one could cope with cold turkey without so much of this theatrical agony and noise – and Julia as Florence Nightingale was frankly unconvincing.

He took off McAllen's shabby mackintosh and returned the shotgun to the gun room. When he returned she was cleaning the hotplate fiercely with a pan scrubber. Tossing it into the sink she turned to him, her back against it. He remembered how her shoulderblades were, and how the ribcage led down to the waist when his hands had been there behind, cradling it.

She said, 'I've been thinking, about the partnership.' Of course she had; so had he.

'Thinking what?'

'Charles, we don't really work in the same way, you and I. We don't share the same approach. I feel we ought to split up now. It's time we did.'

He recognised this for what it was – a counterattack

designed to injure him. She knew him better than to expect a raw protest, but no doubt she wanted him at least to urge caution.

'Fine,' he said, 'as long as I can get my capital out. And something for the goodwill I have helped to build up.' She had offered, he had accepted and that was that. He felt a burden lifted from him.

She said nothing, of course, because he had taken the wind out of her sails, had conceded defeat before the attack had really got started, which spoilt the operation.

She shrugged. 'Well, that's it then. It's settled – if that's really what you want.'

'Yes, it is,' he confirmed, grateful to her for making such a clean break possible. And if he were careful she wouldn't be able to open up on the other front, labelled Margaret Johnson. He was luckier, he knew, than he deserved.

The partnership had looked good but it wasn't working. He had to write it off.

'So we have to see the lawyers again, do we? It's going to be like a divorce.'

'It doesn't have to be,' he said. It was essential to involve his solicitor as soon as possible. He would get in touch with him that afternoon and establish what he could do to protect the capital that he had tied up in the business. The best thing would be to agree to take stock in lieu. It was readily saleable. Without it to work with, however, she was liable to go under even more quickly; he doubted if she would last more than a year in Chelsea without his expertise. That was a matter of indifference

to him after the discoveries of the last twenty-four
hours.

James McAllen put his head round the door.

'I put the gun back in the gunroom,' Ramsay reported,
more brusquely than he meant to, but James didn't
notice.

'She's a lot quieter,' he announced. 'My treatment is
working. Drastic but effective.' He looked from Charles
to Julia, inviting their approval and not really getting
it. They were dubious, unhappy. At least the screaming
had stopped – that was something.

'Certainly drastic,' Julia managed to say at length.

The telephone on the kitchen wall chirped. Julia
reached it first. 'Glengarrick. Yes, he's here.' She
handed it to McAllen. 'It's for you. Cameron Rae.'

Ramsay watched the man, his face intent, concentrating on what his solicitor was saying.

'It can't be done today. That's absolutely out, I'm
afraid.' His mouth pursed at the response he got – Rae
was obviously protesting. 'They'll have to wait. Even in
a case of accidental death ... yes, accidental, surely ...
what do you tell them? You're my solicitor, you think of
something. Very well, tell them that Caroline's ill. She
is ill, in fact. Fraught. She's not made of stone, you
know. Forsyth's sudden departure from this life was a
shock for all of us, me included.'

Then James was briskly overruling him. 'Look, we'll
meet them at your office tomorrow. What time will suit
you? Two. Very well, tell them two o'clock... I've
already told you that is out of the question... It would
look better! What's that supposed to mean? We aren't

suspects, we're witnesses, doing our civic duty. No, I should bloody well hope not. At two tomorrow, then. Goodbye.'

James hung the receiver back on its hook and turned angrily to them. 'I don't know what Cameron is thinking of. He wanted to send the police here today to interview us. I told him no. If the constabulary want to come here to take statements from us, they're welcome. We'll give them a cup of tea and our undivided attention. But not today.'

He clapped his hands, suddenly sanguine, resuming command. 'Look, folks,' he said, 'it seems as if Caroline is really getting through this thing. You've been wonderful, both of you. Your support has been much appreciated. Now I need some more help from you. Will you give me a hand clearing up the mess in the treasure room? If you, Julia, would take Caroline under your wing, Charles and I can tidy up.'

As they clambered up the stairs once more he threw back over his shoulder, 'I warn you, Charles. It looks as though a smart missile has hit it.'

It did indeed. Caroline had destroyed everything that could be smashed or torn. Ramsay's gorge rose at the smell. She was sitting in the only chair she hadn't managed to break. Her eyelids were swollen and her eyes red with weeping, her face was pale, the skin translucent.

Julia stepped forward and put her arm round her. 'Come on, Cal,' she said. 'Let's clean you up.' Caroline coughed once – Ramsay thought she was about to vomit again but her throat merely rattled drily. She got to her feet and allowed Julia to lead her away, the two men standing aside to let her pass.

When he and Ramsay were alone James said, 'It's a hell of a thing, but if there's any backsliding she's going through all this again. I've spoken to her seriously. Now then, let's get on with it. I'll deal with this.' Cheerfully he picked up the chamber pot, saying, 'All the cleaning gear we need is in the bathroom. Come with me, I'll show you.' Charles did as he was told.

Donning rubber gloves, they got down to it. First, everything that was beyond repair – ivories, *cloisonné*, most of the prints and watercolours – was consigned to bin bags.

'What do you think the value is of the stuff she's demolished?' James asked as he began gingerly to pick up the glass from the smashed showcases.

'I wouldn't care to jump a figure,' Ramsay said. 'It would only depress you.'

'Cheap at the price,' James grunted, squatting on the floor. He swore as a sliver of glass penetrated his gloves. 'Anyway, we have the medallion to fall back on. That was in the safe. Even Caroline in extremis couldn't get at that. A bit of swift footwork in the stock market and everything will soon be back to normal.'

Charles reflected. If he didn't speak now James would hear the story from Julia within half an hour, which would be worse. It had to be done.

'James. You know perfectly well. The Mary Medallion is not what it pretends to be.'

'Oh no, my friend. I know no such thing.' James's indignation seemed so genuine that for a moment

Ramsay wondered whether he'd made a colossal mistake; feared that Margaret, for reasons of her own, had misled him, that he'd misled himself – and gone out on a limb with Andover. The moment of panic subsided. That couldn't be right.

'You've got it all wrong.' James was emphatic. 'It is not a fake.'

'What is it then?'

'A facsimile,' James said, trying to give the word dignity and managing only to sound pathetic.

'A facsimile meant to deceive?' Ramsay asked without mercy.

James paused for a moment and then said, 'What the hell does it matter? It wouldn't have looked any different if Hilliard had cast the bloody thing.' Now he was aggressive again.

'James, there aren't two separate worlds – one inhabited by you, where the normal rules of ethics and law don't apply, and another for everyone else. In the world I live in what you did is called fraud.'

'Don't preach.' James shook his head as though trying to rid it of the word. He suddenly burst out, 'Christ, I thought we saw eye to eye. You know how things have been here at Glengarrick. I thought you were on my side. All I'm asking you to do is what Nelson did – put the telescope to your blind eye for once. I need the money.' Then he began to wheedle. 'Once they have the medallion in their museum and their expert's given it the OK we're home and dry. Andover has accepted it.'

Charles Ramsay had either to tell him now or wait. He knew Julia might already be telling Caroline that the medallion was exposed for what it was – something with no more significance than a krugerrand and not worth much more. As a piece of history it was dead in the water.

There was something else James had to be told. He was going to find out in the next couple of hours in any case. Charles said, 'Andover knows it isn't right.'

'Nonsense.'

'No, it isn't nonsense. I phoned him half an hour ago and explained the whole thing to him.'

'You bloody did what?' McAllen roared, with all the indignation of someone in authority who suddenly finds himself bereft of power.

Ramsay looked at him unsparingly. 'Of course he had to be told. He would have been compromised; so would his organisation. It could have cost them millions in lost business, legal fees, damages . . . in the USA, remember. You were playing a nice little game with my reputation as well. You asked me whose side I was on. Right, tell me this. Whose side are you on?'

Each of them stared at the other, blind to any view but his own, unable to see past his own preoccupations and preconceptions. Ramsay had enough insight to understand that. He also understood that however much an outsider might sympathise with McAllen in his predicament, the fact was that the Laird of Glengarrick was a criminal – as much a criminal as any bank teller who put his hand in the till, or burglar who made off with somebody else's television set. He wondered how long it was going to take James to come to terms with that inconvenient idea.

Looking domestic and slightly ridiculous with his cardboard box full of shards of glass in one hand and a brush and dustpan in the other, James stormed out of the turret room and slammed the door, leaving Charles more isolated than ever. Not that he minded, when he considered objectively the other three occupants of the house: the owner, who was prepared to stoop to fraud to maintain his position in life; his wife, a hopefully reformed hophead, and a partner who'd let him down and made him look an idiot. If that was the choice of company, isolated seemed like a comfortable thing to be.

He picked up another desecrated woodcut and straightened it out. What was this? Tokoyuni. It had once been a delight to the eye, but in her anger Caroline had ripped it across and he didn't like to contemplate what she had used it for afterwards. What sort of person could do such a thing, even in the throes of drug withdrawal?

And who could permit her to do it? Someone, he decided, who loved her a great deal. And what else would he be prepared to do for her? Thinking back to the sight of Forsyth sprawled on the stage at Steilbow Castle, Ramsay didn't really want to know the answer to that question. Somebody, though, was going to ask it very soon.

Chapter Eighteen

There was nobody in the high-ceilinged entrance hall. Charles imagined that Julia and her patient were still upstairs; James McAllen had disappeared altogether. The house was dark because the cloudbase was now even lower than before, black and threatening, and rain was still pouring down; he went to the front door and looked up at the wide patch of blackening sky between the trees and rhododendrons surrounding the ample sweep of grey gravel in front of the house. It felt as though it had been raining for weeks, and there wasn't much prospect of a change. A heavy gust of wind hit the monkey puzzle tree facing the entrance, and it showered an extra helping of rain.

He heard a woman's voice at the top of the stairs. Julia, in her consolatory mode; not a tone he had heard much from her. Their relationship had been feisty – was that the word? Combative, at any rate. She seemed to have coaxed Caroline out of the bedroom and to be persuading her to come downstairs.

'Come on now, sweetie. You look stunning. You really do. James will be so proud of you.' With foreboding, Ramsay raised his eyes to the top of the stairs. Caroline came round the massive carved newel post. Pale as a ghost, she was wearing a black taffeta dress with a full, calf-length skirt. Her slender arms emerged from short sleeves cut to resemble two overlapping petals. It wasn't everyone's idea of appropriate costume for a wet Scottish afternoon; it was striking, though, that was certain.

Ramsay heard clapping behind him and turned to see James McAllen giving her as she descended not the slow, sarcastic handclap that might have been expected from him in his present mood, but a genuine congratulation for a wife whom he believed was now able to do him credit, and Glengarrick as well. For some reason James had brought the shotgun Charles had been carrying earlier that morning – as though there was a question he needed to ask about it, though Ramsay had no idea what it might be. He had propped it against the panelling.

When Caroline reached the bottom step she made a grand gesture towards Julia and intoned, 'Thank you, madam,' in the ceremonious voice she had used in the part of Devorgilla the previous evening. Julia curtseyed to her before James intervened, seized the extended hand and kissed it.

He said, 'Darling, I have something to give you.' Squeezing past her he went upstairs.

Caroline stood, regal but uncertain, in her new character as queen of Glengarrick, waiting. Giving a small laugh she asked Julia, 'What can it be, do you think?' Charles she ignored. Clearly word of his treason towards both Julia and her husband had reached her and she was reacting to it, despite her disorientation.

Julia replied, also avoiding Ramsay's eyes, 'Let's wait and see, shall we?' Gently she pushed a lock of hair out of Caroline's eyes as a mother does for a child. A minute or two later James appeared at the top of the stairs with something in his hand, a thin gold chain draped over his fingers. He moved quickly down the stairs, undid the clasp of the chain and draped it around his wife's neck. Her white hands flew up to cover it.

'The Mary Medallion,' he said. 'I only wish it were the real thing. It looks like the real thing, exactly like it, so why don't we pretend that it is?' He glanced at Charles, challenging him to speak. It was the first time for several minutes that any of them had acknowledged that he was still around.

Time for Ramsay to bow out, he thought to himself. Get packed and push off.

It wasn't going to be as easy as that, though. That became clear in the next ten seconds when James picked up the shotgun. He issued no threat but simply pointed it at Ramsay's stomach. Was it loaded? The only way of knowing was to provoke James into pulling one of the triggers and he didn't need the information as badly as that.

Julia called out quickly, 'James, be good.' As though he too was a child, one who needed direction.

'Out,' said James, gesturing with the barrels of the weapon towards the door. 'I want you both out of my house. You have abused my hospitality and I'm turfing you out. Now.'

It wasn't clear why Julia was included and she didn't

ask. It was obvious that they had overstayed their welcome. Such things happen.

Edging towards the door, uncertain how far the cone of shot might spread in the short distance available, Ramsay warned Julia, 'Keep away from me. Don't move yet,' which was to his credit in the circumstances, he felt. She understood and stayed stock still. It was only when he had reached the doorway that she began to inch towards it herself. As Ramsay turned the heavy handle of the front door and opened it a scarf of rain blew in from outside making him start with surprise. Luckily it didn't seem to bother James – being on the other end of the shotgun he had less reason to be nervous.

The rain lashing at his face, Ramsay walked slowly towards his car. He didn't look back – simply assumed that McAllen was behind him and kept going. One just had to keep putting one foot in front of the other.

He had reached the car now. He went round to the driver's side, immediately feeling safer, sensing rather than seeing the steel body of the car between him and the gun; partial protection, at least. Keeping it cool, avoiding too sudden a movement but equally not being tentative, he opened the door with a single firm twist of the wrist. It was important not to hesitate or fluff his movements. By now Julia was out in the open, hair buffeted in the wind, halfway between the car and McAllen. Ramsay didn't look at him directly – could only just register him, looking out of the corner of his eye. He slid into the driver's seat, took the keys from his pocket and switched on the engine. Left foot on the clutch he pressed down on the accelerator, gunning the starter motor. It burst into life with its usual dry chattering sound.

The engine didn't fire. He tried again and there was no response at all. Julia was about to open the nearside back door. She had had the sense to avoid the front seat.

Ramsay wasn't going to get out of the car. He leaned over and wound down the window. 'It won't start,' he reported. 'The damp has shorted the ignition. This rain.' It was piling down. With an obscenity, James invited him to try again. It wouldn't work. He was simply going to run the battery down. Ramsay shrugged, then sat motionless, head high, waiting for instructions.

James approached and thrust the barrel of the gun through the open window. 'Get out,' he ordered. Ramsay did as he was told. 'And you,' James insisted, withdrawing to a safe distance and watching while Julia swung her legs out and stood up, the rain soaking her.

Caroline appeared in the doorway, her face stark and pale against the dark hallway. 'James,' she called out in a high uncertain voice, 'what's going on? Why are you pointing that gun at Julia?' He didn't reply because he hadn't an answer. He lowered it at last.

Ramsay said, 'What happens next? We're getting wet. So are you.' It was a calculated risk with one who had lost his mental balance so completely, but it was a fair gamble.

At first it looked as though he had miscalculated because James's grip tightened on the stock of the gun. He didn't raise it again, though – then he relaxed and said, 'All right. But you have to leave, both of you, get right out of the place. I can't have you here.'

Ramsay said nothing – merely waited.

Julia put in, 'You can drive us. Why not? Surely both your cars can't be off the road?'

McAllen seemed to be testing the suggestion in his mind but he was taking time over it so, chancing it, Julia turned to Caroline. 'Tell him, darling. Couldn't we use your car?'

McAllen's voice burst in brusquely, reasserting his authority. 'We'll take mine. And you're coming too,' he called to Caroline, 'I'm keeping an eye on you. I don't know what you may have stashed away in your dressing room.'

That at least was the kind of thing a sane man might say, so perhaps he was recovering his balance, Charles thought. They weren't out of the wood yet, however; he could see that.

Without breaking it open James McAllen threw the shotgun into the back of his red estate car carelessly, saying, 'You see, it wasn't loaded.'

That wasn't true, Ramsay decided; it was said merely to taunt him. McAllen was no actor; if it had been an empty gun he wouldn't have gripped it with such evident purpose. It had been ready for use and James was reckless enough to have used it.

They could collect their luggage later, he told them as he drove, peering through the windscreen with the wipers slashing regularly across it, hurling the streaming water away. He had decided that they should be taken to a hotel on the coast, well away from Glengarrick, out of his sight and out of his mind.

Now that he had a steering wheel in his hands, a gear lever to pull and push masterfully, he seemed to have fallen back into his manic state. He shot straight past the gatekeeper's lodge and turned into the main road without glancing to right or left. Visibility was not more than a hundred and fifty yards and the road was full of bends. Fortunately it was empty – not a timber lorry or milk tanker in sight – as yet. He pressed his foot on the accelerator and Ramsay felt the tyres slip a little on the wet surface of the road before they gripped it.

James turned his head and spoke to Caroline, and only to her. 'Darling, you must telephone these two at their hotel and fix a time for them to collect their belongings so that I can make sure I am well away from Glengarrick when they come.'

Julia put in, 'I don't know why I'm being blamed. I set the whole thing up for you. It wasn't my fault it went wrong.'

Caroline ventured, 'Yes, why are you getting at Julia?'

That question was too much for him as well. Eventually he sighed heavily and said unconvincingly, 'You're his girlfriend, aren't you? His lover. You set it up between you.'

'Why should we do that?' Julia demanded.

'Leave it,' Ramsay warned. 'Leave the man alone, he's trying to drive.'

And not trying hard enough in these atrocious conditions. The trees lining the road were swirling and boiling in the wind. If one had come down further up the road they wouldn't have a chance. The way he was driving McAllen would go straight into it. Bang.

Julia was too angry with McAllen to take any notice. She jeered at the man, 'Tell me. Go on. Try and make some nonsense up. Why should we want to do that? Tell me, why?'

They passed the turning for Carrucate. Was another pressure on James his knowledge of how Forsyth had met his death? Ramsay wondered. Was that the real reason behind his erratic behaviour? Guilt? Complicity?

Julia continued to bait him, 'There, you can't tell me.'

'It isn't that, Julia. He doesn't mean it,' Caroline burst out. 'It's Malcolm dying that's the problem. We have to be interviewed by the police tomorrow. You know, you heard when Cameron telephoned.'

The car was juddering because it was in too high a gear, pushing up the hill. McAllen slammed it into a better gear but by then it was too late – it had reached the crest and begun the descent towards the shore, towards Scaup Bay where years earlier Cameron Rae's father had been sucked inch by inch into the quicksand while David Forsyth had watched with his farm boy beside him, extracting as much pleasure as he could from the spectacle.

Caroline's voice wailed, 'It's terrible. We don't know what to say.'

Whether to confess, was that what she meant? To confess that both of them, husband and wife, had had enough of their double life – of James's humiliation under the constant threat of exposure which Malcolm Forsyth had held over him; of the slavery Forsyth had imposed on Caroline when she could no longer find the money for the drugs he had supplied her with? The answer seemed obvious. Since James was going down anyway he might as well take Forsyth with him. It was the kind of quick way out that a man like McAllen would have taken when he found himself in a corner without thinking through the consequences. Not a stupid man, by any means, but an impulsive one, incapable of playing a long game. A man, too, who had been at Carrucate that night and had seen Forsyth with his wife.

So now they had reached this pass. The two of them were faced with the prospect of an interrogation with scarcely any time to coordinate their answers. Both too drained of emotion to be able to think up a story that would survive detailed, objective police questioning.

Suddenly Julia cried out, 'What are you doing now? Where are you going?' McAllen had driven them off the road and they were bumping over the dunes, across the wind-bleached grass and on to the flat expanse of the Solway Firth towards a gleaming ribbon of tide which they could see in the distance through the mist and a bank of rain hanging in front of them.

'What are you up to now? Grow up, for goodness' sake,' Ramsay shouted, glancing at the back of the car to see Caroline limp in her black evening dress, the Mary Medallion skipping and bouncing on its thin gold chain at her throat. Julia had put an arm round her.

Driving straight towards the edge of the sea, McAllen

kept his foot on the accelerator. Now the spray thrown up by the wheels was splashing the car windows, sand and water mixed. That must have alarmed Julia even more because she screamed at him, 'Slow down. *Slow down!*' The epitome of the male, assertive and past caring, McAllen ignored her and drove on.

Again Julia's voice came from the back. 'The quicksand. You've forgotten the quicksand.' Had he? Or was McAllen deliberately steering towards it? Seeking it out in that flat expanse of sand so that he could bury himself, the three of them, his troubles, the whole tragic story in the quicksand that had engulfed Lennox decades before? It wouldn't take long for a car as heavy as this to sink and be lost. Ramsay put his finger on the button that operated the electrically controlled window on his side and saw McAllen operate the master switch on the steering column to frustrate him.

Suddenly the car began to swing from side to side, slowing down as it did so. Then it slewed round with the back wheels still spinning, now throwing up gobbets of wet sand that slopped on to the rear windows and began to cover them. McAllen rammed his foot down on the gas. It was hopeless – the vehicle was caught – and it was already sinking. Ramsay seized the opportunity and opened the window again, jamming one arm into the aperture to hold it open while he leaned over with his other hand to unlock the door. McAllen punched at his control again and Ramsay felt the pain as the glass whirred upwards into his elbow joint. The door was open though. He managed to get his arm out, calling out to Julia, 'Open your door. Now, now, now.'

While she did so, James McAllen lunged at him, trying to drag him back inside the vehicle. 'You're coming with me,' he shouted.

Ramsay chopped upwards at his nose with the edge of his right hand: a hard agonising blow that jerked McAllen's head back and left him helpless for long enough to enable Ramsay to get out of the car. It had already sunk up to its tyres in a slurry of water and sand.

'Pull Caroline out,' Ramsay shouted and projected himself away from the car, driving hard with his feet against the bodywork like a swimmer pushing himself away from the side of a pool. Under his outstretched hands he could feel a solid edge of sand. The rain was lashing at his face and suddenly he was half immersed in cold water. Was it firm ground; and was he far enough over it to get a purchase and pull himself away from the quicksand which was rapidly swallowing the car? Desperately he kicked out, trying to stop his feet from lapsing into the pool behind him, hitting the body of the car again. He could just see Julia doing the same – scrabbling to reach the lip of firm sand which ran around the edge of the pool. It was easier for her because she was lighter, but she had Caroline to cope with as well, incongruous in that silly black dress, heavy and bedraggled now. He was panting hard, reaching out as far as he could – almost half his body supported but, crucially, his centre of gravity still on the wrong side for safety. Then he realised – he was struggling too much, trying too much, and that was reducing his chances of survival.

He called out to Julia, dragging in air between each phrase, 'Relax – stop moving – try to float – as though it was water.' He followed his own advice and waited for an unbearable moment to see whether it would work or whether he had lost the battle – and the war – and his life – his sweet life. He felt his legs rise to the surface, gave one strong but careful froglike kick and found at last that the ground beneath him was supporting all of his weight. 'It works,' he reported urgently to Julia, feeling as though he had just invented the wheel, manned flight, the petrol engine... 'What you have to do is just to relax and float.'

'Don't be so stupid,' she answered crisply, much more in charge than he was. 'What do you think I am doing?'

Ramsay slewed round to look back at the car.

McAllen had changed his mind about dying. He was halfway out of the car, his arms outstretched towards his enemy, floundering in the water. If he didn't get his legs clear of the car it was going to trap them as it went down and pull the rest of him down as well.

Charles shouted, 'Try and pull your knees up towards your chin, will you? Otherwise you're going to be caught. The car's going down!'

Suddenly much more biddable, McAllen obeyed the instruction.

Ramsay looked behind him. Julia was clear, so was Caroline. They had both made it back to safety. 'Grab my feet, one each,' he ordered, then countermanded the order. They would have no purchase on the flat sand if they were trying to pull McAllen out.

'Burrow!' he said. 'Try and make a toehold for your

feet.' He pulled off a shoe and began to do that for himself. It was no more than six inches deep, but it might just make the difference. McAllen was a heavy man but there were three of them on the other side. Charles lay down on the sand again, fitted his feet into the holes he had dug, and the women dropped behind him and clung to his ankles. Then he elbowed his body round – his head was projecting a couple of feet over the edge, but he was still safe enough with the weight of the two women on his feet. Caroline was sobbing. He reached out for McAllen and felt the sudden weight of the man as his hands grabbed at him. Was he going to drag him back into the quicksand?

'Move your legs as though you're swimming,' Ramsay told him, and felt the weight on his own arms lessen. He turned his head back to his helpers and called, 'Pull. Together now. Pull!'

As they did so he found himself moving back four or five inches, still holding McAllen's hands. 'And again.' After a couple more heaves they had him far enough back to get his knees into the toeholds and McAllen was almost clear. Triumphantly they pulled him the last few inches to safety.

'You bloody well didn't deserve that,' Ramsay said as the rescued man struggled to his feet, his front covered in sand. The others stood up in the rain, with the wind lashing at them. When they saw how close the tide had come they began to run for the shore.

Chapter Nineteen

Ramsay handed Julia into the taxi, feeling her palm still rough with grains of sand. She had brushed aside the hospital's lukewarm offer of an ambulance; after all she was only shaken, not otherwise damaged. He wasn't much worse off than she was, although he did have a graze here and there and a stiff shoulder where it had caught the car door as he had pushed through it. He had felt nothing until half an hour afterwards. He'd insisted that they visit a store in Dumfries to buy something basic to wear before finding an hotel; he couldn't imagine that they would have been accepted anywhere decent in the clothes they stood up in, plastered with sand and mud with the smell of the sea about them. When he'd taken off his shirt in the store's changing room he'd found a huge bruise on his upper arm, almost bigger than his hand.

The last they had seen of the McAllens was when they had been led away to a separate branch of the outpatients' department because she, they said, showed evidence of ... he couldn't remember what now – shock, nervous exhaustion, whatever you will.

Caroline had still been wearing the black dress, but without the medallion at her throat – that had been lost, swallowed up by the quicksand, he supposed.

Had they thought of it then they could have gone back to Glengarrick, collected the car and their luggage and made a clean break with the McAllens, but they had been too disorientated to latch on to that in time. Now their defences were down and they were too tired to face a confrontation. They would have to come to it later on, though.

They walked into the hotel lobby, across the thick carpet to the blue-uniformed receptionist at her counter. 'A double? Twin-bedded?' she asked brightly.

'Two singles,' he replied. The girl took two keys, gave him one and handed the other to Julia, with particular care, in order to emphasise that she understood her status. Then she nodded to the porter who, looking about, realised that they had no luggage – just the plastic bags that held their discarded clothes.

'My car broke down,' Ramsay explained, which was true enough, 'our luggage will be coming through later.'

Julia was shown her room first, given the usual briefing on the bathroom, room service, the TV set. The porter waited, prompting her to tip him, then made for the door glancing back towards Charles, expecting him to follow. Instead he waited for Julia to say something, and she couldn't find the words.

In order to help her he tried a banality. 'Looks comfortable enough.'

The porter was watching them with impatience,

anxious to get on; an unwanted presence who was more than ready to go.

'That was a gutsy performance you gave out there on the merse,' she conceded.

'You too,' he said, ready to give the devil her due – and no more.

But that gave her enough confidence to say, 'I'll see you later in the dining room... When shall we eat?'

He had to kill that idea immediately. It wasn't what he had meant at all. 'Sorry. I'm afraid you'll have to have the meal on your own. I shan't be eating here,' he said and saw the disbelief leap into her eyes. There was nothing to be done and the man was still waiting. Ramsay realised that he should have just taken his room key and told the chap to go, but it was too late now so, obediently, having said less than he had meant to, he followed him.

As soon as he was alone in his room he put in a call to Cameron Rae and started to explain what had happened.

Rae interrupted him. 'James has been in touch already. He told me.'

'About the car journey and where we fetched up?'

'Yes.'

'Everything about it? Did he tell you why he drove us all out on to the sands?'

'He wasn't as forthcoming as that.'

'I bet he wasn't,' Ramsay said; but there was no point in making an issue of that. Rapidly he told what had happened over the medallion. Rae had to know straightaway. As a lawyer he could only approve of what Charles had done. Ramsay concluded, 'You can imagine that we aren't flavour of the month with James at the moment.'

'I can,' Rae said and left it there because McAllen was his client.

A pause. Charles asked, 'Would you do me a small service?'

'If it really is a small one, yes,' Rae said shortly.

'Get someone to collect my car from Glengarrick. It wouldn't start this morning – the rain got into the distributor and it stalled completely. It should have recovered by now, though. If you could send one of your staff over here I'll let him have the key. I don't want to go to Glengarrick; if I do I'll only set James off again. We can arrange the collection of our things later.'

'I'll do it myself,' Cameron offered. 'I need to talk to you anyway, to check up on James's story. When he gets the bit between his teeth like this he's a worry. It's happened before and I'm not sure yet what sort of position he's got himself into this time. If I'm going to help him I need to have your version of what went on at Glengarrick after the pageant. I'll come over.'

'Don't. I have to come into town anyway. I'll drop the key off at your office on my way.'

'Good. Seven o'clock. I work late.'

There was something else that intrigued Charles. He asked, 'You said you need to have my version. Why mine? We scarcely know each other.'

'I trust you,' the solicitor replied.

It wasn't much of a medal but it was something.

Cameron Rae's office was in a smug little eighteenth-century building close to the white marble statue of Robert Burns. Inside it was modern: dove grey office furniture made of plastic-coated metal, the latest personal computers and windows shaded by pale Venetian blinds – all that, the colour scheme, the space, created an impression of calm efficiency. The blinds in Rae's room had been drawn down against the sun which had returned at last, after the soaking of the past day or two.

One surprise that met Charles as he walked in was that Arabella Knight was there, sitting in an armchair absorbed in a journal about interior decorating. Rae was at his desk, a sheaf of incoming letters in his hand, sharply dictating replies. The other surprise was the painting leaning against the wall beside his desk. *Mystery Four* – it had to be, if Ramsay was any judge. There was no attempt to hide that celebration of pure sensuality. Was it waiting to be hung on the wall? Ramsay wondered how the more sober of Rae's farmer clients would take to it. With suspicion, he felt sure – they would feel more comfortable with the usual photograph of the belted Galloway that had won top prize in the show in 1972, or perhaps a picture of the town provost a century earlier.

Arabella had stopped turning the pages of her magazine and intercepted his glance with a welcoming smile.

'Oh, the picture,' she said. 'Don't worry, it's not staying here. It's going into Cameron's flat. I insisted. It's much too good for here. He could scarcely have a picture of his mother as naked as the day she was born on the wall of his office now, could he? Not in that pose.'

Her tone suggested that she had recently been put in charge of Rae's domestic arrangements – that a relationship had come into being. The journal suggested the same thing – nestbuilding in prospect. Ramsay had suspected it ever since he had heard them bickering at the dinner table on the night he and Julia had arrived at Glengarrick. He had guessed that Rae's apparent contempt for the pageant had arisen from jealousy because it was monopolising her time, while her reaction had been no more than a bid for his attention. They would make, had made, a businesslike team, Ramsay thought, and experienced a twinge of envy because he and Julia had failed in that regard. It hadn't been his fault, he told himself firmly; or if it had, he couldn't remember how.

Without thinking he asked the question dealers tend to ask. 'Where did it come from?'

'Don't be silly,' she laughed, 'you know perfectly well.'

Rae's face was still closely engaged with the microphone of his recorder, so Ramsay simply placed the keys to his car on the desktop where he could see them. Rae put them in his pocket without interrupting the flow of his words.

'Forsyth. The police investigation and all that. It's taken up a lot of time today. He has to catch up,' Arabella explained, above the mutter of her new partner's dictation. Her voice had that proprietorial tone that the wives of professional men use when speaking of their husbands. She was already well into her new role. 'And James is a bother. Headstrong and arrogant are the two words I would use.' Another burden laid on her man.

Rae snapped off his little black recorder and said, 'I'll go down to Glengarrick and fetch your car in a minute. Since I don't fancy walking back you'd better come with me. You can stay in my car. There's no need to bother James with your presence.' It sounded almost as if he, Charles Ramsay, was at fault and James the injured party. But then, they were close friends, always ready to help each other out in an emergency. Undoubtedly.

Rae gestured towards the picture. 'He gave me that,' he said. 'It was good of him, wasn't it? Particularly since his father commissioned it and you could say he had a claim on it himself. A very tenuous claim, though, and James recognised that ... which was why he passed it on to me.'

More of a claim than Forsyth had certainly. So it was indeed James who had taken it from Carrucate that night. Not Rae himself, nor some shady associate of Lewis's – Julia had mentioned several characters she knew.

'The police want to interrogate the McAllens, I hear,' Ramsay said.

'That's no problem for him,' Cameron Rae replied. 'He was in the dressing room with two other people when Forsyth fell from the window and Caroline was being sick in the ladies with one of Devorgilla's waiting women holding her head. They are literally helping the police with their enquiries and nothing else. I told James as much on the phone when I rang last night, but he wasn't listening of course. He was too set on being indignant about it.'

Ramsay knew that he should have kept silent but he felt they deserved to be shaken up. They were far too confident. They had to be taught to be more circumspect.

He said, 'It was odd when the lights went out last night. Everything in the castle was blacked out, but I saw that the lights in a couple of cottages only a few hundred yards down the road were still on. I saw that quite clearly.' He spoke slowly, adding, 'If it was a power cut it was a very localised one, don't you think?'

Arabella glanced across to her lover, a momentary alarm in her eyes which confirmed everything Ramsay suspected.

Rae said, easily, 'The power lines down there are a bit of a mix-up, and have been since mains electricity was first brought there in the 1930s. The lines have been replaced of course but the system's still chaotic. They need to heave it all out and start again.'

The two of them had arranged it, of course they had. Arabella had thrown the master switch in the lighting box – that was all there was to the power cut. If it came to it the story would be that she'd done it by accident and the police would never be able to disprove it. So who had been up the ladder standing behind Forsyth and had ensured he made his exit on cue? Ramsay was looking straight at him; but they would have no reason to suspect Rae. There was nothing linking him with Forsyth.

Ramsay replied lightly, 'I didn't realise the energy distribution arrangements in this part of the world were so eccentric,' and left it at that.

Probitas, he thought ... *Probitas*. It was all very well in moderation, and it didn't really cover this situation anyway. Taking even the strictest interpretation his family motto didn't require him to hightail it down to Dumfries police headquarters and voice his suspicions. If they knew that there was a decades-old feud between Rae and the Forsyths it would put a completely different slant on the whole thing, but the number of people who knew that was limited and those who knew, and this included Ramsay himself, were sympathetic to the cause – which had been simply to rid the world of Forsyth because he wasn't an ornament to it.

He looked at Arabella who had turned out the lights so that her lover would not be seen getting in position to give Forsyth a shove. He wasn't going to interfere. A good citizen might have done but he didn't feel like one just then. It was then that it occurred to Ramsay that the moulds for the medallion which Hilliard had wrought in such an exquisite intaglio were worth something significant. He would have a word with Andover in the morning – but now it was time to take his leave.

'Be assured,' he said – just that. It was all he could offer them.

Arabella relaxed, and so did Rae. They had taken a very considerable risk and they were still exposed – to blackmail, to the appearance of an inconvenient and unexpected witness, to something they thought they had kept hidden. Their position wasn't secure and they were going to have to sweat it out for the next few months. There was nothing he could do to protect them from that.

'If you don't mind,' he said briskly, 'let's get over to Glengarrick and collect my car. I have an appointment in town later on.'

Before he went Arabella kissed him, not on the cheek but the side of his mouth, gently. He had never been kissed by a murderess before – he found it a pleasant experience.

It took longer than he expected to recover his car because Cameron Rae was involved and Ramsay wasn't in control of his own schedule. When they reached the entrance of the estate he stayed in the lawyer's car listening to a broadcast of *Idomeneo* while the solicitor walked up to the house. He was gone a long time and they were well into the first act by the time Ramsay saw his car return. Why had Cameron been so long up at the house? What had he been discussing with James and his anxious wife?

Handing him the keys, Rae said, 'I mentioned your point about the moulds to James. He said he would be grateful if you would speak to Sir Anthony and find out if the Malling Trustees are indeed interested.'

'Very well,' Ramsay nodded. 'I shall deal through you, though. Is that in order?'

'Yes.'

It would have been easier to use the events of the morning as an excuse to wash his hands of Glengarrick and the McAllens, but it was just possible that this smaller deal might come off, might be a help to them. It wasn't going to involve much work – a bridge-building exercise with Andover and a fax or two, a few phone calls.

'Thanks for your trouble. I'll be in touch.' He gave Rae a farewell handshake and wished him and Arabella well. He meant it. Of course they were guilty of encompassing Forsyth's death. There wasn't a shadow of doubt in his mind about that. On the other hand he had come to recognise at last that no act could be categorised as good or bad without reference to its outcome – and who could quarrel with the outcome of this act of theirs? Not Charles Ramsay.

He was late when he reached her flat, too late to be comfortable about it because she might not be there. He took the stairs two at a time and knocked briskly on the door. When there was no response he tried again. He was about to try a third time, harder, when the door opened and she caught him with his right fist raised in the air, in the Communist salute.

'Hello, comrade,' she said and smiled. As she ushered him inside and he walked past her she said, 'I was waiting.' There was no reproach in her voice and when he said, 'I was delayed at Glengarrick,' she asked for no more explanation.

The lights weren't on. She had been waiting in the gathering dark for him to turn up. What had she been thinking that had been so absorbing that she had failed to put on the lights? At first she might have used the time to make some slight improvement in the arrangements for welcoming him. Perhaps she had gone to find the white napkin which lay beside the improvised ice bucket containing a bottle that stood on the side table in the window – had given the glasses a final polish. Then, after twenty-five minutes ... thirty-five, forty minutes ... and he still hadn't turned up she might have begun to say to herself, 'He has thought better of it. He remembers what happened before and has decided not to risk the pain of rejection again.'

She said, as she switched on the lamp on the table, 'I was thinking of Monte Carlo.'

So it had been in her mind – the memory of how she had betrayed him. Wanting to exonerate her he replied, 'It wasn't an easy time for you,' and saw the relief in her eyes.

She went on, 'That wasn't the only thing. There was the medallion too.'

He answered cautiously, 'It's possible to take more than one view on that. The end sometimes justifies the means and if one is going to indulge in forgery I can't imagine a better purpose than the rehabilitation of Caroline McAllen.'

She looked at him, confident enough now to tease him a little. 'The end justifies the means? I never expected to hear you say that. I thought *Probitas* was your motto – rockhard Protestant integrity and let the sky fall in – on everybody if necessary.'

Probitas. The word brought to mind his family tree, widely spread with all the names linked in a kind of trellis reaching down to the present day. He recalled some of them:

John Ramsaye married Jeyne Woodrowe – ?1434 ...
James Ramsaye married Eleanor Hooper, 12th December 1525 ...

– and below each name their arms neatly painted by a Victorian artist in colours which were still bright after a hundred and fifty years. Underneath those of James and Eleanor was the name of their firstborn son, William, who didn't survive his teens. Next to him stood his brother Francis, who had two sons and a daughter, Jessica. And so on down the centuries. Charles remembered his father, many years ago – a slimmer, darker version of the Ernest Ramsay who lived at Bressemer now – standing in front of the chart and telling him, not long after his tenth birthday, how all those Ramsays – or most of them anyway – had governed their behaviour by that single idea ... *Probitas* – probity, honesty, straightforward dealing ... and so should he. Yes, his father had conceded, there had been the odd backslider among them, but they had been few and far between.

Few and far between? Really? Could his father have

meant that? He had always respected him as an honest man if not always a wise or far-sighted one. But what about the rest of them? Had James Ramsaye, Francis and his children survived and prospered in Tudor times by always calling a spade a spade? Had they spelt out the precise articles of their faith when the king was busy divorcing Katherine of Aragon and nobody outside the court was at all certain what he wanted them to say? Or when his daughter Mary Tudor was on the throne and burning so-called heretics at Smithfield? In those grim times for Protestant faith had they always stated what their religious beliefs were? Of course they hadn't. He, Charles Ramsay, wouldn't be standing there if they had.

And later on – during the Civil War – had the head of the family come out fearlessly for King Charles when Cromwell's commissioner had asked for his support? No, he hadn't. He had smiled and murmured something vague and hoped for the best. In Victoria's reign too. The Richard Ramsay who had participated so successfully in the railway boom. Had he kept scrupulously to the family motto when seeking local backers for George Hudson's Grand East Anglian Trunk Railway to London? No way. And if all those forebears of his hadn't lived by the slogan why should he? As that question and the expanding light it brought with it grew brighter and brighter in his head, becoming clearer and clearer, he saw that it led majestically to one inescapable conclusion.

Stuff *Probitas*.

That was it. The resolution of the matter. Stark and clear. Looking across at Margaret he saw that she had read his face and guessed what he was thinking. How life was much more complicated than that – just sticking blindly to a motto.

No, when eventually he inherited Bressemer he was going to take down that family tree, treating it with respect of course, roll it up, and place it in one of the rooms at the top of the house where nobody ever went. Having done that he would try to forget where he had left it.

He was certain that Margaret would not go out of her way to remind him which room it was in but perhaps one of their children or grandchildren would find it in the middle of the next century and restore it to its proper place. That was their privilege. As far as he was concerned it was a relic, a quaint bit of family history which might provide a few minutes' conversation at a dinner party, and that was all.

Margaret asked, 'Well, Charles Ramsay, have you seen the light?' She was too tactful to say, have you grown up at last? That was what it came to though, wasn't it? He had grown up, and not before time. He smiled at her with affection but didn't reply. He felt liberated; all his life, up to that moment, he had laboured under this burden and now he found that all he needed to do was to lift it off his shoulders, lay it down on the ground and walk away from it. He was treading on air. In a world where right and wrong were never easy to discern he was his own man, and free to make his own decisions.

Margaret picked up the bottle by the neck, dripping from its bed of ice and water.

'Laurent Perrier,' she said, handing it to him. 'You'd better open it.' She must have caught his look of surprise as he turned away to untwist the wire on the neck of the bottle because she said, 'I found where Ian cached his bankroll, so this comes courtesy of him.'

That was as it should be after the life he had given her.

'Have you had any news?' he asked as he poured the wine into the glasses.

'Nothing,' she replied. 'This time I think he's vanished. I shan't be wasting time on searching for him.'

'You know,' he said, 'Julia and I...' He tried the name out on her experimentally to see if she was ready to accept it.

'Yes,' Margaret answered with patience. 'You and Julia?'

'We were supposed to be visiting Scotland for a break, a holiday. It doesn't seem to have worked out.'

'That's an understatement...'

He went on, 'I think you and I should try again and see if we can be more successful. Where would you like to go?'

She needed no prompting to reply. 'Paris,' she said, 'for at least three weeks. There's a lot I've been longing to see. And then another fortnight in the Loire Valley.'

'I'll fix it,' he said as she took the glass from his hand. He knew of a modest-looking hotel which had a cool garden where you could sit over an aperitif in the evening before sampling the excellent dinner menu. It was an ideal place to restore their relationship.

They stood together looking down at the street below them, the occasional car passing in the road. She was close to him – he could feel her warmth beside him.

'Here's to us,' he said, draining his glass.

'To us,' she agreed.

Epilogue

The large man with the naked woman tattooed on his arm handed Ethelred the delivery note. 'Just sign here, chief, if you would be so kind,' he said elaborately, giving a sideways glance at his young companion, a look that said, 'one of those', as clearly as if he'd spoken the words. Ethelred had sensitive antennae and picked up the message immediately though he had seen too much warfare and was too far advanced into middle age to let such a small thing bother him.

He studied the yellow slip of paper, with its small print and the scarcely decipherable scrawled address. His sight was not what it had been. 'Are you sure it's for me?' he asked sharply. It was some elaborate joke of course but he couldn't imagine who had played it on him – who would know. Anny wouldn't have done it; she had more sense than that – the thing was valuable.

The asperity of his question had the man worried. He looked at Ethelred's crisp white shopfront, the large Georgian-style window, and the sign that said, in restrained lettering:

ETHELRED LEWIS
Antiques Bought and Sold.
Late of The Arcade, Bond Street, London W1

Nowhere was there a street number.

'This is Montacute Walk,' the man asserted carefully, looking down at his copy of the delivery note, 'number eleven.' Now he was unsure of himself.

An ox, Ethelred thought and answered, 'Yes of course,' dismissively, determined to give him a hard time – to go down fighting.

'Then it's yours,' the man concluded. 'Sent by a Mrs Arabella Rae, all the way from Scotland. So, where do you want it?'

'Well it's nothing to do with me,' said Ethelred trying to remember who Mrs Arabella Rae was. He wasn't going to admit ownership of it, not until he'd made enquiries. It could be awkward.

The man sighed. 'Do you want us to take it back then?'

'No,' said Ethelred, quite ready to be accommodating now, since it was worth money. After all the cheque had bounced, been stopped rather, and there was just a chance, when he thought about it, an outside chance that he might recoup that money, or some of it.

He ordered, magnanimously, 'You'd better leave it here. Outside in the street here. I'll see to it.'

They lowered the tailgate of the van, put the ramp in place and trundled it down, its iron wheels rushing the last few inches when they almost lost their grip on it, banging onto the cobbles.

The Drumpagan cannon. Ethelred reached for his

wallet and then, remembering that glance, he thought better of it. Instead he thanked them effusively. 'Thank you. Thank you so much. You have been very patient,' he gushed enthusiastically. It was a great deal cheaper.

He looked at the powerful barrel ready to belch fire, the great iron undercarriage, the wheels. Splendid. But he couldn't leave it there, it was causing an obstruction. It might be towed away. Where the hell was he going to put it?

Looking disappointed, almost as if they wanted to take it away again, they left it there next to the pavement.

Ethelred went into the shop, put on his glasses and telephoned the number on the docket – Mrs Arabella Rae. The name Arabella rang a sort of bell. He waited patiently.

'Rae,' a woman's voice said.

Ethelred decided to play it very cagily. He started, 'I'm phoning from Brighton,' he said. 'My name is Ethelred Lewis.'

'Oh but we have met, Mr Lewis. Don't you remember? At Steilbow Castle. The pageant.'

'Oh, Arabella *Knight*,' he exclaimed as the penny dropped. 'Your married name.' He congratulated her, he felicitated her because he did know his manners. After a polite exchange he got down to business again.

'Two men have just been here and delivered a cannon. The cannon. The one I procured for the pageant.'

'Good,' said Arabella.

'I don't quite understand.'

'Well I don't know if you heard, but there was

something of an excitement up here because our benefactor Mr Forsyth died suddenly during the first night.'

'I did hear something,' he admitted. The circumstances of Forsyth's death had been so bizarre that they had found their way into the English newspapers, though not on the front pages.

'A very strange accident,' he added.

'Wasn't it?' Arabella agreed. 'And of course all the other performances had to be cancelled. After all those rehearsals. We were all terribly put out.'

Ethelred said nothing. He hadn't liked the man either.

'Then afterwards we had to sort out the accounts and everything, a horrible job in the circumstances, with the lawyers who were winding up the estate, because Mr Forsyth had guaranteed our loss, you see. Anyway, we found that he'd never paid for the cannon and we knew you'd supplied it so it belonged to you and had to be returned. That was obvious. I was going to write and then there was so much to do – our wedding, all the arrangements. Then I meant to phone you but I forgot, I'm afraid.'

'No problem. No problem at all,' Ethelred assured her hurriedly. He didn't want her wondering why he hadn't laid claim to the cannon. 'But where did you get my address?'

'From Julia, Mr Ramsay's friend. We knew she was a friend of yours as well...'

When she rang off Ethelred went outside and inspected the cannon, trying to assess its potential. Where could he dispose of it? Julia. Why didn't he ask her? It would give him another chance to sympathise with her about Ramsay's defection. Julia needed advice herself, of course, now that their partnership had broken up. He hadn't broached the subject yet but if she was looking for another partner he knew just the person. Himself.

The bell on the shop door chimed melodiously. It was Mrs Blennerhasset.

'A cannon, a genuine cannon,' she exclaimed, sailing into the shop. 'I don't know if I've ever mentioned it before, Mr Lewis, but I was born in a castle, you know. And we had a cannon like that on the west rampart. Do you know, my father used to fire it off whenever he'd made a really big coup on the Stock Exchange...'

KATE CHARLES

Appointed to Die

A clerical mystery

Death at the Deanery – sudden and unnatural death.
Someone should have seen it coming.

Even before Stuart Latimer arrives as the new Dean
of Malbury Cathedral shock waves reverberate
around the tightly knit Cathedral Close, heralding
sweeping changes in a community that is not open to
change. And the reality is worse than the
expectation. The Dean's naked ambition and ruthless
behaviour alienate everyone in the Chapter: the
Canons, gentle John Kingsley, vague Rupert
Greenwood, pompous Philip Thetford, and Subdean
Arthur Bridges-ffrench, a traditionalist who resists
change most strongly of all.

Financial jiggery-pokery, clandestine meetings,
malicious gossip, and several people who see more
than they ought to: a potent mix. But who could
foresee that the mistrust and even hatred within the
Cathedral Close would spill over into violence and
death? Canon Kingsley's daughter Lucy draws in her
lover David Middleton-Brown, against his better
judgement, and together they probe the surprising
secrets of a self-contained world where nothing is
what it seems.

FICTION / CRIME 0 7472 4199 6

Shroud For The Archbishop

A Sister Fidelma Mystery from the author of
ABSOLUTION BY MURDER

Peter Tremayne

Wighard, archbishop designate of Canterbury, has been discovered garrotted in his chambers in the Lateran Palace in Rome in the autumn of AD 664. The solution to this terrible crime appears simple as the palace guards have arrested an Irish religieux, Brother Ronan Ragallach, as he fled from Wighard's chambers.

Although Ronan denies responsibility, Bishop Gelasius, in charge of running affairs at the palace, is convinced the crime is political; Wighard was slain in pique at the triumph of the pro-Roman Anglo-Saxon clergy in their debate with the pro-Columba Irish clergy at Whitby. And there is also the matter of missing treasure . . .

Bishop Gelasius realises that Wighard's murder could lead to war between the Saxon and Irish kingdoms if Ronan is accused without independent evidence. So he invites Sister Fidelma of Kildare and Brother Eadulf of Seaxmund's Ham to investigage. But more deaths follow before the pieces of this strange jigsaw of evil and vengeance are put together.

'The Sister Fidelma stories take us into a world that only an author steeped in Celtic history could recreate so vividly – and one which no other crime novelist has explored before. Make way for a unique lady detective going where no one has gone before!' Peter Haining

FICTION / CRIME 0 7472 4848 6

A selection of bestsellers from Headline

OXFORD EXIT	Veronica Stallwood	£4.99	☐
BOOTLEGGER'S DAUGHTER	Margaret Maron	£4.99	☐
DEATH AT THE TABLE	Janet Laurence	£4.99	☐
KINDRED GAMES	Janet Dawson	£4.99	☐
MURDER OF A DEAD MAN	Katherine John	£4.99	☐
A SUPERIOR DEATH	Nevada Barr	£4.99	☐
A TAPESTRY OF MURDERS	P C Doherty	£4.99	☐
BRAVO FOR THE BRIDE	Elizabeth Eyre	£4.99	☐
NO FIXED ABODE	Frances Ferguson	£4.99	☐
MURDER IN THE SMOKEHOUSE	Amy Myers	£4.99	☐
THE HOLY INNOCENTS	Kate Sedley	£4.99	☐
GOODBYE, NANNY GRAY	Staynes & Storey	£4.99	☐
SINS OF THE WOLF	Anne Perry	£5.99	☐
WRITTEN IN BLOOD	Caroline Graham	£5.99	☐

All Headline books are available at your local bookshop or newsagent, or can be ordered direct from the publisher. Just tick the titles you want and fill in the form below. Prices and availability subject to change without notice.

Headline Book Publishing, Cash Sales Department, Bookpoint, 39 Milton Park, Abingdon, OXON, OX14 4TD, UK. If you have a credit card you may order by telephone – 01235 400400.

Please enclose a cheque or postal order made payable to Bookpoint Ltd to the value of the cover price and allow the following for postage and packing:

UK & BFPO: £1.00 for the first book, 50p for the second book and 30p for each additional book ordered up to a maximum charge of £3.00.

OVERSEAS & EIRE: £2.00 for the first book, £1.00 for the second book and 50p for each additional book.

Name ....

Address ....

....

....

If you would prefer to pay by credit card, please complete:
Please debit my Visa/Access/Diner's Card/American Express (delete as applicable) card no:

Signature .... Expiry Date ....